Midnight Song

ISBN: 0-9855-4950-5
ISBN-13: 9780985549503
Library of Congress Control Number: 2012922086
Beachbooks Entertainment, Inc.
Lake Worth, Florida and New York, New York
www.beachbooks.co

Midnight Song

J. E. Laine

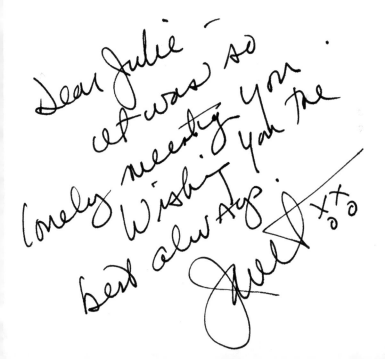

Dear Julie ~
It was so
lovely meeting you .
Wishing you the
best always .
Jxx
oo

The body was found huddled in a corner of the elevator, its eyes staring hysterically looking like a frightened child pleading for its mother.

At first it looked like the antique red walls had just been touched up with an animated modern enamel paint. But the double take that the scene commanded confirmed that newly splattered blood was dripping to the floor, and that the shiny charm peaking out of the shirt was the point of a knife.

chapter

ONE

The party was to be given by Claudia Banks, the classically beautiful heiress to the Chappel-Banks textile fortune. The occasion was to celebrate the success of a song about the splendor of women, a song that was titled "Claudia."

Everyone knew that the song was about this particular Claudia. Just the mention of the long blonde hair, fabulous blue eyes, her tantalizingly long legs, which were all legend, would not have been enough to point to only this Claudia. No, it was the line about the baby blue Lamborghini that gave it away.

It had been in the press all over the world. Claudia's father had had her eye color matched precisely. The car's paint, the leather seats and the lushly carpeted floors were Claudia's eyes, a blue so pale and mesmerizing that they were hard to look at while you were talking to her. Men would perspire at the realization of her eyes. Most were intimidated enough already by just who she was.

The party was going to be at her gracious home, a fourteen room Fifth Avenue co-op, which was the ideal setting for entertaining. But tonight she was attending another party.

Claudia, Evan and Marni arrived at the thousand dollar a plate dinner for the Environmental Society at the Edinborough Hotel dressed to the nines. Evan, the song's writer, was tall, tan and resplendent in a chocolate silk Italian loose fitting suit, which perfectly offset his seductive eyes and lush chestnut hair. Claudia and Marni were each wearing dresses by Larenge. Claudia's was a pale yellow strapless long liquid chiffon, and Marni's a spaghetti strapped to-the-knee pale rose organdy and chiffon flowy skirted A-line. All heads turned as they walked through the lobby.

Marni's lustrous dark mink brown hair, which had always been one of her most complimented features, was newly trimmed and shiny, falling ravishingly just below her shoulders, with her wispy bangs French cut unevenly dipping into her eyebrows, crowning her large almond eyes. Her long, thin still teenage-shaped body had always been easy for her to maintain, and she moved with an elegant grace.

At thirty-six, she had hit her stride as a deal maker in the record business and she completely, and unashamedly, enjoyed the many perks that came with her hard won success. Claudia had never had to work a day in her life. While Marni Kendell had toiled hard for so many years, she wasn't jealous of her best friend Claudia who, at thirty-five, was in her prime and always looked perfectly coiffed and rich. No, she couldn't envy a woman who had had to spend so much of her growing up in the public eye.

Claudia's family had been racked with scandals, really juicy scandals that Marni remembered hearing about when she was a teenager. Claudia's father, Jordan Alexander Banks, had become one of the wealthiest men in America. He was an impeccably dressed, fiercely handsome, well built virile man with thick black hair, manicured nails, and he was a womanizer. His stunning wife Tabatha was known for her exquisite taste, her closets full of to-die-from clothing from the couturier houses of Paris and her salon pampered long multi-platinum mane. When she and Jordan entered a room together, stares and flashbulbs followed their every move.

They were without a doubt one of the most striking couples in the society columns. The press never tired of wondering why in the world this handsome man, who seemed to have it all, could play with the feelings of the two women he clearly cherished the most, and with whom he was otherwise intensely protective. But he did, and these captivating women were photographed when the family vacationed together in the South of France, the Caribbean, Hong Kong, the Hamptons, and they were photographed when they were abandoned, however temporarily, by their scion of a patriarch.

"I wonder who she's seated us with this time?" Marni was referring to Carlotta Hindsberg, the wealthy multiple divorcee who never tired of organizing charity events for the New York moneyed crowd so that she could find herself another suitable husband.

"Ladies, if you'll pardon me, I will be delighted to register our presence with our hostess' assistants and get our place cards while the two of you scan the situation. Be right back." Evan made a grand gesture of a small bow, kissed Claudia's hand, and turned to walk towards the gala's reception desk.

"She's had her allotment of husbands for both of our lifetimes combined, Marni," Claudia said. "It's definitely our turn. We're long past due to find our prince charmings and, you never know, maybe this will be our lucky night."

"From the looks of you and Evan lately, my dear, it appears that I'm about to be the lone spinster among us, and the two of you will be my escorts for the rest of our lives."

"Now now, a beautiful, young and talented girl like you should be swooped up any minute now."

"Claudia, we've been saying that to each other for years. We're both so ridiculously picky. I swear, sometimes I think we'll be having this same conversation when we're seventy."

3

She gave her friend one of her 'I mean business' looks that never failed to crumble anyone's resolve at meetings.

"Okay, what do you want to ask me?"

"Claudia, we haven't spoken about this in awhile. But Evan's been seriously pursuing you for months now. If you don't make a decision soon, it's clearly going to break his heart, but he will give up."

"I know what you're saying, Marni. I know, I know. I just don't know what to do. Quite frankly, I haven't been able to get used to his suddenly thinking of me romantically. We've been warm friends, but I've never thought of him, you know, that way. And I don't know if I ever could."

"You know what they say, Claudia. Friendship is the most important part of a marriage. And he's handsome, rich, a sweetheart, fun, and he absolutely adores you. I wouldn't let him go that fast."

"The worst part is now that the song is such a success, and it's been all over the press that he wrote it about me, whatever we decide is going to be in front of the entire world. And this is such a personal decision. It's so embarrassing. But more than anything else, I just don't know, Marni. Sometimes I think..."

Marni gave Claudia a nudge when she saw Evan approaching them.

"Ladies, I'm sorry to break up your little tete a tete, but I have our place cards with our table number, and I would be honored to escort you into the grand ballroom." He linked arms with them.

As the great brass-handled twenty foot oak doors to the Governor's Ballroom were opened by gloved butlers, they heard Senator Delward making his closing remarks.

"So, ladies and gentlemen, I ask you to support..."

Evan grimaced and whispered, "I'm glad we didn't rush. I know he's a friend of your father's, Claudia, but he's such a painfully boring speaker."

"Please Evan," Claudia giggled. "Don't make me laugh. Of course you're right, but it's so rude to be rude, and it will definitely get back to my father. Let's just find our table."

The ornate room was decorated like a forest, an arboreal delight festooned with eucalyptus, hemlock, juniper, maple, magnolia, palm and oak trees, ferns, shrubs and flowers.

Each of the imposing trio was stopped and greeted a dozen times as they wove their ways past the already seated guests.

"Oh look. There's Matty." Claudia led them to their friend's table. Matty Fellstein dressed like a country bumpkin, albeit fashionably, for every occasion. Her book *Primal Evergreen*, about man's abuses to the environment, had been on The New York Times best seller list for almost a year. Her proficiency with money-raising, in dealing with potential investors, and her tie-in successes with celebrities were legend.

Evan was the first to hug her. "Bet you're doing a lot of business tonight, Matty. You certainly have a captive audience here."

"At least everyone here got a free copy of my book just for attending. If only half of them read it and send donations, I'll be thrilled. Have you seen Eric? As always, he has done a wonderful job of publicizing this event. We've just got to keep educating everybody about this issue."

Eric Stanton was the mercurially handsome publicity genius whose bi-coastal public relations firm had worked with every celebrity and every cause of national and international import.

"No," Claudia answered. "We haven't seen him yet, but I'm sure we will. Is Susan here?"

"She sure is. She wants to do a project with Eric and I, somehow involving her company. I'll let you know what we come up with."

Susan Bergman was a co-owner of Crown Jeans, a company that had held a position of prominence for so many years that their jeans were valued as the sign of ultimate American culture and style with the fashion conscious all over the globe.

As they approached table number three, Claudia motioned for Marni to catch up to her.

"There's somebody I want you to meet, Marni. He owns the Majestic Modeling Agency. You two should do business with each other. He's very successful and, as you can see, quite good looking. Come with me."

Before Marni had a chance to respond, Claudia said, "Bon soir, Henri. It's so nice to see you again." The gentleman she was speaking to pushed back his chair, stood up and shook Claudia's hand, then gave her a peck on each cheek.

"Claudia, how wonderful to see you. I didn't know you were a patron of the earth, although I should have guessed."

"But of course I am, Henri. And I know that you always like to meet brilliant and stunning women. A propos to that my dear, there's someone I'd like you to meet right now." She reached for her friend's hand and moved her next to Henri.

"Henri, I'd like you to meet Marni Kendell. Marni, this is Henri Beauvais."

"Miss Kendell. I am charmed to meet you. Your work in the record business is well known."

"As is your work with the most beautiful models in the world. I'm delighted to meet you too. Perhaps you'll have the chance to stop at our table."

"The pleasure would be mine."

"Please excuse us for now," Marni said as she permitted Henri to kiss her hand. "I'm famished."

The threesome finally found their table and exchanged looks between themselves that only long time friends understand. At the table for ten, there were already six other people, all obviously couples, and all B list people.

"Carlotta isn't being very generous with the single men or the VIPs tonight, is she?" Claudia was angry on Marni's behalf, and secretly for herself, at least until she decided how she felt about Evan.

"She knows we're her biggest competition. Isn't she something. Not even the pretense of courtesy. And she'll have quite an excuse, I'm sure, because she also wants to stay on your good side. But Claudia, it doesn't matter. This is a worthy cause. Let's just make the best of it."

"I'm with the both of you tonight, my two luscious creatures." Evan's dimples were in full regalia. "Neither of you need the attentions of other men." The women returned the compliments.

"Marni," Claudia changed the subject. "You were awfully abrupt with Henri."

"Look, my dear friends. Henri seems like a lovely man and we could potentially do business together. And I thank you for trying to make this a double date. But let's just enjoy the night and see what happens naturally."

The salmon fillet appetizers were served.

Evan tickled the bottom of Claudia's back and looked adoringly into her eyes. "My dear Claudia. Marni will find someone. Look how long it's taking for us to make any progress. Obviously, these things can't be rushed."

"Evan, I'm sorry, but I..." Claudia signaled a quick SOS to Marni which Evan caught.

"It's okay, Claudia. Marni, do you know how I realized that I was in love with Claudia?"

Marni sat there, speechless, as she saw her friend's face pale. This was Claudia's moment, and all she could do was see how her friend wanted to handle it.

Claudia simply looked at the two of them, her great eyelashes soaring from their follicles, and then put her arms around Evan's neck. "Evan, you are an exasperating man. How in the world am I supposed to keep up with you?"

"This is really embarrassing, you two. I'm leaving." Marni pretended to get up.

"No you don't," insisted Claudia. "You have to protect me from my friend who has turned into a Romeo."

"You haven't seen anything yet, Claudia. Marni, let me ask you something. Why would a woman as beautiful and intelligent as Claudia even try to resist a man like me?"

"Oh no you're not. You're not putting me in the middle of this."

As the appetizers were cleared from the table, the orchestra started to play "Claudia" and the crowd stood to applaud the famed songwriter and his vision of the perfect woman.

"Let's give them a thrill, shall we?" Evan said as he reached for Claudia's hand. "May I have this dance?"

"Of course you can, silly. But when we come back, we all have to talk about the party I'm throwing for you, Mr. Hit Maker. There are still so many details. Marni, we'll be back soon."

A few moments after Evan and Claudia left for the dance floor, Marni felt a tap on her shoulder. She shuddered at the sudden physical intrusion and turned abruptly to see who it was.

"Excuse me, ma'am. But would you care for some wine?"

Before she could stop shaking enough to respond, she saw Henri motioning to her from the dance floor. She extended her hand to him, and let the chill she felt melt into the music.

chapter

TWO

With only two more weeks until Claudia's party, she and Marni spent hours going over lists of names to make sure they hadn't left anyone out. The invitations had been mailed weeks ago, but they kept coming up with people that they didn't want to exclude.

Mostly they wanted to make sure that the three guests of honor were properly feted. Of course Evan, the creator of the hit song they were celebrating, was the evening's number one man. The hit record was performed by the second honoree, Trace, the internationally adored recording artist signed to Marni's management company. The third beneficiary of the kudos was Hal Kinsberg, the owner of both Motion Records, the company that released the hit single, and the publishing company that Evan Strang was signed to. Between the three roastees and their coterie, they could already fill a small hall. But of course there were to be dozens more.

They went over the menu with Tommy Laten, the caterer, who thought of himself, and rightly so, as the Caterer to the New York Stars. They met with the florist. Everything was going perfectly and on schedule.

Claudia and Marni were to meet for an early dinner at L'Etoile to again determine that they had covered everything. After all, they were celebrating Claudia's song, written by one of her friends, and, seemingly, her potential husband. She intended this to be her best party ever. And if anyone was capable of throwing the party of the year, it was Claudia.

By 2:30 in the afternoon Marni had finished reviewing her notes on the script for the new Argon Film "Wake Up," which was to star the box office rage Pamela Baker. The film's music director wanted Trace to perform the soundtrack music and to make a cameo appearance, his first role in a major motion picture.

Because of Marni's persistent management style, her long held contacts and impeccable reputation in the music business, she had succeeded in getting Trace some of the sweetest deals in entertainment. But everybody, the industry and fans alike, knew that Trace deserved every bit of the money and renown that he now had. When she first heard his demo tape and saw him perform live, Marni knew that his vocal style pulled her heartstrings the way her older brother's 45's from the 50's did.

She loved doo-wop music, the girl groups, every A minor chord change. With this artist, she had finally been able to put at least a hint of the 50's into the contemporary music psyche. Trace's music was the most soulful, heartfelt, free and fun music she had heard in years, and, over the last two years, he had become one of the most popular recording and performing artists in the world.

Admittedly, the enormous amount of money that she earned with Trace was reason enough to have pushed him as hard as she had. But perhaps the truly big thrill came from knowing that she had played a part in bringing a generation musically full circle so that they could relive the passions they had when their teenage feelings of love were new and pure. And, she knew just as well, that she had helped make a new generation aware of this very special kind of music. So much of contemporary music was so angry.

Her thoughts were interrupted when the phone rang. Of course it was Claudia, and probably with a new list of pre-party plans for them to go over.

"Marni, can you meet me earlier than 6:30? I'm frantic."

"Claudia, relax. If there are any details that we've left out, they can't really be important. Your party is going to be wonderful."

"No, that's not it, Marni. I have to talk to you about Evan."

"What is it? Did he propose?"

"I almost would rather that were the case. Marni, we had planned several days ago to have lunch today. Usually he checks with me the night before, or that morning, when we have a lunch date. But he didn't do that this time. Every time I called him, his voice mail picked up. Well, that's not that unusual. But it is odd that he just met me at the restaurant without confirming first."

"I'm not sure I understand what the big deal is, Claudia."

"Let me finish. We met at Grenadines, his favorite. He acted strangely. Oh. I don't know what the right word is. He just kept glancing away from me. He was very quiet. I asked him if he was feeling ill, and he insisted he was fine. But he wasn't his usual warm, funny, kissy self. Actually, he was quite fidgety. We ordered. When the food was served he said, 'Claudia, I'm sorry. You're right. I really don't feel very well. I'll call you tomorrow.' And he left the restaurant."

"So Claudia, he didn't feel well. That sounds pretty typical of how people act when they simply don't feel well. Maybe he had a fever. Why are you so upset?"

"It's just not like him. I've known him, how many years? I've seen him sick before. He was never off-putting like this."

"Well, Claudia. He's also never been in love like this. Maybe he was going to break off with you. Maybe he was going to tell you that he gives up. And maybe that thought made him ill."

"All right. I suppose I would just let it pass if something like this had only happened today. But, actually, the last few times we've had plans, he's been...not unfriendly, but chilly towards me. Even when we were 'just friends,' he'd hold my hand when we crossed a street. He seems suddenly so...so deep in thought all the time. Really uncharacteristically introspective. Something is eating at him, and I don't have any idea what it is. I hope he's not in trouble of any kind."

"What even makes you think that?"

"Oh, I don't know. He knows a lot of high rollers. I don't mean that he's a gambler. You know he's not, as well as I do. But maybe he got involved in a bad investment with bad people."

"I think you're reading into it too much, Claudia. And I still think it's that he's simply trying to resolve his feelings for you."

"I hope you're right, but honestly, I don't think so. Today was...too strange. He's never been shy about discussing anything with me. And if it was just about us, I don't think he'd hold back saying anything that was on his mind, be it good or bad."

"Claudia, he might be trying to make *you* think that his feelings have changed so you'd wonder what's going on. Did you ever think of that? And if that's what he's trying to do, I'd say it's working."

"No. That never occurred to me. Let me think about that for awhile."

"So, what else is new?"

"If I make one more list for this party, I'm going to scream."

"Claudia, you are known around the world for your glorious parties. And it's because you pay so much attention to detail. So, scream if you must, but remember. He who raises a voice wants to be heard."

"Well, that was deep. Who in the world said that? And what made you think of that now?"

"That's from a poem by Gaston. Mortimer Gaston. Fifteenth century. I think you have feelings about Evan that you're not admitting, even to yourself."

"All right, Marni. Enough from you right now. I'll see you at 6:30. And thanks for raising my spirits. You're a wonderful friend."

"One more thing, Claudia."

"What?"

"Is this an A or a B outfit dinner we're having tonight?"

"Let's do B's, Marni. We've been wearing too many A outfits lately. We need to relax a little."

"Right. I'm with you there. See you soon."

FRIDAY

chapter

THREE

Jordan Alexander Banks sat in his wood paneled office on the 43rd floor, the top floor, of the Tanser Building that he and his father had purchased from the bankrupt family three decades ago. His spacious office was windowed on two sides and gave him a panoramic view of Central Park.

His secretary, Sarah Leber, who had been with him for twenty-three years, had just left for lunch. He had asked her to have his calls held by her young new assistant Julia.

Jordan took the note out of the envelope and read it for the third time. He could feel his muscles stiffen and the pulse in his temple pound on his head. This was not the first time that he had received threatening mail or letters pleading for money. A man in his position expected to hear from crazies on occasion. After all, his picture was in the society and business columns regularly, and his philanthropic contributions were known all over the world. Everybody knew that he was filthy rich. But this was the first time that he could not make any sense out of a message in one of these letters.

> I have information on you.
> It's about the biggest deal of your life.
> I think it should be worth about a mill
> but I'll let you have it for half a mill.
> I'll contact you again soon for the details.
> But remember, you can't own everything that you buy.

The letter was handwritten, so the police would be able to do a handwriting analysis. Maybe there were fingerprints, so he purposefully touched only the corners.

He carefully folded it again using the creases that were already there, slipped it back into the envelope and returned it to his locked desk drawer.

After a man threatened his life years ago in an attempt to get $150,000.00, Banks had taken advantage of his political connections and was assigned a personal detective through the local precinct's Special Investigations Department. He'd given their Detective Colter dozens of letters over the years. The investigator had easily tracked down all of the writers through their PO boxes, addresses, fingerprints or handwriting. Only two of them turned out to be a potentially dangerous kook with a record. The rest were just trying to get something for nothing.

Jordan Banks knew what poverty felt like and smelled like, and he remembered the night that changed his life. Sometimes it seemed like only yesterday that he was sitting with his parents, Frederick and Hannah, on the lower East Side listening to them argue about the only things that ever made them upset and raise their voices: money and guilt. More than anything else in the world, his parents wanted to be able to give him the best, send him to good schools, raise him in a nice home, and leave him a business that he could pass on to his sons. But no matter how hard his father tried, he couldn't expand his business.

Mama Hannah would tell Frederick not to worry so much, that they could do just fine with what they had. She hated their tiny two bedroom railroad apartment as much as he did, but she always managed to feel thankful for their blessings. She could ignore the filth on the streets, the noisy crowded neighborhood and create wonderful meals on her small budget. And she spent every extra penny for her Jordan.

Then came the nights that his father wouldn't come home until long after Jordan was put to bed. Some nights Jordan would hear him bumping into furniture. He had never before experienced such a feeling of gloom and foreboding.

Late one evening, when his agitating dreams wouldn't let him sleep, Jordan saw his mother sitting alone in the armchair in the living room. She was pretending to read the newspaper, but she was really crying. For the first time in his life, Jordan was truly frightened.

Just then the old grandfather clock chimed ten on the hour and, as if on cue, the door opened and in stumbled Frederick, who attempted to sober himself when he saw his son.

"You should have been in bed by now, young man."

"Are you sick, Papa?"

"I promised my father that we would have a wonderful life here in America, and that I would carry on the family name with pride and success and riches. I was so sure that I would do better than he did. Oh Hannah, I was so sure."

"Oh my dear Freddy," Mama said to him as she pulled herself wearily from her chair and cradled her husband. "We came to America with nothing and you started a business that puts food on our table and has given us a nice enough home."

"But Hannah, I must keep my promise. I must..."

From that moment on, Jordan realized that he was not going to get all of life's answers from within these walls. And so he watched everything around him to find the secret to avoiding the sadness that he saw in his father.

The day he turned ten, Jordan made an announcement to his parents. He told them that he would one day be rich and that he would take care of them and his own new family. His parents looked at him and at each other with pain and adoration in their faces.

"That's wonderful, son," his father said. "I know you can always do anything you want to do. But you really mustn't pressure yourself this much. You will do in business what you will do, and I am sure you will one day meet a young woman and marry and give us grandchildren."

He heard his Papa tell Mama that he would never forgive himself for burdening his son with his own problems. That he wished he could erase the night he drank and said too much.

But as the years went on, they marveled at Jordan's ingenuity. By the time he was fifteen, it was clear that Jordan Banchleman was driven. He already had proved himself to be a very clever and enterprising young man with his newspaper delivery routes and the help he gave to his father's friends in their stores and businesses.

The teenaged Jordan liked to spend his free time uptown, where all the wealthy people lived, took their strolls, went to the theater and to dinner so that he could watch the way they dressed and acted. He was taken by the quality and design of their clothing. Mostly he noticed that they didn't seem to have a care in the world. He promised himself that he was going to be one of them some day.

He convinced his father to let him take several dozen silk flowers, feathers and little ornaments he was selling from his shop so that he could personally present them to the owners of the expensive apparel stores.

Jordan would dress in his only suit, polish his shoes and put the samples in the brown leather case that his mother had brought here from Europe. Introducing himself as Jordan Alexander Banks, he talked his way in to the buyers' offices, sold to them and found out who else they were buying from. He soon expanded his sales calls to manufacturers, and within ten months the newly named Banks and Son had become one of the primary suppliers of hat and clothing accessories and ornamentation. Within two years they owned a small building that housed their manufacturing plant and showrooms, and they renamed the company Chappel-Banks so that they could honor also Mama's family.

When he was twenty, Jordan was having lunch with one of his clients at The Plaza when he saw the most beautiful girl he had ever seen. She was sitting just a few tables away having lunch with a woman he assumed was her mother.

"Tabatha," he heard the woman say. "You must finish schooling in Europe. It is what all the fine young ladies do today. Just one year. That's all I ask of you. And when you come home, you will be old enough to think about a husband. Right now, you are just a little bit too young, my dear."

"But mother," Jordan heard the young girl say. "I'm in love with Jeffrey. I'm seventeen now and that's old enough to know what I want."

As Jordan watched this auburn haired beauty with her enormous green eyes and her steady delicate voice, he knew that he was looking at the girl who would be his wife.

Since his success he had been out with some of the prettiest, wealthiest and most exciting girls his age. He had moved his parents up-town into a fine two bedroom apartment in a building with a doorman a few blocks from his own three bedroom home. They had all adjusted easily to a life of many luxuries.

He knew that this young girl was spoiled. But there was something about her look, about her childish insistence, about the glow of her cheeks that made him excuse himself from his client and walk over to their table.

"Pardon me, ladies. I couldn't help but overhear your conversation, and I thought that perhaps I could be of some assistance."

They both looked at him with wonder, and certainly had they not been at The Plaza, the women might have told the intruder to simply leave them alone. But they were both taken by the man's charm and striking good looks.

Tabatha looked in to his eyes, delightedly realizing that his attentions were on her. But her mother, while clearly amused, quickly interrupted the spell. She wanted to know immediately who this young man was, what he could possibly want, and insisted as always that her daughter understand that one must be careful when speaking to strangers, especially strange men.

"Please introduce yourself, and tell us what you would like to say, young man."

"My name is Jordan Alexander Banks, of the Chappel-Banks Company." He could see that the mother was instantly impressed and attentive, and so he continued easily.

"It is probably impolite of me to intrude, but I have never seen a girl as lovely as you, Tabatha. And I am certain that the love you have for Jeffrey must certainly seem real. But if you will go to Europe as your mother says, well then, if your mother allows it, I will take you to lunch when you return."

When Tabatha looked into Jordan's eyes, she knew, too, that this is what was meant by love at first sight. She looked at her mother, and then again at Jordan and said, "This might be the most childish or the most grown-up decision I've ever made. I suppose I won't know its certainty until I return. But...yes, mother, I will go to Europe for a year. And yes, Jordan, I would be happy to have lunch with you when I return."

Jordan gave them each his business card, a small bow, and explained that he had to return to his business luncheon. They asked him to join them in the sitting room after his meeting and he politely accepted their invitation.

By the time Tabatha was half-way into the two months of preparation for her trip to Europe, both families knew that there would never be a reason for Jordan and Tabatha to be far away from each other. They were married fifteen months later in what was one of New York's most talked about events of the season.

Jordan always had to have the best. They bought a wonderful townhouse on East 68th Street between Fifth and Madison Avenues. For the first year their families waited excitedly for the announcement that a baby was on its way. But Jordan had to spend a lot of time in Europe with his clients, so they postponed their hopes for the next year. During the following two years he insisted that Tabatha join him on most of his trips abroad, and so they sailed back and forth on the Queen Elizabeth in the ship's most luxurious stateroom, staying away for months at a time.

While they dazzled European society and made many friends in England and France, Jordan was never far from the inner panic that he felt. He knew that he would never be totally happy until he fulfilled the promises that he had made to himself and to his family.

How the time goes by so fast, he thought to himself. They had loved his choice of Tabatha as a wife, and they were smitten by their darling granddaughter Claudia.

After his father retired, Jordan continued to expand the business to reach every major city in the world. He supplied the top clothing designers with high fashioned ornamentation and accessories. His parents had been proud of his successes, well, most of them anyway. Jordan and Tabatha had a weekend house in Great Neck, Long Island. He had bought a summer cottage for his parents there too. The Banks family had earned all of the comforts and extravagances they had dreamed of. At least, he thought, his parents died knowing that their ten year old had been right, and confident that the Banks' fortune and name would be passed on to other generations. They couldn't have known that Jordan would never have a son.

Only he and Tabatha knew how hard it had all been. And now there was a song for their beautiful Claudia. He looked at his watch. Her party was tonight, and he wanted to be in a happy mood for her.

Just then the buzzer on his desk rang.

"Yes, Sarah."

'No sir. This is Julia. Sarah is out to lunch. I'm just calling to remind you that you are supposed to meet Mr. Taylor and Mr. Lawrence in the executive dining room in five minutes."

"Thank you Julia. Please arrange my mail for Sarah to go through. But if I should get hand delivered envelopes or packages, or special delivery or certified letters, hold them unopened for me. And tell Sarah to do the same."

By the time he arrived in the executive dining room, his two senior vice presidents were already seated at his table.

Within seconds the head waiter was handing him the day's menu. "Can I get you a drink before lunch today, Mr. Banks?"

The Chappel-Banks executive dining room was run like a very exclusive and expensive small restaurant. The top company men usually ate there, as did the managing directors from companies around the world who did business with Chappel-Banks. It was convenient and tasteful. Tabatha had overseen its decor and menu with the help of her famous decorating friends and chefs. She often ate here with friends, as did Claudia.

"Yes, thank you Thomas. I'll have a bubbly water." He turned to the others. "Gentlemen, please order what you would like."

Thomas took their orders and left them to discuss their business. As Warner, the assistant waiter, placed their drinks on the table, Thomas handed them their menus that always contained a beef, fish, chicken, salad and pasta dish.

"Our special today is smoked lobster with artichoke hearts, Mr. Banks. If there is anything special we can make for you, please let me know."

They placed their orders and exchanged the usual pre-meal pleasantries. As they finished their drinks and began discussing their primary reason for this meeting, the entrees were served.

"Thank you, Warner. Please bring our salads in a few minutes."

"Yes, sir." Warner knew that Mr. Banks liked to be served his salad just as he was finishing his main course.

Jordan addressed his executives. "Gentlemen, I am delighted with the progress of our new Miska line. I must hand it to you. I wasn't sure if Europe would like this design. I thought that we could start a new division for accessories of this sort. What do you say?"

As he spoke to his vice presidents, one phrase kept going through his mind. 'You can't own everything that you buy.'

Who the hell could have sent him a note with such threatening, confusing undertones. Most letters that he received mysteriously like this fit one of only several patterns. There was the 'give me money or else' letter, the 'we are honest hard working people, and if you could just send us $5,000 we could' whatever, and the 'I promise I'll pay you back' version. He'd heard it all. But this letter did not fit into any of those patterns.

By the time he returned to his office, Jordan was in turmoil. He had managed his business and personal lives so carefully and thoroughly. The thought of an outsider distracting or interfering with his hard work was infuriating. He tried to calm himself by remembering that this was just the game of a deranged mind.

He had been so cautious and discreet in covering every possible loophole. There was nothing untoward anyone could ever find. He had important decisions to make for his company over the next few weeks, and he didn't need to be sidetracked by a sicko.

He wanted this out of his mind for Claudia's party tonight and it was already 3:15. He wasn't in the mood for the questioning and the tension, but he finally decided that if he called in Detective Colter, he would probably feel a lot better.

chapter

FOUR

"Detective Colter here."

"Colter. This is Jordan Banks. I've gotten another letter, and this one is really strange. I can't figure out what the man is trying to say."

"I'll be over in a little while, Mr. Banks. Don't worry. We'll take care of it for you. What does it say?"

"You've taught me well about fingerprints, so I don't want to touch it again. I just keep remembering one line, though. 'You can't own everything that you buy.' I'll be honest with you Colter. This one has really made me feel uncomfortable." He couldn't hide the strain in his voice.

"Okay, take it easy. Will you be there in half an hour?"

"I'll make sure that I am. See you then."

Within twenty minutes Detective Lenny Colter was in Jordan Banks' office. With his thick dirty blond hair that constantly fell on his brow, blue eyes, tan pants, plaid shirt, blazer and loafers, he looked and dressed like an ivy leaguer, but he wasn't one.

Colter put on plastic gloves and put the envelope in a protective bag. He studied the handwriting and the return address through the clear glassine. He slid the note out. There were six lines, neatly written and with a period at the end of each sentence. There was something sinister about the left-leaning scrawl, and the double line exing the 'x' in 'Alexander.' He decided not to mention those thoughts for the time being.

He took a seat usually reserved for the prosperous Chappel-Banks clients and the glitterati, a cushy oversized high-backed chair, upholstered in deep blue leather, directly across from Jordan's desk.

"Had any problems with clients or employees lately, Mr. Banks? I know we've been through this kind of questioning before, but it's either someone near you or a total stranger in the public who wants to see you squirm for some unfathomable reason."

Sitting behind his desk turning his Mont Blanc pen through his fingers, as if that could some how soothe him, Banks stared at Colter hopelessly.

"Not a thing, Colter. I've been going through every possibility and I can't come up with anything at all."

"Well, I'm gonna run this by the lab and have a few of our boys study it. I'll call you when we have something. It's probably just a nut, but we'll get to the bottom of it."

"Do me a favor. Can you have your lab men make a photocopy of the note so that I can look at it again? Maybe something will click."

"Sure, Mr. Banks. We can fax it over to you by around 6:00, 6:30. We'll call you first so that you can make sure that you're at the fax to receive it. By then probably everyone in your office will have gone home, and we wouldn't want anyone else seeing it at this stage."

Colter got up and walked around the room. "On second thought, I better have someone hand deliver it to you. I don't want to take any chances."

Jordan looked at the Cartier clock on his desk. It was 4 o'clock already. He had wanted to go home no later than five so that he could relax for a little while with Tabatha before he changed his clothes for Claudia's party.

The men shook hands. As Colter was about to open the office door he turned back towards Jordan.

"I'm sure I don't have to say this, Mr. Banks. But I wouldn't say anything about this note to anyone, not even to Mrs. Banks."

Jordan gave his assurances. He had to call Tabatha and tell her that he'd either meet her at home later than they had planned, or he would meet her at Claudia's.

With two hours to wait for the copy of the note to arrive, Jordan occupied himself with paper work, interrupted only by the phone calls that Sarah buzzed in to him.

Good, reliable, trustworthy, hardworking, gray hair bunned, homely looking Sarah, he thought. He was able to run his company smoothly because of her efficiency, and he knew that. When his first secretary left the company twenty-four years ago to care for her family, he had determined to at last hire a secretary who was both professional and good looking. But Tabatha would not allow it. She was confident when they were together within their international circles of friends, but she knew how her husband conducted himself when he traveled alone. And she would absolutely not tolerate him having a great looking secretary in his midst all day.

In truth, it had been many years since his sex life with Tabatha had been anywhere as lustful and loving as it had been in their early years together. When they were first married, he made love to her every day, and sometimes several times a day. He adored her, and her elegant feline beauty had mesmerized him from the first time he had seen her having lunch with her mother at The Plaza.

But after their first year together, when she hadn't gotten pregnant, he had begun to get angry at her and annoyed with himself. Between the business, their parents always winking at them about babies and their social calendar, he thought that perhaps there were too many pressures in the city. He had felt certain that spending a lot of time in Europe together would relax them both.

Just then the buzzer on his desk switched off the day dream. He hoped it was Detective Colter with some news. He really wanted to get home and had promised his daughter that he would arrive at her party early.

"Yes, Sarah."

"Mr. Banks, I just want to let you know that Julia and I are leaving now. You did not receive any new mail this afternoon. Just the interoffice memos that I brought in to your office earlier. I'll have your calls switched to the evening receptionist. Is there anything else?"

"Thank you, Sarah. That will be fine. Enjoy your weekend. I'll see you Monday morning."

"Enjoy your weekend, too. Good night, Mr. Banks."

Jordan pushed the button that would automatically call Tabatha. He prepared himself for her disappointment concerning his change of plans. She had been so proud of the song written about Claudia, and had wanted them to arrive early to help her greet her guests. And, of course, she had wanted to recommend different wardrobes for him for this night, as she often did. Tonight she wanted them to look their youngest and most vital.

"Jordan, I'm sure your meeting can wait until Monday. This is Friday night. How could you have a meeting scheduled this late, dear? After all, it's your company. You really should be able to schedule things your way."

He knew that he couldn't tell her about the note. It would upset her unnecessarily, especially since it's mystery would probably be solved within a week.

"I know Tab. And, of course, you're right. But I promise that this meeting is unavoidable. You know that I have also been anxious for us to have some time together, and to get to Claudia's early. Why don't I phone you as soon as it's over and we'll see what time it is then. If I have to meet you at Claudia's, I'm sorry, but I am sure the evening will be a big success for her, and you, no matter what."

"All right, Jordan. If this is how it must be, then that's that. I'll probably leave here by six to arrive at Claudia's by six thirty or so. If you're not home by then, I'll just leave and see you there. Have a good meeting." And she hung up.

Jordan could tell from her tone that she didn't at all think he had a business meeting planned. Heaven knows what she thought, and how often she had been right. But this time, he was truly protecting her, and he couldn't tell her the truth.

It had been a long time since she trusted him, and for good reason as he well knew. At the beginning of their marriage he had had every intention of being true to her. But, for as fortunate as they had been, their lives had been filled with far too many frustrations. And, as controlled as he usually was, there were times when he just couldn't subvert his demons. Yes, he usually tried to be discreet, but he was often found out by the press. Tabatha and Claudia always bore the brunt of it, and for that he was truly sorry. But he couldn't help himself. Sometimes things just ate at him.

It was 5 o'clock. He really had no more pressing work to do, it was far too late to call Europe, and Sarah and Julia had already left so he couldn't dictate a few letters. He dialed extension 547.

"Karen Gladstone."

"Miss Gladstone. This is Jordan Banks. How lucky I am that you haven't left yet. I wonder if you could bring in today's computer printout from Les Champs."

"Of course, Mr. Banks. I have to return a few calls right now. Would about ten minutes be all right?"

"That would be fine, Miss Gladstone. I'll see you then."

He had used their code. When he said he wanted this week's printout, it meant that he had a lot of time. Today's printout meant that his time was limited.

For many years, Jordan had managed to have at least one woman on his staff who understood his needs. Karen had been with them for eight years now, and she had become a widow two years ago. She didn't think that she would ever want to get married again, or if she was even emotionally ready to seriously date. But she was a woman, and she had desires that were left unfulfilled.

Jordan had been exceptionally kind to her when she lost her husband. He had attended the funeral and had sent beautiful flowers to her home weekly during the two months that she could not bring herself to go to work. When she returned to the job he had held for her, he had taken her to lunches and dinners. Conversations between them were comfortable and animated, and the sexual feelings between them were evident. She welcomed their easy undemanding relationship.

Jordan turned on the television to the news.

When he heard the four knocks, he jumped to his feet and opened the door. Karen walked in, dutifully holding the Les Champs printout for today, fulfilling the meeting's stated purpose just in case someone had overheard them on the phone and followed her down the hall. Her rust layer cut wavy hair highlighted the most enormous sea green eyes he had ever seen, and her olive short jacketed skirt suit allowed her long legs their full display.

"Here are the printouts, Mr. Banks." Karen used her most professional demeanor and tone of voice, until Jordan closed and locked the door behind her. Once safely inside the room, she carefully put the stack of papers on his desk, took his hand and led him to the couch.

Without either of them saying a word, she put his hand on her breast, moved her arms around his neck and kissed him. They kissed for a long time, and held on to each other as if they were life savers that they were each clinging to.

"This is a nice surprise, Jordan. It's so rare that we can see each other on a Friday evening."

"I know, Karen, but I don't have much time. To be truthful, I'm waiting for a letter to be delivered between 6:00 and 6:30, and then I'll have to leave right away. Claudia's having a party tonight for the people involved in the song that was written about her. I'm sorry that our time will have to be so limited."

"Well, then, let's just make the best of it," she whispered, as her hand moved down his body to just below his belt and she rubbed him there until she felt him getting hard in her hand as he moaned with pleasure.

She took off her jacket and he pulled her silk tee shirt over her head. He rubbed her large firm breasts over her bra as he kissed her lips. As he moved his hands around her back to unhook her bra, his kisses made a warm and wet path down her neck and to her breast, sucking each nipple until she whimpered for him.

Within seconds, they both had their clothing off and they lay on the floor facing each other.

Their hands searched each other's bodies as if they had all the time in the world. But they knew each other's rhythms so well, and they knew how it had to be when they only had a short time together. She kissed him from his head to his feet, and then up again until she had his throbbing penis in her mouth. He groaned and writhed, lifting himself to her.

And then he held her shoulders and laid her back on the floor and kissed her from her head to her feet, and then up again until he reached the center of her spreading legs and he kissed her there. And then he put himself in her and they rolled back and forth on the floor together until he was on top of her and he pushed and pulled himself in and out of her until they both collapsed into each other's arms.

"Sometimes I don't know what I would do without knowing you were here, Karen." Jordan spoke to her as he let his hands roam over her body that was now so calm.

"And I definitely don't know what I would do without you, Jordan. If it wasn't for you, I would feel like I was living in a convent. And I'm too young for that. I am thankful for you every day. We better get dressed now. It's ten of six."

As soon as they had their clothing on, the buzzer on Jordan's desk blasted into the room through their sweet serenity. He pushed the intercom button.

"Yes. Can I help you? Yes, this is Jordan Banks...yes, send him right to my office. Thank you."

He turned to Karen and they kissed each other lightly.

"I'm sorry that we have to say goodnight so abruptly Karen. I'm truly sorry."

"We both knew it would always be this way, Jordan. And the day that it's not okay, we'll stop seeing each other. But in the meantime, I'll just say goodnight, Jordan. Until next time." And then she was gone.

Within a few minutes there was a knock on the door.

"Who is it?"

"It's Colter."

Jordan opened the door and Colter walked in with a manila envelope and a two foot long Kraft paper wrapped cylinder under his arm.

"We made you the copy, Mr. Banks. And then the lab men made enlargements for themselves. When I saw what was on them, I had them make one for you, too."

As he said this, he took the letter sized copy of the note out of the manila envelope and put it on one edge of Jordan's desk.

"Can you clear the top of your desk for me, Mr. Banks. We're gonna need some room for this."

As Jordan moved aside his Cartier clock, Mont Blanc pens and pencils, the silver frames holding the pictures of his family and a few files, Colter took the paper off the cylinder and spread the map-sized copy of the letter over the middle of the desk.

There it was. The source of Jordan's afternoon nightmare. He didn't even bother to look at the smaller copy. The enlarged version made the whole thing more ominous and frightening. And suddenly he knew why. Something was different.

"What is it Colter? It looks different now."

"Look at this," Colter said as he pointed to what had, in the smaller copy that Jordan had received, seemed like either someone had tested a pen or smudged a dot on each of the lower corners of the page.

Jordan bent over the paper, and there were the words "tell her" on the bottom left corner, and the numbers 16659 on the bottom right corner, that he hadn't realized were there before. How could he have missed that? And what could it mean?

"Does this mean anything to you, Mr. Banks?"

Jordan stood there, a stunned look on his face. There were those lines of words again. And now, if he added the words and numbers that had just been discovered by enlarging the note, it still didn't make sense. Or did it? He read it again before he said anything.

"I'm not sure what it means, Colter, but I can guess. It hasn't exactly been a secret that I have had my share of affairs, as you know. It sounds like somebody wants me to admit to my wife what she, and everybody else, already knows."

"That's what I thought too, at first. But what about the numbers? It's not any of your phone numbers, or a part of any of your addresses or any other numbers that we know are connected to you. Could it be part of the phone number of somebody you've been seeing, or some kind of secret message they're trying to send you?"

"It's not something that I recognize. There uh...there've been a few, Colter."

"I know, Mr. Banks. My wife reads all the society columns and the gossip magazines, and she always shows them to me when you're in them. Especially, if I may be so personal, when you're not with Mrs. Banks."

"I don't think it would do us, or this investigation, any good for us to feel embarrassed speaking about this subject. I've obviously gotten myself into some kind of mess, and it seems that it's because I've been so..." He couldn't think of the words to say what he meant. At this moment, he didn't know what he meant.

"Where would you have those phone numbers, Mr. Banks? I think it's best that we check them out as soon as possible. I don't mean to alarm you, and probably there is no reason for alarm. But we want to make sure that we've covered everything, and that there are no dangerous people involved in this."

"I can tell you with absolute confidence that nobody that I have ever been involved with is even remotely connected to anyone that you or I would consider dangerous."

"You're probably right, Mr. Banks. But we're the police, and we have to do everything that we can to be absolutely sure. Where would those numbers be?"

"I'd have to look in my rolodexes and computer. They're right here. My God, I don't know where to start."

"Start from your most recent affairs, Mr. Banks, and work your way back. It will be easier if you make a list of the names, and then write down any numbers connected to them. Home and office phone numbers, fax, email, summer homes, hotels you stayed in together, any clubs they belong to. I know you're not going to have all that, but whatever you do have could be a potential lead for us. And of course business situations too."

"This will take more than all night, Colter, and I don't have all night. My daughter is having a party tonight, and I was supposed to be home changing two hours ago. I should be at her apartment now. I can't do this tonight."

"I understand. Really I do. Listen. Give me just an hour or so now so we can have something to work on, then we can deal with this some more tomorrow."

Jordan knew that he had to stay for awhile. What if there really was a nut involved? He had to do this for his family.

"All right. Let me call my wife." He called his home and the butler told him that Mrs. Banks had already left. He hung up the phone and looked at the detective.

"Damn. Tonight was going to be a wonderful family night. Damn it. And I can't even allay her suspicions with anything remotely resembling the truth."

"Not this time, Mr. Banks." He thought of asking why this time should be that different from most other times when he'd had to lie to her, but he didn't say that. Instead he said, "It still could be a wonderful family night, Mr. Banks. Just give me something to start working on. I'll call you here tomorrow, late morning."

chapter

FIVE

How could he have an affair on the night of Claudia's party? He was not usually this reckless with his indiscretions. And why was she so forgiving, Tabatha wondered. Perhaps, deep inside, she knew that she knew him too well. Then again, maybe, just maybe, he was telling the truth this time.

"Mrs. Wilkens. Would you please fix me a pot of tea with..."

Then she remembered. Mrs. Wilkens was already at Claudia's helping with the final preparations for the party. Dear Mrs. Wilkens, she thought. She had been with the family for thirty-two years now. My, how time has sped by. Mrs. Wilkens had initially worked for the Banks five, sometimes six days a week as a housekeeper but, over time, she had become an invaluable aide to Claudia's ever changing nannies. She had grown deeply attached to little Claudia and would have been the perfect help to Tabatha if only she could have lived with them in those years. But of course, she had a husband and children of her own that she had to be home for.

Just then a voice bellowed from downstairs.

"Mrs. Banks. I would be happy to prepare your tea for you. Mrs. Wilkens has already left for Claudia's." It was Albert, the butler, assistant chef, driver and all-around house helper.

"Thank you, Albert. I've changed my mind. There will be plenty to eat at the party."

"Well then. Let me know when you're ready to leave and I'll bring the car around."

"Thank you, Albert. I'll be leaving here before six."

Tabatha wished that Mrs. Wilkens was with her right now. Over the years she had become an integral part of the family and like a second mother to Tabatha. She certainly knew more of the family's secrets than any other person and, those she didn't know, she seemed always to sense. Tabatha needed her warmth and understanding now. More than her own mother ever had, Mrs. Wilkens often held Tabatha in her arms and let her cry like a baby.

The Wilkens were fiercely loyal and devoted to the Banks, and their children and Claudia were like cousins. After all, they had known each other practically all of their lives. Just a few years after Mrs. Wilkens' children Kyle, Roger and Polly became teenagers, her husband died suddenly. Jordan had helped her with their doctor bills, the children's schooling and had sent them on several family vacations. When the children moved out on their own, the Banks had insisted that she live in the main suite in the servants' wing, and her children visited with her often.

Polly was happily married now, and lived with her husband and their two small children in New Jersey. Both Kyle and Roger worked for the State, and Mrs. Wilkens found comfort in the secure medical and retirement benefits that their jobs guaranteed. Even with their busy schedules, the boys' attachment to their mother and the Banks found them helping around the house and attending various business and social functions that the Banks were involved with.

Of course Mrs. Wilkens was at Claudia's now, Tabatha thought. She was greatly attached to the whole family and would never miss the opportunity to help Claudia with anything at all. Truly, their lives would have been very different without that dear woman.

Tabatha picked up the phone and dialed Claudia's number. It was 5:19.

"Let me speak to Claudia, please. This is her mother."

Now that she had no intention of waiting for Jordan, she had to make sure that everything was going smoothly at her daughter's apartment. She knew that Claudia would bristle at yet another call from her. How had she become such an overbearing mother? It was small wonder that she was taking so long to pick up the call. Finally, she heard her daughter's exasperated voice.

"Hello, mother."

"Claudia, sweetheart. Tell me how everything is going, dear. Has the champagne been delivered, and are you sure you want to wear that Verretti? I like the Louis Frere. It brings out your beautiful eyes so much more."

"Oh, mother. Everything is exactly on schedule. Honestly, there is nothing at all for you to worry about. The cooks are almost finished with their preparations, and the waiters and bartenders are setting up their stations now. And I do have my heart set on wearing the pink. I know you'll love the new shoes that Marni and I found for it at Lally's when we went shopping last weekend."

"It's just that the song, about your blue eyes...well, yes, of course, Claudia. I know that you know what's best to wear. I'm wearing the green organza. I hope you think that's all right. I certainly don't want to embarrass you in front of all of your friends. Do you think that's too dressy or too flashy?"

They had gone over their outfits, and every other detail for tonight, a million times already. She couldn't understand why her mother was so unable to just take life more in stride. Everything was such a big deal that had to be gone over time and time again. Claudia faced every day with a much calmer attitude than her mother seemed to be capable of, while her mother seemed to have insatiable needs that Claudia had never been able to understand. Organizing events, overseeing the most intricate plans, had always come easily to Claudia. Then again, she thought it rather amazing that her mother was as controlled as she was, considering how much father ran around with other women.

"That outfit is perfect, mother. I've always loved you in it."

"I had my hair and nails done this morning. Did the rest of the RSVP's finally come in?"

"Everything's all set. I promise you. And Hal is going to bring over several boxes of CDs so that there will be plenty for all the guests."

Here it was again. Claudia knew that she and her mother could talk endlessly about clothes, hair, friends, decorating, politics, gossip and everybody else's problems. But throughout her whole life, whenever Claudia wanted to talk about things that were on her mind, her real feelings and fears, her questions that woke her in the middle of the night and filled her dreams with shadows, her mother changed the subject. When she had grown in to an adult, Claudia reasoned that her mother was so absorbed with her own problems about father that she didn't have the capacity for any more. Maybe some day, she always hoped.

"You have wonderful friends, Claudia. You're the luckiest girl I've ever known, and I love you so very much."

"I love you too, mother. When will you and father be here?"

"I'll be there at about six-ish. Your father will probably meet me there. He had a last minute meeting at the office that he couldn't reschedule."

"A Friday night meeting? He knows how much tonight means to me. Is everything all right?"

"I'm sure that it must be about one of those big European deals he's been working on. Well, whatever it is, he said that it was absolutely unavoidable. You know how much he adores you, Claudia. I know he'll be there as early as possible."

There was a silence on the line for a few seconds, and both knew what the other was thinking. Claudia considered herself a modern woman. But to imagine her own father seeing other women was awful, embarrassing and, most of all, she couldn't bare to know how hurt her mother must be. She couldn't remember exactly when it had happened, but at some point she knew that she and her mother had reversed roles, and she had become her mother's protector.

"Please try and get here as early as you can mother. You know that nobody can handle the finishing touches like you can. How soon can you leave?"

"Oh, I can leave in about twenty minutes, Claudia. Is there anything from here that you need?"

"Just you, mother. I've got to go now. There's a lot to do. I'll see you soon. Bye...oh, hold on for a sec. Mrs. Wilkens wants to talk to you."

Tabatha held back her tears as Mrs. Wilkens got on the line. That woman had a way of knowing all of her moods.

"How are you tonight, Mrs. Banks? You were bathing when I left the house. I hope Albert told you that I had left already."

"I'm fine, Mrs. Wilkens," she lied. "I've just got to slip on my outfit and leave. I'll be there soon."

As she put the finishing touches on her make-up, Tabatha admitted how she tried so hard to cater to Jordan's peccadilloes, or whatever it was that made him run to other women. How had this happened? They had had the most perfect love. I need you now, Mrs. Wilkens, she thought. I need you now.

chapter

SIX

The stars of the party arrived early so that they could greet the guests with Claudia as the song played in the background.

This hit song was yet another success for Hal Kinsberg's record label, Motion Records. Hal had landed in Claudia's elite inner circle fifteen years earlier when they were both vying for the same Pierre De Long painting at the Bostic Gallery. Claudia and Hal arranged to meet for afternoon cocktails at the Carlton so that each could attempt to convince the other to end the impasse, which didn't work. Luckily the gallery's owner, Jacques, phoned them the next day with the news that a new De Long had just been delivered. Hal fell in love with it, they were both happy and their friendship was sealed.

Hal was dressed in his usual very expensive European black silk pants, black silk shirt, no tie and a black silk loose jacket which perfectly complimented his charcoal eyes and his still very full and thick silver streaked black hair.

Tonight Hal shared the celebration with, of course, Evan, the song's creator, and for many years the most successful writer in Hal's publishing division. Claudia had first met Evan when she accompanied Hal to a BMI awards dinner that honored million selling songwriters. And now his song for her had already topped five million in sales.

When the guest of honor arrived he gave her an affectionate greeting, but to Claudia, it felt like his warmth was really for public consumption, and not sincerely directed towards her. Evan still couldn't seem to look her in the eyes. Maybe, she thought, Marni was right and he was trying to make her feel that she was losing him. And maybe, she thought, his ruse was working.

"Claudia" was now Evan's fifth multi-million seller, and he owed this one to the song's extraordinary vocalist, the internationally adored Trace, who made the song a worldwide smash.

Trace's charismatic presence was magnetic and highly stimulating to men and women alike. He was a man of commanding charm and intelligence, he was blessed with a velvet voice and he looked like a god. Tonight he wore a pale green loose fitting silk suit without a shirt under the jacket. He looked dazzling with his tan and his long blonde hair that melted into his golden chest hairs. He gave Claudia a warm hug and an innocently mushy kiss. They looked like each other's gender counterparts, and had always felt a tremendous affinity for one another.

The next to arrive were Claudia's closest friends. Besides Marni, there was the perfectly manicured Carl Hoenig, an internationally respected multi-media deal making attorney who wore only Armani. Tonight he wore a navy suit with navy and white Italian shoes. Matty Fellstein arrived in her long flowered dress and several cartons of her *Primal Evergreen* book.

The famed entertainment industry publicist, Eric Stanton, who knew everyone's secrets and who wore a tuxedo whenever he attended any event, had represented most everyone that was going to be here tonight, or a project that they were involved with, at some time. He arranged for the photographer for the evening, and it was he who would assure that the society columns and magazines had the pictures they wanted from the affair.

And last but not least was Claudia's friend Susan Bergman, who always stood out in a crowd with her nearly six foot tall trim figure and long red hair. She was the driving force behind the success of Crown Jeans that used celebrities in their sexy ads and that sponsored many rock tours.

Eric, Matty and Susan had been toying with the idea of starting a line of green Crown Jeans so that, like the red ribbons for AIDS and the pink ribbons for breast cancer, wearing green jeans would signify support for environmental concerns. Crown would manufacture the jeans, Eric would publicize the issue internationally, they would arrange for celebrities from all over the world to wear the pants and get involved, and Matty would be the cause's spokesperson. It was a great idea, and it seemed like this night offered them an unpressured opportunity to develop their vision.

Marni knew that she looked particularly fetching. She had just recently bought the Clarez eggshell white silk slack suit that she was wearing this warm spring evening. After all the work she had put into planning this night, she was ready to have an engaging evening.

Ida Wilkens spotted Tabatha coming through the door. When Tabatha was worried, her brow wrinkled vertically as it did now. Mrs. Wilkens noticed immediately and, as sympathetic as ever, greeted her as if Tabatha were her own dispirited daughter. They walked through the various rooms together.

"Oh, Tabatha, you look so beautiful tonight."

"Thank you, Ida. Where's Claudia? Everything looks so enchanting. Oh Ida, Claudia utterly knows how to put an evening together. We taught her well, didn't we?"

"Yes, we certainly did, Mrs. Banks. We certainly did. And, may I ask, what time will Mr. Banks be here?"

Tabatha's head dropped a bit, and then she snapped out of it, knowing that Ida understood. "Oh, I'm not sure. He had some last minute business to take care of at the office. I'm sure he'll be here soon. Let's look around some more and sample the hors d'oeuvres. I want to see who's arrived."

Frank and Jackie Strang arrived. They were the proud parents of the successful songwriter, and they brought with them the framed platinum record that had been presented to Evan by the Recording Industry Association of America.

By nine o'clock, there were just over a hundred people at the party. Of the fourteen rooms in her co-op, Claudia always had at least four or five rooms open for the guests to wander around in so that they could meet with new groups of people in different settings. On this balmy night she had the screened sun-room, the sitting room, the living room and the den filled with pale yellow flowers, bowls of shrimp, fruit and nuts. Formally uniformed waiters unobtrusively served delicately sumptuous hors d'oeuvres and champagne in Claudia's gold rimmed Baccarat flute glasses that had soaring birds etched into the crystal.

Claudia loved birds, especially gaily colorful birds. Live, embroidered, etched, painted or woven stunning turquoise and yellow macaws, peacocks, blue jays, red breasts, yellow canaries, sea green parrots, flamingoes, white cockatoos and doves adorned her world. Birds were everywhere, incorporated into her home's decor, as her personal logos on stationary and she wore a gold and diamond necklace shaped like a bird in flight. Claudia herself had taken up painting in acrylics, and there were her canvases throughout the apartment, all featuring her cherished birds.

Marni first saw Craig sitting with a group of guests in a corner of the sun-room that perched twenty stories overlooking Central Park, a spacious room that Claudia had filled with plants and exotic birds in white cages. She wasn't sure why this man struck her so immediately, but she made a quick mental note of his casual elegance and easy conversational style. Although she tried to file the information away as having merely sited yet another of the many fascinating men in Claudia's life, she knew that she felt drawn to this man.

Even so, she was not prepared for the expression Craig had on his face when he suddenly turned and saw her standing with

Claudia as she was being greeted and escorted into the room. His soft brown eyes and warm smile made her blush, so much so that she forced herself to concentrate on Claudia's forbidding eyes so that she wouldn't look at him again. A self-possessed woman, Marni was not used to being caught off guard. There was something deeper about that look, something that was beyond a standard admirer's glance.

For the next two hours, Marni thoroughly enjoyed herself speaking to the myriad of guests scattered throughout Claudia's home. It was clear that Craig was not able to take his eyes off her. He watched her as she seemed to so enjoy, and seamlessly succeed at, socializing and doing business at the same time.

She sensed him watching her, and every once and awhile their eyes would meet. Even while he was rapt in conversation, he watched her.

Jordan Banks had finally arrived with heartfelt apologies, which his daughter and her guests accepted and made light of. And truly, most everyone there was accustomed to absurd schedules.

The glitterati were roaming the rooms. There were celebrities and executives from the entertainment industry's highest echelons in Claudia's orbit, and she had a knack for inviting just the right mix to her parties, which always resulted in the beginning or sealing of professional relationships or the opening and closing of deals.

The elegant Earl and Babs Hothington, with their coincidentally matching straight silver hair, were the money behind television's latest conglomerate, the Alpha Network. They were sitting with the home video king Clyde Castle, his new girlfriend, the Eurasian model Ariel and her accomplished agent Henri Beauvais.

Phyllis and Bob Nuestein, who usually dressed very Ralph Lauren, were the owners of one of the largest and most successful stables in Saratoga who made their nouveau fortune from the patent on an indestructible vinyl for record manufacturing. They were sitting with Mel and Tina Carter, the owners of Vanderlin Jewels, who everyone adored, but who came to parties like this extravagantly wearing what looked like the crown's jewels.

J. E. Laine

Sipping champagne with them was Connie Larson, an incredible flirt who only stayed with a particular group of people at any given party for a few minutes until she flitted on to the next crowd. She was the very beautiful and desirable widow of Steve Larson, one of the early executives of the record industry who, when everybody else thought it was a short-term fluke, had the ears and the foresight to invest Laredo Records' vast resources in the new sound that became rock and roll. And then there were the usual smatterings of politicians, film moguls, internet billionaires and major money blue bloods.

Evan found Claudia holding court with a group of her guests who were moaning with delight at the taste of the shrimp dumpling hors d'oeuvres. He begged their forgiveness and asked to speak with her alone. As they walked around the party together, Claudia was hopeful that Evan had finally snapped out of the mood he had been in.

"Claudia, you've put together the most incredible evening. I can never thank you enough."

"Well. Evan, this is really all your doing. You wrote the song. You're the reason for these festivities. Have I told you a million times yet how proud I am of you, and how very flattered I am that you wrote this song about me?"

"Claudia, you deserve this, and so much more. So very much more. But listen to me. I have to talk to you. It's very important. There's a lot that I have to tell you, but we can't do it now. Can we spend some time together after everyone leaves?"

"Of course we can, Evan. I haven't understood your moods lately, and, more than anything, I want to talk to you and find out what's been on your mind."

"Good, Claudia. I'm sorry for the way I've been acting. Everything has been so confusing lately. I can't explain now. I'll tell you everything later. I promise."

"I'll be here, Evan. Now, let's mingle with the guests. They're here for us, you know."

As they kissed each other on the cheek, Claudia realized that he still couldn't look her in the eyes.

48

chapter

SEVEN

Marni could not forget the look in Craig's eyes, but for the rest of the evening she occupied herself speaking to all of Claudia's guests, most of whom she either knew from business or had met socially at other events. For Marni, meeting new people and absorbing herself in conversation at large parties had always been easy and something she enjoyed immensely. As the evening progressed, it was obvious that she and Craig had purposefully avoided any real contact, except tangentially when they found themselves in the same grouping.

The party started to break up at around 11:30 and, as far as Marni could see, only a handful of people were left. Except for Craig, it was their usual core crowd, the chronically unmarried but ever so interesting and successful group that usually found themselves together after events. They could spend hours adding up and ripping apart the evening's fare. Claudia was taking care

J. E. Laine

of some closing details with Tommy the caterer, while Hal, Eric, Susan, Matty and Carl were gleefully finishing the shrimp on the serving table in the sitting room.

It was then that Craig reached out his hand to introduce himself to Marni. As their eyes met, this time only a short distance from each other, and their hands touched, their first touch, electricity ran through both of them. Marni took back her hand, at the same time trying to hide the blush that she felt taking over her face by starting an admittedly silly conversation about what a lovely party it had been. As she spoke, Craig just stared at her with kind amusement.

"Let's sit down," he said gently as he took Marni's hand again and led her to a love seat covered in a fabric hand-painted with birds sitting on tropical trees. In front of them was a gold leaf coffee table with a white marble top surrounded by several groupings of over-stuffed chairs beautifully upholstered in garden colors, each with a different exotic tropical bird embroidered on the backs and seat cushions. A fresh bottle of champagne was served, poured by the ever gracious waiters. Craig handed Marni a glass, and they wordlessly clinked and took a sip.

"At last we have a chance to talk. You know I have been looking at you all evening. Who was it that said 'save the best for last'?"

"You are most flattering, kind sir. But you know, we don't even know each other's names. And that was Vincent Yardsley who said,

'In the morning when I wake,
through the day my soul you take to bed
I love you through the night,
Oh mourn what past
then save the best for last,
lest the fright of time gone by
stalk the road to midnight.'"

Craig had chills as Marni spoke with such a quiet, insistent passion. He froze, staring at her, any words that he might have said suspended somewhere deep inside of him. How could she have known those words, those thoughts, that he had so long ago tried to forget? He shuddered as long buried memories flooded into his mood. Why had he said those words to her now? Did he know that she would know where they had come from?

This woman had just read further in to his being than his conscious intentions would ever have allowed. He had expressed himself so innocently, but she knew where it came from, what it said, what it meant. She knew it, as if it were a part of her heart.

After a marriage that ended in tragedy, and through a series of girlfriends since then, Craig had grudgingly expected that he would never find a woman who he would want to settle down with. He had assumed that the hopes and dreams from that part of his life were over. The flash of sudden feelings and possibilities were too much to deal with all at once, so he attempted to continue the conversation as if there hadn't been this profound pause and seismic occurrence. He began simply.

"I'm Craig. Craig Harris. And you're Marni Kendell. Everybody here knows you, and throughout the night I've heard purely unsolicited references to the many successes you have had. Here I thought I was looking at a woman who had inherited a fortune, as did Claudia, but instead your friends and professional acquaintances only rave about how very hard you have worked and how well you have succeeded. I must say, I am very impressed."

Marni was surprised that he had learned so much about her. It was almost unsettling, but she chose to ignore the feeling. Who was this man, and why hadn't Claudia told her about this unattached male in her circle as she usually did?

It was as if they had both known, all evening, that they had been savoring the anticipation of these moments when they could just concentrate on each other, when the necessity of other conversations was satiated.

"Well, Craig. I'm clearly at a total disadvantage. I know absolutely nothing about you, except that you are also a friend of Claudia's. But now tell me, what would you like me to know about you?"

Craig's eyes twinkled. He liked her spunk. He had only just had a few words with this woman and he knew that he was crazy about her. But how much should he tell her so soon, and where in the world should he start?

As Craig was agonizing over where to begin, the remaining guests, not realizing the synergy, began to join them in the nesting area that they had chosen. But even as conversations were carried on around them, in a very private and unspoken way, it was as if they were the only people there.

He looked into her eyes. "I'm forty-three years old. I am a non-practicing attorney who has had surprising successes with investments, primarily in the entertainment industry which is why I was invited here tonight. I love to go to fabulous restaurants and have wonderful meals with the best wines. The only sport I watch on television is baseball, but I would rather play it than watch it. The only other sport that I would rather play than baseball is tennis. I was raised on Long Island. Like you, I take full credit for my successes. And I admit that I am so very happy that we have met."

She loved the sound of his voice. It had a calming effect on her, but it also made her tremble. "You are ever the charmer and flatterer, Craig, although I do believe, my new friend, that you are sincere. So I accept your compliments and the champagne."

She was starting to feel tired from having talked so much tonight, and the bubbly was beginning to make her sleepy, but she was not yet ready to end this conversation. Something about this man was so compelling, she just had to know more.

"You describe yourself as just a regular guy who has had fantastic luck, Monsieur Craig. But if I were to read between the lines, what would I find?"

Marni had taken off her heels and Craig, in an action that probably should have startled her, started rubbing one of her feet, as if they had known each other intimately for years. But it wasn't unnerving, and, curiously, it felt perfectly right and comfortable.

For an instant, Claudia caught Marni's eyes in female acknowledgment of the obviously cozy new liaison. Marni wondered what was going on between Claudia and Evan.

From another room a clock that had long been in Claudia's family chimed midnight, in deep dulcet tones and reverberations that brought the echoes of centuries into these new millennium New York City rooms.

And then there was a horrible gut wrenching scream, as if an animal was in agonizing pain. Craig's hands, which had been gently massaging Marni's foot, froze in mid-movement as Marni's leg tried to reflexively kick away with fear. Claudia's eyes moved with questioning shock to Marni's and, at what would have been the count of three, they both looked around in utter horror.

chapter

EIGHT

For a moment no one was able to move, trying to process the sounds that so inelegantly ripped through the cozy gathering.

And then another piercing sound, a voice screaming for help.

"That...that sounded like it came from the hallway outside," Claudia stuttered, her face white with fear. "What...what in the world...?"

"Let's go...now!" Eric yelled with a shriek, which made everyone jump out of their seats and follow him.

The seven of them ran through the sitting room, through the gallery past the library and into the vestibule that lead to the front door, with a few of the waiters that still remained falling in behind them. As they reached the outside hallway, they saw Connie Larson shaking and whimpering, her body limp against the elevator door frame while her foot was firmly planted on the door's path so that it could not close.

Eric reached her first.

"Connie, what's wrong, what..." and those were the only words that came out of his mouth as he followed her stare into the elevator.

The body was huddled in a corner of the elevator, its eyes staring hysterically looking like a frightened child pleading for its mother.

At first it looked like the antique red walls had just been touched up with an animated modern enamel paint. But the double take that the scene commanded confirmed that newly splattered blood was dripping to the floor, and that the shiny charm peaking out of the shirt was the point of a knife.

Within moments, everyone had witnessed this unbelievable sight. As Claudia's shrieks echoed through the long corridor, they all looked at each other incredulously. It was Evan. But how could that be? He had just left a party in one of the safest buildings in the city.

"Ok. Don't touch anything," Eric said evenly. "I'll stay here and keep the elevator on this floor. Craig, call 911. Tell them the body's...he's...tell them they can't take one of the main elevators, so they have to take the other one or the service elevator or the stairs. Somebody buzz the front desk and tell them...tell them something, but don't panic them. Susan, take Connie inside and...oh my God...this is impossible."

Someone yelled, "Push the emergency stop switch." Eric forced himself to take his eyes off Evan and looked furiously for the switch.

Claudia just stood there, ashen, trembling and in shock. She had seen Eric take charge at so many different events. But this was surreal. Everything in her sight started to swirl in front of her eyes, beautiful colors going around and around, and then they turned into a spinning black, gray and white spiral. She wavered, eyes fluttering, and Hal checked her fall just as she slowly crumpled down the wall to the floor.

Hal smacked her face lightly with his hand as his other arm held her.

"Claudia...Claudia...wake up...it's Hal, honey."

"What...why...what happened? Oh, Hal...who would want to hurt Evan? Why Evan? Why...I love you...Evan...." Great sobs heaved from her pain wracked senses as she struggled to lift herself up through Hal's arms.

"I have to go to him...I have to...Eric...why is this happening?"

"I don't know. The police will be here soon, and then it will be in their hands. There's nothing we can do in the meantime except wait."

Eric was just about to reach out for Claudia but suddenly stopped in mid-movement.

"I hear something...what the..." A siren was approaching the area, and he thought he heard footsteps, far away, a faint padding sound in 4/4 time muffled and fading further away. He was just about to say something when another noise jolted him from out of how he had started straining to hear. A raspy gurgling sound was coming from within the elevator.

"What's that...he's breathing! Oh my God. Look! Look Claudia. I just heard him. Look! His chest is moving. Somebody get an ambulance! Oh my God hurry."

"Do something! Please do something!" Claudia was screaming uncontrollably. "We can't just let him stay like that. We have to help him. He must be in so much pain. Oh, Evan...Evan...can you hear me? Oh please...Evan."

"No, Claudia. We can't touch him. We have to wait for the police and the ambulance. It's late. There won't be a lot of traffic. They'll be here soon."

Eric was used to hyping, having everything under control and making schedules for dozens, sometimes hundreds of people. He had a reputation for organizing the most complex worldwide events and for making quick, correct decisions. He prayed that he knew what he was doing this time.

"Who could have done this, Eric? Why would anyone want to hurt Evan?"

"We'll find out, Claudia. The police will figure it out." Could some nut have broken into this building, he wondered. Their whole crowd lived in luxury doorman buildings except, of course, the ones who owned townhouses. But they had elaborate security systems. This building was particularly strict. Delivery boys were never even allowed into the elevators unless the concierge at the front desk knew them. Eric didn't have any answers. He just knew that he had to stay strong, at least until the police got here and took over. That's what they would do. Then he could collapse.

Every second seemed like an eternity. He didn't know if they'd been waiting a minute or an hour.

At the end of the long hallway the service elevator door started to open spewing forth two policemen who raced down the hall towards them, followed by two uniformed emergency medics carrying equipment, medical bags and a rolled up stretcher.

The police ran towards them with their guns drawn against dark blue uniforms. To the shocked and weary onlookers it could easily have been an hallucinogenic vision with quick laser beams of light reflecting off the badges and gun tips. As the policemen ran, their eyes rapidly scanned the scene and they holstered their guns. The first to arrive took charge.

"I'm Lieutenant Fazio. This is Officer Ragney. What happened here?" By the time the last word had come out of his mouth, he had followed Eric's stare into the elevator.

"In here!" he barked to the medics, then to the others, "Let's give them some room."

Fazio talked and looked like a Marine with his no nonsense six feet of solid muscle evident even through his police uniform, his brown crew cut hair and his air of rugged authority. His slightest gesture was a command to move everyone ten feet down the hall while Ragney checked the elevator controls to make sure the car was secure.

As the medics practically dove in to the elevator, leaving only the stretcher in the hallway, Fazio turned to the shaken group.

"Everybody just keep calm and let them do their job."

The team worked on Evan as if they had done this type of thing a thousand times before. In a fast forward ballet of arms and hands they made his body the recipient of tubes, syringes, gauze and an oxygen mask worming out of a machine that beeped green and white lights.

"Can they help him? Please make sure they can help him." Claudia clutched Eric's arm as she pleaded to Lieutenant Fazio.

"Give them a minute, miss. Please. They know what to do." Whenever he said this, he hoped with all his heart that it was true. He pulled his radio from his belt and spit a string of orders into it.

Fazio turned to Eric. "Do you know this man? What happened here?"

Eric made an enormous effort to collect his thoughts and express them in a rational way in this, the most irrational moment of his life.

"His name is Evan Strang. We...Claudia...Claudia Banks, this lady...had a party tonight. It was just a party. We were honoring him..."

Fazio was used to hearing people talk when they were in shock. But he hadn't seen an attempted murder in a high society situation like this in years. And these people, except maybe one of them, had never seen anything like this in their lives, although he'd seen men in tuxedoes and women in gowns who were guilty as hell.

The hall was getting crowded again as Marni, Craig, Hal, Matty, Carl and a few of the evening's help made their way back into the hall when they heard the commotion. Marni rushed to Claudia's side and held her friend's arm.

"He left about a half hour ago." Eric kept talking. "A group of us were just talking in the sitting room when we heard a scream from out here. When we got here, this is what we saw."

"Did anybody touch your friend or try to move him? Did anybody touch anything like the knife, the elevator walls, anything?"

"No, Lieutenant, no. We didn't touch him or anything in the elevator, I'm sure of it. I was just standing here keeping the elevator door open and Craig went inside to call 911. This is Craig, Lieutenant. And this is Hal..."

The thought crossed Eric's mind that nobody shook hands. How could he think of something like that at a time like this? He felt alert, but it was more like he was watching a police show on TV and he was in it. How many television shows and specials had he arranged for over the years, and how many plum parts had he gotten for his celebrity clients? He was used to being on television and film sets. That's what this was like. But there was no script and...

"Connie was here before we were, Eric. What about Connie?"

It was Hal who interrupted his bizarre thoughts. He had forgotten about Connie.

"Where is this Connie?"

"She's inside, Lieutenant," offered Hal. "She's been hysterical and throwing up since we found her screaming out here."

"Did she say anything?"

Just then one of the medic's heads peered out of the elevator. "He's alive, Lieutenant, but he's just holding on. We better move fast. We'll take him to Springhurst. It's the closest. Can you radio it in for us so we can get him out of here?"

Marni looked at Claudia, trying to muster the strength to help her friend through this. She had an idea.

"Claudia, let's call that doctor, that doctor you told me about, your father's friend, who's a specialist in violent injuries. Do you have his number?"

Claudia looked to Marni as if she had taken a powerful sedative. She just stared, dazed, towards the elevator door, not able to move. Marni wasn't even sure if she had heard what she'd said. Then, unsteadily, Claudia turned to Marni.

"Yes, yes, he'll help us. I know he will. I've got to find his number. I have to remember his name. What is his name? Oh, Marni, what is his name?"

"We'll find it, Claudia, don't worry. Come inside." Marni led her by the arm towards the opened apartment door. "We'll remember it, I know we will. Everything will be all right, Claudia. But we have to hurry."

"I want to stay with him. Marni, I have to go to the hospital with him."

"Let's call the doctor first, Claudia. We have to make sure he gets the best treatment. Come on. Hurry up. Then we can go to the hospital."

Fazio and Ragney surveyed the crowd in the hall. Fazio directed himself to Eric.

"How many more people are still here, Mr., eh, what's your name?"

"Stanton...Eric Stanton. I don't know who's still here besides me, Claudia, Hal, Marni, Craig, Matty, and Carl. Susan's inside with Connie. I don't know how many of the cooks, or waiters or bartenders or maids are still here. They had a lot of cleaning up to do."

"We'll put him sideways on the stretcher." The medics were talking to each other and to Fazio at the same time. "We don't want to take out the knife and cause any more damage. Let them do it at the hospital. Don't worry Lieutenant. We've already bagged it on him."

Fazio lead them to the service elevator as he spoke.

"The service elevator is yours. Ragney will stay with you till you get into the ambulance. We've got two more guys in the lobby, maybe four by now. One of them will ride with you in the ambulance to the hospital. And there'll be two police cars downstairs when you get there that'll flank you with all sirens to get you to Springhurst fast and safe. Ragney, wait down there till the detective gets here so you can bring him up."

As the elevator door closed behind them, an eerie silence filled the hallway and all, except Fazio, stood still as if in freeze-frame.

"Okay, everybody. Let's go inside. I'm sorry, but nobody can leave here. A detective will be here in a few minutes and he'll have a lot of questions to ask. Eric, are there any other exits from the apartment?" He had noticed two other apartment doors on the floor and added, "and who are the neighbors?"

Just then the other passenger elevator let out four policemen, a man in a trench coat and three men in jeans, sweatshirts and police wind breaker jackets carrying equipment bags.

The man in the trench coat said, "Detective Grange, Lieutenant." They shook hands. "Good seeing you again. I saw the medics downstairs and I took a look at the victim. What's going on?" As Grange asked this, his large brown eyes, set under thick brown uncombed hair and a day's worth of beard stubble, squinted as they took in the scene. He removed his coat, which had cloaked his tolerably rounded middle and rumpled suit.

Before Fazio answered him, he had one of the officers find and secure the service entrance to the apartment, told another to guard the front door and had the other two search the building. Then he and Eric told Grange what they knew.

SATURDAY

chapter

NINE

"Where could that number be? Oh, Marni. I've never been so frightened in my life."

"I know, Claudia. I am too. But we'll get through this. Let's do this in some kind of logical order. I know you wrote it down somewhere because you told me you had his home number. Where's your phone book?"

"I know I didn't put it in there yet. I've been so busy getting everything ready for the party. This damn party. It's all my fault. If I hadn't had this party, this never would have happened. He can't die, Marni. He can't."

"He won't. He can't. Let's look through these scraps of paper. It's got to be here."

The desk in Claudia's study was strewn with notebooks, yellow legal pads, blue stationary, RSVP cards, all different sized little scraps of paper, fountain pens, ball point pens, felt tipped pens and pencils. This wasn't one of the rooms opened for the party.

"You take that side of the desk. I'll look through these. Do you remember what you were doing when you wrote it down? Maybe that will tell you what you might have been writing on. Or with what color pen."

They spent the next few minutes furiously shuffling through the mess that Claudia had intended to straighten up the day after the party. There had just been no time for it before. They didn't notice that a guard was watching them.

"It's no use. We'll never find it. Evan must be at the hospital by now. Marni, I have to be with him, and I have to make sure he has the best doctor."

"Springhurst has excellent doctors on staff, Claudia. It's the best hospital in the city." Marni stopped sorting through the papers and looked at her friend.

"Claudia, why didn't we think of this before? We're both so out of our minds right now. Why don't you call your father and get the number. Your parents should know about what's happened here anyway, and I'm sure they'll want to meet you at the hospital."

"Well, if I have to I will, but I'd really rather call them from the hospital once we see how Evan is. I don't want them to have to go through this. They've had enough scandals, Marni. I want to be able to spare them for at least a few more hours and let them get a decent night's sleep. After this, they're going to be more over-bearing about me than ever. They'll have guards at my door twenty-four hours a day."

"We might not have a choice if you want Evan to have that doctor, Claudia. I think it's time we call them." Then she realized, "Oh my God, Claudia. What about Evan's parents? We have to call them right away."

"I remember! I remember! Yes. I was on the phone with my father just as I was about to leave for the La Doria fashion show last week. I must have stuffed it into my pocketbook. What was I wearing? Red. The red suit. It's in the red pocketbook. I know that's it."

She ran to her bedroom with Marni close behind. When she grabbed for her red snakeskin purse, everything in it fell to the floor. They both got on their hands and knees, sorting through the make-up, keys and pocket notebooks. Claudia opened a matching red purse and sifted through her cards and receipts.

"I've got it. Here it is." She dashed for the phone, a white and gold copy of a turn-of-the-century phone with a push button panel hidden under the decorative old fashioned dial disc that opened like a little door.

"It's almost one in the morning. But he's a doctor. He must be used to this." The phone rang five times before a man's sleepy voice answered.

"This is Dr. Perlstein."

"Dr. Perlstein, please forgive me for calling at this hour. This is Claudia Banks, Jordan Banks' daughter. There's an emergency." She told him everything she knew. He assured her that he would contact the chief of staff right away, and that he would get to the hospital as soon as he could.

"Let's go. Wait. Oh my God. His parents. We have to call Evan's parents. We'll call them from the hospital. No, we have to call them now. How do we make this kind of call, Marni? They are the sweetest people, and they're going to be so frightened."

"Ms. Banks. Would you and your friend come in to the living room, please." It was Fazio.

As the two women walked into the living room, it looked like there was still a party going on. Most of the food was still on serving platters, every table had several partially filled champagne glasses and little hors d'oeuvre plates and napkins. There were people sitting on every sofa, chair and ottoman and policemen were everywhere. The yellow flowers that filled the room gave the scene a bizarre air of celebration.

At Grange and Fazio's request, Eric had gathered all of the remaining guests and workers and had asked one of the cooks to replenish the large silver coffee urn in the living room. At Fazio's order, no one was to speak to each other until all had been questioned.

Detective Grange was talking to the men who were taking blood, fiber samples and fingerprints from the outside hallway, elevators, stairwell and instructing them on which rooms in the apartment needed their attention. He looked like the disheveled detective from central casting. His brown hair speckled with gray should have been cut two months ago. His ill-fitting beige cotton gabardine jacket, matching slacks and baby blue shirt should have been replaced three springs ago. But his brown eyes were intense, and they were an interesting counterpoint to his over-sized lips that stressed his smiles and frowns with dramatic effect.

Grange and Fazio had put in a silence order and forty-eight hour till-further-notice press freeze on the incident and investigation. They didn't want the city to panic about a possible maniac on the loose in New York's luxury buildings. And they had gotten heat from on high to try to keep the Banks' name out of the papers for as long as possible.

Detective Grange looked past the opulent surroundings and studied the stricken faces. There were fifteen in all, and he doubted that any of them had actually done the stabbing but it was possible that one of them at least had information that would help lead him to the wacko that did this. There was always the chance that an outside intruder did it, but his every instinct told him that the victim knew his assailant. He also knew that people who were tired when they were being questioned tended to have less energy and imagination to tell convincing lies.

As he looked around, he realized that he couldn't imagine another occasion that would put this diverse group together. Wealthy men and women in evening clothes sitting in an Upper East Side living room with the help, albeit silently. He addressed the crowd.

"I'm sorry that all of you have to stay. I know it's late, and we'll get through this as fast as we can. I'm sure you understand that I must ask each of you a few questions, and I'll need your names and addresses and phone numbers in case we have to get in touch with you again.

"And one more thing before we begin. It is very important that you do not speak of this to anyone. We don't want the press to hear about this until we're ready to tell them. We don't want the city to panic about a lunatic on the loose. When we're ready for it to hit the papers, it could help us find who did it." Of course he knew these last were pretty empty words. There's no way to keep fifteen people from talking, but he had to try.

"I have to go to the hospital. I have to be with my friend." Claudia was trying to subvert her hysterics, but at this point she had very little control over herself. Her pink sequined silk outfit, that had been so gorgeous and sparkling just a few hours ago, looked like it had been stuffed in an overnight bag for days.

"Yeah. Okay. Of course. I'll talk to you first, Miss Banks. I want to use the kitchen for the questioning. My men should be finishing up in there now."

She led him into the kitchen, but the forensic men and cameras were distracting and intrusive. They sat instead in the adjoining breakfast room.

"I understand that you are very close to Mr. Strang, Miss Banks. Who do you think would want to kill him, and why?"

Claudia tried to answer him, but she couldn't. Kill Evan. Somebody had wanted to kill Evan. She felt the blood drain from her face, and her head was moving from side to side saying, 'No... No.'

"I'm sorry, Miss Banks. I know you're upset. I'm with the New York Department of Law Enforcement, Division of Criminal Investigations. Someone wanted to murder your friend." It was always hard for him to invoke a nice bedside manner at a time like this, when he needed information fast.

"Tell me about him, his friends, his work. Then I'll have someone drive you to the hospital." He saw that these last words noticeably calmed her.

They spoke for nearly an hour. She told him everything her distraught mind could remember about Evan, except why they had practically stopped talking just before they might have made love for the first time. She gave him the guest lists, and the name of the catering service which had also supplied the waiters, bartenders and maids.

"Can I go now, Detective? Every minute that I'm here, it's another minute that I can't help him."

"Just one more question, Miss Banks. I hate to ask you to do this but please, if you would, picture Evan as you saw him on the stretcher. Can you do that for me?"

"Oh, why? Why do you want me to do that?"

"Because I need you to picture the knife. Did you recognize the handle of the knife?"

"The handle of the knife? I don't remember seeing it. I was just looking at him. Lying there like that."

"Did the handle of the knife look long or short to you?"

"It was a long handle. A long shiny handle. A shiny metal... well, partly shiny. It wasn't all metal."

"You're very observant. Okay. Do you remember what color the part that wasn't metal seemed to be? Was it dark or light?"

"It was...it was dark."

"Did the handle look familiar to you?"

"Familiar to me? Why would I have ever seen that knife before? Why are you asking me this?"

"I'm just wondering if it could have come from your kitchen."

"From my kitchen? How could it have come from...from my...I don't understand what you're saying."

"Miss Banks. I'm just wondering if someone from your party, or someone who worked here tonight, could have taken a knife from your kitchen and used it to stab your friend."

Claudia responded with a dazed and beaten look on her face, which he understood as her total inability to process what was happening. Detective Grange thought she was going to faint.

"Can I get you some water?" He didn't wait for her to answer. "Wait here. Okay? Let me get you some water."

When he returned with the water, in less than a minute as the breakfast room was just a few steps from the kitchen, Claudia had not seemed to have changed position by a molecule. She took a few sips of the cool refreshing liquid.

"I don't understand, Detective. I don't understand how you can think somebody from my party could have done something like this. And the caterer, well, I know the caterer, Tommy Laten, for years. He does most of my parties and he works for most of my friends. He would never use workers that were criminals. Somebody must have broken into the building. Surely you must know that. There is nobody who would want to hurt Evan. There simply is no reason for it. Please, we have to find out who did this, but it has to be some crazy person who somehow got into the building."

"Did you recognize the knife, Miss Banks? Did it look at all familiar to you?"

"Well no. I'm sure I've never seen it before. But also, you see, I don't cook very much. So, even if it was here, from my house, I might not even know it. And really I still don't understand what you're saying."

"Right now we're not sure what to think, Miss Banks. But we have to cover every possibility. We already know that the knife does not match any from your kitchen. But it could be one that's not part of a set, or it could be one that the caterer brought. Think about it, if you would. If anything comes to mind, please call me." He handed her his card. "I'll have someone drive you to the hospital now."

"Please. Please find out who did this."

"Thank you Miss Banks. I am sure that we will. You take care now."

He had an officer take her to the hospital and promised to arrange for a ride for Marni, too. The maids were not to clean up, and the caterer would have to pick up his equipment when the police were ready to release them from the apartment. Eric volunteered to stay there until the morning shift of police arrived.

It was six in the morning when Grange finished questioning the last person.

chapter

TEN

The knife had missed Evan's heart by mere centimeters, but had maliciously grazed the lower lobe of his right lung. When Dr. Perlstein arrived at the hospital within thirty minutes of Claudia's call, he had expected Evan to be dead.

By the time Claudia arrived at 2 AM with her police escort, Evan had been in surgery for over an hour. His parents, both dressed in beige linen slacks, khaki cotton knit pullovers and sneakers, were conferring with the head nurse. As she ran over to them, she silently thanked Marni for having had the presence of mind to call them amidst the tension and disruption of the detective's questioning.

"Jackie...Frank..." She hugged them both. "How is he? What are they saying?"

They both looked appropriately exhausted but bolstered by caffeine and mortal fear. Frank had tears in his eyes. "They're still operating. They say it's minute to minute. I just want to be with him."

From where they stood, they could see the operating room doors with a police officer standing guard in front of it. Another policeman stood near the stairwell door, and yet another paced the hall. The Banks name had clout, but so did the potential fear of an entire city.

"Can you make sense of this, Claudia? Why did this happen? Who could have done this?" Jackie was pleading for logical answers.

"I don't know. The police and detectives are still at my apartment questioning everyone who was still there when we found him. He looked so..." Claudia collapsed sobbing into Jackie's arms, and they tried to console each other.

"I think we'd better sit down. Come with me." Frank led them into the Intensive Care sitting room. "All we can do now is wait."

Evan's parents wanted to know everything that had happened since they left the party, and Claudia told them what she could remember except, of course, how their son looked when they found him. How do you tell someone's parents that their child looked dead.

When Marni arrived at 3 AM, she arranged for Claudia and the Strangs to use a private suite, the room that hopefully waited for Evan, so that they could try and get a bit of sleep and privacy. But of course, no one could sleep. So they talked.

The Strangs talked about Evan as a child, and how creative he had always been. They had started him on piano lessons when he was only four, and he had given his first recital when he was five.

"I'm sorry that I gave this party tonight," Claudia sobbed. "We should have just gotten a group of friends together and..."

"Oh Claudia. It was lovely of you to give this party. I can't imagine your having done any less. And I know that Evan adored you for it." Jackie was trying to stay strong and positive. She knew she would need all the strength she had to get through this.

"But I must ask you," Jackie continued. "What has changed between the two of you lately? I thought you were getting pretty serious. And you know I liked that, Claudia."

Claudia had first met the Strangs five years ago, soon after Hal had introduced her to Evan. She and Evan had become good and amiable acquaintances, but not particularly intimate. But Claudia and Jackie Strang had discovered an instant and warm rapport. They could always speak freely and effortlessly with each other, and Claudia knew that she could easily confide in her about anything in the world. She knew she could have the relationship with Jackie that she always longed to have with her own mother.

When Evan made it clear that he wanted the relationship to turn into a romance, Jackie had held Claudia in her arms and told her that there was no one else that she would rather have as a daughter-in-law. And when that didn't progress the way she had hoped it would, Jackie had tried to stay neutral. And then there was the song that Evan wrote about this fabulous girl.

Claudia kept repeating that she couldn't believe that just a few hours had passed since they all had been celebrating and having the best time. They all vacillated between sitting, pacing and generally babbling to pass the time.

Claudia's parents arrived at around 4 AM. Marni had called them too. Claudia almost knocked over her coffee when she saw them, impeccably dressed amidst the madness, and ran down the hall to greet them.

"Sweetheart. Oh, Claudia. This is terrible. Are you all right?" Tabatha hugged her daughter, trying not to let her sense of absolute alarm derail them both. But Tabatha was truly frightened. She was sure that there was a murderer lurking in her daughter's life, and she was certain that it was because there was so much money in the family.

"I'm all right, mother. Really I am. It's Evan. You should have seen him. Oh, my God. It was awful."

Jordan took his daughter in his arms, and it gave her the first feeling of absolute protection, warmth and security that she'd had all night.

"Claudia, I've sent two of my security men to your apartment. Don't worry, baby. Everything is going to be fine. You'll see."

"Oh, daddy. I've never seen anything like this in my life." She had not intended to tell them everything. She had wanted to be cool and strong so that they wouldn't be overly overbearing with her, as was their habit. But her emotions were unplugged.

In great sobs and gulps, she told them everything. "There was a knife in him. There was blood everywhere. And the police. And the emergency medics. The detectives..." At that moment she almost fainted again, but her father held her up, walked her to a couch in the waiting room and had someone bring her a glass of water. Tabatha stroked her back, and when she felt better, she clutched her daughter's hand as Jordan asked more questions.

"How's Evan doing? Marni only told us a little bit on the phone. Oh, there she is." Marni was walking down the hall from the ladies' room. She gave Mr. and Mrs. Banks a hug and gave the answers that the Banks were clearly looking for.

"He's still in the operating room. We just don't know anything yet. We're waiting for a doctor to come out and tell us something."

"Where are his parents? Aren't they here?"

"Of course they're here. They just went to get some more coffee and rolls. They can't sit still anymore."

Jordan was finding it hard to believe how traumatic this last day had been. Between this incident and the note, he accepted that he was to have no peace for awhile.

"I'll get the Strangs, Mr. Banks," Marni offered. "I'm sure they'll be very grateful to see you here." Claudia tried to ask Marni not to leave her alone with her parents, but no words came out, and she was not able to summon the strength to make the meaningful eye contact that Marni would have understood.

Tabatha assembled the courage she needed to ask the questions that were haunting her. "Claudia, dear. Do you have any idea who could have...who could possibly have been sneaking around your building?"

"Of course not, mother."

"I just meant, my dear, you know, with all of the people you meet. Possibly there is someone who is jealous of you, or who you didn't invite to your party that held a grudge, or who you didn't hire for the night for some services you required."

Jordan understood where Tabatha was going with her questions and he didn't want Claudia to have to deal with it.

"Claudia, your mother is just concerned. And, of course, so am I. I am sure you told the detectives everything that could be helpful. But if you think of anything else at all, just tell me. You probably don't need to talk to them again. I can tell them anything that you want me too."

Claudia had regained a little of her stamina, and she did not want her parents to think that she was in danger. In fact, she didn't think she was.

With all the conviction she could muster, she told them how she felt. "I think it was just a deranged man who got into the building. Maybe the concierge closed his eyes for a few minutes too many. Maybe the janitors forgot to turn on the alarm system in the basement. Maybe one of the regular delivery boys just went crazy. And I know with all my heart and soul that there is absolutely no one in my life who could do something like this. No one."

Just then Marni returned with the Strangs, who exchanged warm hugs with the Banks. They had seen each other only hours before, each with champagne glasses in their hands, and smiling proudly about their children. Before last night, they had only met a few times.

Jackie reached for Claudia's hand. "Thank you so much for being here. I must tell you that Claudia and Marni have been wonderful friends to Evan and to us."

They all saw a doctor walking towards them, his white coat stained with blood. He told them that they were still operating, he wasn't sure how long it would take, but that it would be at least a few hours. He suggested that they all try to get some rest.

"I'm staying here with you," Claudia told the Strangs. "Why don't we all get something to eat."

Marni hugged her friend. "I'll stay here too. I wouldn't be able to sleep now if I tried."

"We're going to go home now, Claudia. I have a few people to call that might be able to help. By the way, I compliment you for calling Dr. Perlstein. It's just lucky that we had just been talking about him. He's the best, and so are you."

With that, Jordan Banks gave his lovely daughter a kiss on her cheek. He knew that there was nothing he could help with here, and that his time would be better spent making sure the security on his daughter's apartment, and her life, was the tightest money could buy.

After hugs and kisses all around, the Banks left the hospital.

The doctors worked on Evan through what was left of the night, and although the five hour operation was a success in terms of that he was still alive, he could not breathe on his own and had lapsed into a coma.

His body was hooked up to beeping blinking machines, pumps, and liquid dripping into his arms. Police officers were assigned to guard his room around the clock.

chapter

ELEVEN

Detective Ted Grange left Claudia Banks' apartment at 6:15 Saturday morning. He'd been on the force for almost twenty-seven years now and had hoped his schedule could be a little less ball-busting while he was working out his last few years before retirement. Especially right now this minute. This was not how he had expected to spend his weekend. Spring had finally arrived, and he had intended to meet his new girlfriend, Martha, for lunch and a walk around Central Park. She had complained that all he ever did was try to go to bed with her and never take her out on nice dates. She was right, of course. But unless he took her out once and awhile, he'd never be able to get her into the sack.

The detective that normally would have gotten this shift, Tyler, was out on special assignment. Shit, he thought. This was New York, and if it wasn't this case, it would have been another.

But the usual mugging and shooting would have gotten him home at a decent hour, and he wouldn't have had to go to the office until nighttime.

Sorry, Martha, he thought. Our little day in the park will have to wait. And I'll have to wait too. Damn it, she was a cute one. Chicks. They all wanted you to get serious with them. And you had to do a lot of work to make them think you were thinking that way. Suave and handsome he wasn't, and he knew it. He didn't exactly have women begging to go out with him. What a price.

He had time for a quick shower and a couple of hours sleep. By the time he went to the office at noon, the lab might have something. He fell into a deep sleep and dreamt that sirens were getting closer and closer to his building and he was panicking because he couldn't figure out what the emergency was and the fright jolted him upright until he realized the phone was ringing.

"Grange here," he growled into the phone.

"Grange, it's Detective Lenny Colter in Special Investigations."

"Yeah, whad'ya want Colter. I need some sleep." His eyes were sticky with morning eye dew as he tried to focus on the clock. Eleven o'clock. Not that bad.

"I'm not sure. Your guys just started entering some lab reports into the computer, and when they tried to open a new file under Banks, a report that I filed last night kept coming up. So they called me."

"What are you talking about? What report did you file last night?"

"Jordan Banks gets threatening letters every couple of months. He showed me a new one yesterday, and I brought it down to the lab."

"What did it say?"

There was silence at the other end of the line. Oh, the new protocols in action. They weren't supposed to discuss the details of a potential criminal case that could have ominous qualities from a home phone ever since the bomb threat on the Micronics Building. There was too much phone tapping and surveillance equipment out there for practically anyone who had enough money to pay for it. Just precautions, boys.

"Okay, Colter. I'll meet you in my office in twenty minutes."

Colter had checked into what happened at Banks' daughter's last night with forensics, and he had spoken to Jordan Banks. Could be just a coincidence. Mr. Banks had gotten so many of these weird letters and there was no immediate reason to believe that this wasn't just another crank with a new angle and bad timing. Then again.

He hadn't gotten that feeling of his hair at the collar tingling, the sign he often got just as he hit on what direction a case would take. He knew that he and Grange were among the best detectives in the force. They'd figure it out.

They both arrived at Grange's office at the same time. Colter made himself comfortable as Grange headed for the coffee machine.

"I gotta have some coffee. This one is a no sleeper. Want some?"

"Sure. Black."

Grange's office looked like it belonged in a B movie. The light gray walls were peeling, the gray speckled linoleum floor was so old and porous that the red wine stain from six years ago never came completely out, which wasn't so bad because at least, he joked, it gave the room a little color. There was a brown naugahyde couch with four matching chairs that had so many cracks on it that it looked like it was designed that way. Two of the matching chairs were near the couch, and the other two were in front of the old gray metal desk. Two 5 drawer gray metal file cabinets stood separated against one wall framing maps of the country, New York, the subway system, a bulletin board and a blackboard. Except for the calming panoramic view of the Hudson River, the disordered room belied Grange's incredible sense of organized sleuth.

When they were facing each other across the desk, they reviewed everything that had happened so far. When Grange finished telling him about the questioning at Claudia Banks' apartment, he added, "Now we've got men all over the tri-state area interviewing everyone on her guest list who had left the party already. The lady sure knows a lot of important people."

"They're in that other stratosphere, Grange. I've worked on a few things for her father. They all live like urban royalty. He's going through a lot right now between the note and the stabbing taking place so close to his daughter. This is not the best time for this family. Something strange is going on here."

Colter showed him the photocopies of the letter in the actual size and the enlargement.

"Look at this." Colter was getting pumped up. "Whoever wrote this really likes his games. He plays hide and seek with these little messages here. Colter pointed to the spots that magnified the smudges into 'tell her' and '16659.'

"I don't know what to make of it off hand," Grange said. "Has this one written to him before?"

"No. This seems to be a new one. We're running all the tests on it. Prints, DNA, particles, ink, paper...the usual. And Banks has been combing his files for any number that might relate to any of his girlfriends or deals. He's a rich man, and he usually makes time with rich women. You never know what he might have confided to one of them in the height of passion. One of them could be getting really greedy, maybe one of them fell in love with him and wants to make his life miserable. Maybe one of their boyfriends found out and is going bananas."

They both looked at each other. Neither of them were the type to be taken in by the gossip columns, but this Mr. Banks was about as blatant as a man could get with the ladies. Neither of them could figure that one out.

"For all we know there could be something really strange about him," mused Grange, "but then again a lot of the rich and powerful men play around. Look Colter, I'm just thankful this Evan Strang is still alive. At least I hope he still is. Better attempted murder than murder any day. I have some men guarding him."

"So what do you think about this note, Grange?"

"Well okay. The way I see it, it's either that whoever wrote it thinks he's got Banks on cheating, like you said, or he's pretending he knows about some shady business deal. And why not? You said Banks gets lots of threatening letters, people asking him for money for all kinds of reasons. It's a fair guess that some of his deals were a little, ya' know, under the table or not made with the most reputable characters. So, the guy's making a good guess, and hoping that Banks'll be nervous and just pay him. That's all I read into it. Look, the man's known for his big business deals. All over the world deals. He's in the paper for it all the time, he and that pretty wife of his."

"Sounds logical, Grange," Colter said. "I agree with you at this point. Those seem like the only two possible motives."

"Let me find out what's happening over there at the hospital." Grange yelled to the nearest desk outside his office. "Reiss, come in here."

In two beats Assistant Detective Reiss stood in the doorway, his youthful pink cheeked face camouflaging the sixth sense that won him his title faster than anyone in the force's history. "Yeah, Grange"

"What's the word from the hospital and the lab on the Banks situation?"

"The lab just called. They should have something for us in a couple of hours." He filled them in on the all-night hospital reports. "And as of about forty-five minutes ago, Strang was still in a coma. They're gonna keep us posted, and, except for the doctors, you're the first person they'll allow to talk to him."

Colter and Grange were thinking the same thing. The doctors couldn't guess when he would pull out of the coma. You never knew about these things. Could be minutes, could be weeks or more.

"Look," said Colter. "You've done a great job of keeping the press out of this so far. But once word gets out that someone is running around New York stabbing people in luxury apartment elevators, everybody's going to panic."

"I know, Colter. I know. We questioned fifteen people at that apartment. Not all of them will be able to keep this a secret. I wish we could privately weed this one out like we did with the Stromberg case. But these people are too well known. When it hits the papers and TV, it's gonna hit big. Look, I'm gonna just sit tight until the lab reports come in."

Grange yawned. "I need more coffee." He could have used eight hours more sleep, but he knew that the adrenaline would start to bubble when he had to concentrate on solving a crime. It was like a button was pushed and he went into automatic. It amazed him every time.

After he poured himself another cup, Grange told Colter he'd be right back and left the room to talk to Reiss. When he returned, he looked pumped-up and satisfied.

"Okay, Colter. Between us now we got men on twenty-four hour surveillance at Banks and his daughter's apartment buildings, and at his office building. They're watching the entrances, exits, stairwells, elevators, the reception area...anywhere someone would have to go to deliver something to Banks. We even got a man on as an elevator operator in his apartment building so we don't miss anybody going up and down."

"But they don't have manual elevators there."

"Yeah. I know it's an automatic elevator, but they're telling the tenants that there's a mechanical problem so it has to be run manually till it's fixed. Whatever that means. With the kind of tenants in those buildings, they'll probably want to have an elevator man on permanently."

"Good, Grange. Now all we need are a few healthy leads." As Colter pushed his chair back to get up, its aluminum legs made a squeaking sound on the linoleum floor.

"They'll come. They always do."

"Yeah. They usually do." Colter let out a sigh. "I'd say we have a far better chance waiting for that than waiting for them to redecorate for us." They both got a little chuckle out of that one. "I'll leave the xerox of the note here. Call me when you have something."

When Colter left, Grange ordered a roast beef sandwich on a hero, two apples and a cream soda. His doctor had told him to cut down on his cholesterol. Well, he was trying, but he was starving. And this was going to be another long day.

chapter

TWELVE

Jordan didn't get to his office until close to noon and wondered that he had been able to get there at all. He could always handle five hours' sleep, but not two or three. After spending a good part of the middle of the night at the hospital, he had not had much luck falling back to sleep again. He was going to have to make the list for Colter fueled by caffeine. Within an hour the phone rang.

"Glad to hear from you, Colter. I feel like I'm in Fort Knox here. Are there any policemen left on the streets?"

"Between that note you got and what happened at your daughter's party last night, we thought we ought to beef it up around your family for awhile."

"I do appreciate that, Colter. We've always been a pretty blessed and lucky family. This is really a double whammy, but I'm grateful that only you and I know that. If my wife knew about the note I think she would go mad. She's already so distraught over what happened at Claudia's. We've never had anything like that happen in such close proximity to any of us."

"I know that, Mr. Banks. I'm hoping that we can get to the bottom of all of this pretty fast. I just finished meeting with the detective that was assigned to the incident at your daughter's. Detective Grange. Believe me, he's leaving no stone unturned."

"Do they have any leads yet?"

"No. Not yet. He's waiting for the lab reports and the results of all the interviews. Unless there's a really strong piece of evidence from the scene like, you know, a clear print, fibers we can connect to something, blood samples we can link to someone, it's gonna take a little time. Maybe we'll get some kind of damning remark from one of the guests, you know, or some follow-up incident that ties something together. From here on it's a crap shoot. We know something will come. We just don't know when or from where."

"I know that every one is doing all that they can. I can't ask for anything more. Just please, keep me informed."

"Of course I will. How are you doing with that list?"

"I can tell you that I'm not very happy about this homework. I feel like I'm doing a term paper for school, and truthfully I had more fun writing about igneous rocks for earth science class. But, I am making progress."

"Do you have a time frame for when you might be finished with it?"

"At least another hour or two. The names that have been entered into the computer take time, but they're easy to cross reference by number. But I've never kept everything in the computers. I'm too old fashioned and still like my privacy with some matters. Will you be in your office later?"

"You can always reach me through my office. If I'm not there, they'll know where to find me. I'll have someone pick it up from you. That way you can just go home when you're done."

"Thanks. I can use the sleep, although I'll probably stop at Claudia's before I go home. Colter, let me ask you something. What do you think this was? Random? Just some crazy person who got into her building? Or do you think it could be someone who knows her?"

"I really can't conjure a guess yet. It's too soon. I can let my imagination go in a million directions right now, but I gotta wait for the reports to come in. I can tell you one thing, though. There's no telling how long her friend's coma could last. I understand they're pretty close so this must be rough on her. I hope she's handling it."

"She's got a lot of good friends, and she's very close to Evan's parents. They all seem to be holding up as well as can be reasonably expected."

When they were off the phone, Jordan resumed his list making. The process, or maybe it was the memories attached to this list of names and numbers he was putting together, was making him nauseous. He could not fathom one of the women he had been involved with being in any way the cause, or a link, to any of this insanity. Or someone involved with one of his old business deals. But maybe he had hurt someone and never suspected it.

By two o'clock he had seen nothing that related to the number on the note and his list was as complete as it was going to get. Maybe the detectives would see something that he couldn't see. He called Colter but he wasn't in his office. They'd find him and have him return the call in a few minutes.

Jordan switched on the TV to CNN. There had been nothing in the papers yet about any of his problems. If word had gotten out about the stabbing, he knew that CNN would have it right away. In the fifteen minutes that he waited for Colter's call, there was nothing.

"I don't know how you guys keep these things away from the press. I know a few politicians who wish they had your resources."

"We'll see how long our luck will hold out on that account, Mr. Banks. You're a pretty famous family. This silence isn't going to last very long, so enjoy it while you can. Are you done with the list?"

"Yes. I'm finished and I'm leaving my office. What do you want me to do with the envelope?"

"There's an Officer Perelli in your building. He should be knocking at your door any minute now. Give it to him. He's got very dark hair and eyes and olive skin. If anyone else comes to your door, I'll be on the phone with you and I'll know it. So let's just keep talking. I don't want you dealing with any strangers today. I know your driver brought you to the office. We had an unmarked car follow you there. And it will be the same thing when you go home, unless you just want an officer to give you a ride. I know you sent Albert home so he could be in the house with your wife."

"You don't miss much, do you Colter? Yes, I would like to let Albert stay home with her. I'll take that ride to my daughter's apartment. If the driver can wait for me, he can take me home, too."

"That'll be Officer Terso. Blonde hair, blue eyes, built like a twig but don't get fooled. He can kill three people without your hardly noticing that he moved. I'll have radio contact with you on your way."

"Thanks Colter. I really don't think there's that much to worry about, but I do appreciate the protection you're giving me and my family."

"What time did you leave your daughter's party?"

"Well, thanks to you I didn't get there until almost nine. I'd say that Tabatha and I left at around eleven, eleven-thirty, in that area."

"Did you notice any unusual conversations? Or any strangers in the hallway when you were leaving?"

"No. Nothing noteworthy at all. Really, I've gone over every detail since I got the call to go to the hospital. Tabatha and I discussed just that, and she doesn't remember anything unusual either. And believe me, she'd be more observant than I when it comes to something or someone looking out of place. No, I can't say that either of us can be of any help to you with that. You can tell that to your associate, if you would. It would probably be better if we can avoid one of your men having to interview my wife. She can be a bit fragile and high strung in upsetting situations."

"I'll see what I can do there. That shouldn't be a problem."

"Your man's at my door. Hold on a second."

Jordan asked who it was before he opened the heavy metal enclosed wooden office door. The man said he was Officer Perelli, so Jordan let him in and went back to the phone.

"There's someone on the line who would like to speak to you, Officer."

Just as Jordan picked up the receiver to hand it to the man who identified himself as Perelli, he froze. Another policeman entered the room. All he could think of was that two young thugs had somehow stolen police uniforms and were about to beat him up or kill him. He was too old for this, he thought. If one of them made a move, he'd be finished. He was about to scream something into the phone when the most recently arrived officer started to speak.

"I'm Officer Terso. I'll take you wherever you need to go, Mr. Banks."

"You almost gave me heart failure, young man. Give me a minute to catch my breath." In the meantime, Perelli took the phone, talked to Colter, and handed it back to Jordan.

"I am clearly not cut out for your world, Detective Colter." Jordan was still panting. "I guess I haven't admitted to myself how unsettling all of this has been."

chapter

THIRTEEN

At 2:30 Grange looked over the second delivery of preliminary lab reports that Reiss had just brought in. So far they were just doing basic tests. If more detailed analysis were needed in any of the categories, he could always order them.

The knife was definitely a kitchen knife, not a hunting knife or one of those Swiss Army fold-ups that a lot of New Yorkers carried around with them. Looked like a fancy imported chef's knife with a black onyx-like handle and a slightly undulating serrated edge. It was either a gift to Claudia Banks that she never knew she had, it was part of the caterer's gear, or some loony cooking freak carried it around with him and broke into the building. If it was Claudia's or the caterer's, then the assailant was someone who attended the party, either as a guest or as part of the help. If it was a non-invitee, then it could be anyone for any reason.

Looked like strands of hair from everyone at the party, and all of their relatives, were in that elevator and the hallway. That wasn't helpful, but that wasn't surprising.

Nothing notable with the fibers. Except for pieces of carpet that everyone dragged around with their shoes and that clung to clothes, there were some very colorful pieces of women's outfits and a lot of black strands from men and women's evening clothes.

The fingerprints were smudged. Whoever did it made a quick and successful effort of removing anything that could have been run through the computer.

They had enough of Evan Strang's Type O blood to do every blood test that had ever been conceived of, and then some. No other blood types were in the area.

The hallway showed some evidence of Type O blood tracking. And so did the stairwell. Nothing big enough to get a shoe or foot size. Somebody he interviewed after the party said they thought they heard footsteps far away. Padded like sneakers or some sort of rubber sole. But it could also have been bare, stockinged or socked feet. That means it could have been a man or a woman.

The first part of the report that grabbed Grange's attention was what they found under Strang's fingernails. Black fibers, a bit of dark brown shoe leather and food. There was a lot of finger food at the party, so that part could be explained logically. But whose shoes was he gripping onto and why? It must have been a strong hold for him to get black fabric under his nails, he thought. Was it the same person who was wearing the brown leather shoes? He'd be a lousy dresser if it were. And why would he have a fragment of shoe leather under his nail? He must have scratched at one of his attacker's shoes when he fell to the floor of the elevator.

When forensics came in with their findings and compared them to the hospital x-rays and interviews with Strang's doctors, they'd know about the angle of entry, which would then determine the force needed to inflict the injury. The shape and direction of the blood splats would tell them a lot too. If the poor guy was for some reason crouched lower than the attacker, it would open the door again for it being a man or a woman.

Then there was the trace of cologne. Men's or women's? The chemical analysis might tell them.

There were always so many variables. This is what he loved about his work. From nothing, all of a sudden you had a card table topped with hundreds of little pieces of all different shaped and colored puzzle parts. At first the sheer number and initial indistinguishability of all the pieces was overwhelming. But then you saw how you could begin to fit a few of the shapes together. Some over here, some over there. And then you got a corner. And then you filled in some sky. And then more, until a whole picture was right in front of you. On the other hand, right now it looked like a lot of nothing.

"They're all still at the hospital, Grange."

"Huh? Oh, hi Reiss. I didn't know you were in here. Anything from the guys in the field yet?"

"Too soon."

"We gotta know what everyone was wearing. The type of fabric and the color. And shoes. All the guests and the workers. Everyone."

"You know they're thorough."

"Yeah, I know. I'm just thinking out loud."

"They should be back to us in a few hours. Did anyone at the party take pictures?"

"Yeah. There was an Eric Stanton there. Big in entertainment publicity. He had someone with a camera on the scene. We had the rolls of film picked up from him early this morning when he was being interviewed. We'll have the shots from the lab soon."

"What do you want to do about talking to Claudia Banks again? And her family? Or Strang's parents?"

"I want to give them till tomorrow after they get some sleep. I don't think any of them'll make any sense right now. Anyway, we got orders from above to be real respectful to the families and to make this a very comprehensive investigation. Seven days a week, twenty-four hours a day. Whatever it takes. It's a priority. Colter's used to mingling with people like this. I'm not. This is like dealing with the aristocracy, ya know? And everybody's watching us."

chapter

FOURTEEN

If it weren't for all of the equipment attached to him, Evan looked like a sleeping young child, but hardly recognizable as the same Evan who had been so animated and happy less than a day ago. Only two people at a time, with a doctor, were permitted in his room and, until he woke up, and had spoken to the police, his visiting list was limited to the four people who had been keeping vigil at the hospital.

Frank and Jackie Strang had spent as much time with their son's near lifeless body as the doctors would allow. Even though they knew he was still heavily medicated and sedated from the operation, they stroked his arm, held his hand and tried desperately to make contact with him through their warm loving words. Marni held Claudia's hand as she sat by Evan's bedside and talked to his sleeping body.

By 2 o'clock Saturday afternoon, Claudia and Marni were having trouble keeping their eyes open and thinking clearly. Their make-up had long been scrubbed off their faces and their gorgeous clothes were wrinkled and disheveled. The doctors had told them all to go home. There was nothing anyone could do but wait till there was some kind of change in Evan's condition.

Jackie and Frank insisted on staying with their son and intended to make the hospital their home until Evan woke up. If Evan woke up. Claudia and Marni were to be driven home in an unmarked police car. Except for the police guards that hovered nearby, the girls were left alone for the first time since they had arrived at the hospital.

"So, if this is what running on empty feels like, I think it's time we both thought of going home and getting some rest. If there is any change with Evan, we won't be able to deal with it properly without a little sleep. What do you say?"

"I'm exhausted, but I don't think I'm ready to go home yet. I don't know what my apartment is going to be like. A war zone, probably. Let's get some soup or some tea first, all right?"

"Sure. Let's do that. You know, you can come to my house. I have plenty of clothes that will fit you, and maybe it's better if you're not alone. Or, I'll come home with you. Whichever you'd prefer."

"I think we both need our own homes, our own beds, and our own bath tubs after a night like this. And my parents will go crazy if I don't stay in my apartment with all of the security they've arranged for me."

"Whatever you want. Unless you're stalling and you think there might suddenly be a change in Evan, even though the doctors insist that nothing is going to change that fast."

"No, it's not that."

"All right then. Let's get something to eat, and then let's leave this depressing place. This has all been a bit overwhelming."

The posted sign said that if they followed the yellow stripe down the corridor, they would arrive at the hospital cafeteria in just a few minutes.

"Of course you're right, Marni. This has all been too much. It's bad enough to see Evan in his condition, but his parents. I've never seen two people so distraught. I care for them both so dearly, and I feel so helpless."

"All you can do is be there for them. You know that. The rest of it, his recovery, is out of our hands. We have to trust that the doctors are doing all they can for him."

"You know, Marni. I've been so used to having practically unlimited amounts of money. I can always buy anything I want. Fix anything that needs to be fixed. And yet there's nothing I can do for Evan. What good is having so much money if, when it really matters, it doesn't make a difference anyway?"

"You have made a difference, Claudia. Don't forget, you made sure he had the best doctor in New York. And you're the only one who could have consoled his parents. They so clearly adore you."

At the end of the yellow stripe they found a surprisingly busy dining room filled with doctors, nurses, and tables of people so sad and scared they could hardly speak. They each took a tray and silverware. The smells from the food cauldrons had a calming effect. They both chose pumpernickel rolls and the hearty vegetable soup and plopped into their chairs.

Claudia was relieved to be able to speak privately to her friend. "I need to talk as if everything is going to be fine. I have to figure everything out now. And I have to admit I'm terminally confused about my feelings for Evan. Marni, at the party he told me that there was something very important that he wanted to talk to me about. He said we would wait until everyone left, and then, if we still had the energy, we would talk."

"Oh Claudia. It sounds like he had finally made some decisions. You must have been a wreck all night. I'm sure he was going to propose."

"I'm not so sure. Because I asked him if what he was going to tell me had anything to do with how cold and distant he had been lately. He said it had everything to do with it, but he wouldn't give me even a clue as to what he had on his mind."

"You want to know what I think? I think he was going to give you an ultimatum. I think he had finally accepted that you were having trouble letting yourself fall in love with him. I seriously don't think he could take the indecisiveness anymore."

"You're probably right. And I don't have the slightest idea how I would have responded if he had done that. I don't know why I haven't fallen in love with him. He's certainly everything a girl could want. But there's something. Oh, I don't know. Maybe it's that I think we were meant to be only friends, and it's as simple as that. Or I'm not used to someone insinuating themselves into my life so intimately and so publicly with a song that everybody in the world knows that he wrote for me."

"Or, maybe you have the kind of relationship that you've always wanted, and you're frightened. Look, Claudia. We have both lived on our own and by ourselves for so many years. If the possibility of a wonderful relationship appears, maybe neither of us would even recognize it. Or maybe we're more terrified of the big commitment than we've ever admitted."

The soup had started to make them both feel better. Half way through the large sized bowl, Claudia took a deep breath. "Let's get the subject off of me for a minute, can we?"

"All right. What?"

"You and Craig seemed to have a lot to talk about. The two of you looked quite cozy together."

"You know, just before we heard that horrible scream, I was going to drag you into another room and ask you about him. I guess now's my chance. Why have you kept him such a secret?"

"Purely unintentional, I assure you. I've known him only medium well for a few years."

"So, tell me something about him." Marni was only too glad to get both of their minds off the immediate crisis, if only for a little while.

"Well, of course. Let's see. I know that he made a small fortune in the stock market. He used the profits he made after he sold most of his shares in a film company that he had invested in. You know the company, Marni. A small one, but it surprised everyone when it had a number of huge box office successes."

"Pandalay?"

"That's it."

"It was the hottest independent film company for years."

"Right. And Craig sold out after it had been on top of its field for about five years. One year later, the company was out of business. Craig had been on Pandalay's board of directors with my father. That's how I first met him."

"Now this sounds familiar. I remember reading about that in the trades. I certainly never related it to the Craig I met at your party. Actually, he seemed to know a lot about me, and I knew absolutely nothing about him. Hmmm. I remember now that there was a mini scandal about this story. The company went under. I remember reading that your father had held onto his stock until it was too late. Right. The press had said something like 'not that a few million really mattered to Mr. Banks.'"

"So, what else is new? They always say something like that when he invests in something that goes bad, although that rarely happens."

"I remember reading that insiders had speculated that somehow Craig knew when, why and how Pandalay's lucky streak was going to end. For awhile, there were all kinds of rumors. Then there was an investigation, and it was determined that Craig Harris had no way of knowing. He just had good investment instincts, and knew the right time to get out."

"That's him, all right. But, now do you see why he and I hadn't stayed friends for awhile? It was a little touchy between Craig and my father. And then, frankly, I had forgotten about him until I heard that he wanted to make some investments in the music business. That's why I invited him to the party."

"Oh, now I get that picture. But what about his personal life? Do you know anything?"

"Hmmm. Actually, yes, but just a few things. I know that he had been married. I'm not sure, but I don't think there were any children." Claudia's brow wrinkled.

"What is it? He is divorced, isn't he?"

"Yes, well...I know he's not married now. He was dating someone when I first met him, and that was about three or four years ago. But you know, I think I remember knowing that his wife had died. I...you know, I'm too tired to think. But I promise I'll figure it out for you."

"My brain feels fried, too. I guess it's time to go home now. Are you sure you'd rather be alone?"

"If I don't feel totally self-conscious having all of those security people around, I'm sure that I'll be asleep so fast that it won't matter. Of course I'll be all right. Come on. Let's get them to take us home."

The unmarked car dropped Claudia off first, and a policeman was waiting in the lobby to escort her upstairs. When Marni finally reached her building, she was so exhausted that she could hardly walk. The plain clothes police driver took her upstairs, checked her apartment and made sure that she was securely locked in before he left.

This was a nightmare, and she was drained. All she wanted right now was a long, hot perfumed bath. Then sleep.

It was wonderful to be home. She had created a beautiful haven for herself and she treasured every moment she spent there. It was her cozy retreat from the intensity of everything else. During an experience like this, she felt like it was hugging her back into familiarity.

She looked around her apartment and felt proud, and relieved, that she had worked so hard and had earned so much. She now owned a three bedroom condominium on New York's Upper East Side. She opened the sliding doors in the living room and went out to the terrace where she invariably found the most peace.

Her sprawling terrace was lovingly filled with colorful flowers every spring, emphasizing those that would bloom well into the fall. Pink, white and scarlet begonias, hanging baskets of delicate cascading purple browalias, tubs of red dahlias, rose pink petunias, cherry dianthus, lavender pansies, pink and lilac impatiens, white daisies, red and pink geraniums, miniature pink roses, deep rich violet morning glories and walls strewn with ivy. But never yellow flowers.

Flowers were Marni's passion, and she never tired of planting new ones from seeds or bulbs throughout the year, or from finding wonderful fabrics from all over the world, and from years ago, with floral designs.

Her master bedroom suite was lovely, warm and cozy with her bedspread and curtains of lilac-blue with tiny little white flowers, lilac-blue carpeting and two dark carved wood white marble topped dressers. Her second bedroom was the guest room done in wonderful pink and white fabrics, and there were paintings and pillows with every imaginable kind of pink flower. The third bedroom was her at-home office, with a periwinkle blue sofa, a matching marble coffee table and a glass topped desk. The fax, phone, scanner and computer were hidden behind a gorgeous French white stained cabinet, as were the file cabinets.

The large living room curved into a nice size area that Marni made into a wonderful combination of den, television room and library. The wood paneled dining room abutted the sizable kitchen that had a breakfast nook that looked like an outdoor French bistro. Yes, after so many years of struggling, she had created a home that she truly loved.

Except for her adored fluffy white Maltese named Flower, she was alone. In her wildest thoughts, she could never have imagined still being single and alone at thirty-six.

She was just starting to get ready for her bath when the phone rang. She didn't think she had the energy to answer it, but the fear of receiving bad news about Evan forced her to pick it up quickly. It was Craig.

"Hello, Marni. I just wanted to see if you're all right."

She was astonished by her reaction to his voice. She was very happy to hear from him, but that wasn't it. His voice had an immediate and incredible effect on her. She hoped that she was able to conceal her bewilderment at least a little bit.

"That's very sweet of you, Craig. Actually, I've just returned from the hospital, and I'm exhausted."

"How is Evan doing?"

"Not very well, I'm afraid. He's in a coma."

"That's horrible. I'm sorry for him and for all of you who are close to him."

"Thank you, Craig. That's really very kind of you." Marni wondered how his wife had died. Could it have been something like this?

"I'd like to spend some time with you, Marni. But I'll be patient. Of course you're tired. Please, give my love to Claudia. I'll phone you tomorrow."

She felt like his voice had cast a spell on her. "I'd like that," she finally said.

When they got off the phone, she remembered feeling this way only once before. The first time a boy kissed her.

chapter

FIFTEEN

At 3 o'clock Saturday afternoon Reiss walked in to
Grange's office with a sheaf of paper in his hands.

"We've got the first ream of reports in from the party
guest list interviews. They haven't been able to get to everyone
yet. Some of them just haven't been home."

"Anything there?"

As Reiss answered him, Grange looked through the
papers to see for himself.

"The one that needs your attention right away is this one."
He pointed to the top sheet. "We definitely confirmed that
the knife belongs to the caterer, Tommy Laten. They brought
him down to the lab to verify it in person. The poor guy almost
fainted when he saw it."

"I wanna see him."

"He's downstairs now."

"Okay. Bring him up here. While we're talking to him, have the guys do a check on him."

"Got it."

"What about prints on the knife? Still not even a portion of one?"

"No. There was nothing. Whoever did it either wore gloves or wiped it clean before he left the scene."

"This Tommy Laten was one of the people who was still at Miss Banks' when the body, I mean the injured party, was discovered. I interviewed him myself. Can't be him, unless he's a real snake and made a quick and seamless return without anybody noticing he was gone."

"The only other enticing item was something a few of the guests and help said."

"Yeah? What was that?"

"Seems that Miss Banks, and her guest of honor, the victim Evan Strang, were acting strangely towards each other."

"Oh yeah? What's that supposed to mean?"

"Well, you got the history. Friends for five years, then he falls in love with her and writes a song about her that becomes a big hit. She's not in love with him. He goes through changes and by the night of the party they're hardly talking to each other. They just seemed to be acting cordial to each other, you know, for the sake of the guests. Except once he took her aside to have a private chat. But they supposedly still didn't seem right after that."

"Yeah, I got that too from some of the interviews. Could be something there. We need a little more solid stuff before we jump on that one."

"Want them to talk to Miss Banks?"

"No. I did a pretty thorough with her after the incident. And nobody talks to any of the Banks except me and Colter."

"I figured that."

"I'll talk to her and her friend Marni Kendell again if we need more from them. I'm sure they're both traumatized and exhausted from being up all night. They'll probably sleep till the middle of the day tomorrow. In the meantime, let's talk to the guy who made all of that delicious food. That and her French roast coffee is what kept me going all night to do those interviews. Damn he made some good stuff. Too bad you missed it."

"You forget to invite me to the fun things."

"Some fun. Okay, bring him in here. See what the guys can find out while he's here. Have them bring the report in or call me so if there's anything at all, we can pin him on it while he's in our face."

Tommy Laten walked in to Grange's office with red splotched eyes framed by bags, and a look on his face as if he had just seen a ghost. Except for his depleted appearance, he looked like he could be a model, with his thin muscular body topped with a luxurious head of blonde and brown streaked hair which crowned enormous angelic blue eyes and a ruddy peachy complexion.

Grange reintroduced himself and offered him a seat across from his desk. Reiss sat on the other chair next to Tommy.

"This is the most awful experience of my life. Please, I just want to go home. I've got to be able to sleep this away. I can't believe you see things like this every day and you can still breathe."

"Yeah Tommy, this is what we do. I know you've been through a lot, but it's your knife so there has to be some kind of a connection there. So we have to talk about it until we can figure out what it is. Then you can go."

"Ask me anything you want. I'm too freaked out to be able to think of anything to say."

"How many people did you have working for you at Miss Banks' party?"

"You already asked me that when we spoke last night."

"I know I did. But just in case something new comes to mind, we're talking about it again."

"Jesus. This is like the movies. All that's missing is a bare light bulb swinging over my head. Do you have a two way mirror here so people can watch us talk?"

"Okay Tommy. Don't be a wise guy."

"Hey, listen. I'm not trying to be smart. I'm just more tired than I remember being tired in years. These kinds of hours are for kids. After seeing what I saw, I feel like I'm delirious and I'm still walking in the nightmare. Please be a little gentle with me."

Grange and Reiss looked at each other. Neither of them could decide if this guy was for real.

"Let's get the names down again."

"I'll do the best I can, but I don't have my work sheet for the night with me. Do you have some coffee? And a piece of paper and a pen? I'll reconstruct the list as best I can."

"That's fair enough."

Reiss left the room to get coffee, and Grange gave Tommy a legal pad and a black felt tipped pen. While they were waiting for Reiss to come back with the wake-up juice, Grange kept the conversation going.

"So I hear that you're called the 'Caterer to the Stars' Tommy. Why is that?"

"Look I've been in this business for about fifteen years, the last ten on my own with my own company. I had worked for a few famous and wealthy people when I was with my last job years ago. We got along great and they loved me and my work. When I went out on my own, a lot of the people I had met hired me. Then, you know how it is. Word got out, and I've been lucky to be recommended for a lot of the important society parties."

"You make a lot of money doing catering?"

"I'm not usually asked questions like this. But, I'm in a police station, so I guess anything goes. Well, yes. I've been fortunate. I make very decent money."

Reiss came in with the coffee and put it on the desk in front of Tommy with two miniature cups of half and half, a couple of bags of sugar and some wooden stirrers.

Grange caught Reiss' eye and spoke to Tommy. "Sorry. I know this is not the kind of gourmet coffee you're used to, but this is what our budget gets us. We'll leave you in here a few minutes to work on those names. Be right back."

When they got to the outer office, Reiss told Grange that nothing was coming up on a Tommy Laten that was at all unusual. Everything checked with everything he'd said.

"Okay. We'll just have to make sure that no one saw him leave except to go to the bathroom. And that means the guys might have to talk to his help again. Did they get to his whole list yet?"

"No. You had twelve names on that list including Tommy's. Of the three cooks, five waiters and three bartenders, only four had already left when you went up there. They've interviewed all of yours and got one of the guys that you missed. The other three weren't home when the guys went to their apartments, and nobody answered the phones either. They're either asleep or they're just out. I got men watching their buildings so we won't miss them when they come home, or if one of them sneaks out."

"Or maybe some of the addresses are bogus. You did good Reiss. Can you give me a copy of the names so I know who we missed, and so I can check it against the one he's doing now. And tell the guys in the field to check if anyone saw Tommy leave that god damn party. A stab like that doesn't have to take very much time. He seems too light weight for it, but right now, he's a contender. I'll meet you back in there. And see if there are any more lab or hospital reports."

When Grange returned to his office, Tommy's head was being held up by both hands and he was obviously trying to focus on the piece of paper.

"How are you doing with those names?"

"I almost have them all, but give me another minute. I'm having trouble remembering a few of the names. Some of them were regulars that work with me all the time, and some are just from the bunch of names that are usually in the circuit, or referrals, you know, depending on availability."

When Tommy was finished, Grange compared the new list with the one he had given him before that Reiss had just brought in. It was all the same names, but some of the spellings didn't quite match. The ones he misspelled were the Italian and Spanish names, but it looked like they'd be pronounced the same. The guy seemed to be making an honest effort.

"Tommy. Did you leave the party at all?"

"Did I what?"

"Did you leave the party? You know, go onto the terrace to get some air, or into the hallway just to get out of all the pressure for a few minutes. You know, everyone deserves a break when they have to work for hours."

"Hey. I don't know what you're trying to get at, but no. Of course not. Anybody that knows my work knows that I'm a perfectionist. Mr. Grange. I'm sorry. I mean, Detective. I would never ever leave a job until it's finished, and I know that all the guests, and especially the host and hostess, are happy. No. I don't take those kinds of breaks. Ever."

"You mean to tell me that if we asked anybody that was working with you, or any of the guests, no one, not a soul, would have seen you leave? Even for a minute?"

"I went to the bathroom once. That was it. That was the only time I wasn't working. There is no one who could tell you any different than that."

"Let me ask you about some of these people who were working for you that night."

"As I told you last night, and when I got here today, you can ask me anything you want. I have nothing to hide."

"Which ones on the list are your regulars, which have you worked with at any time before, and which were new hires?"

They spent about an hour going over all the names. Tommy told Grange everything he knew about each one of them. Just like he had the night before.

SUNDAY

chapter

SIXTEEN

At 10 AM Sunday morning Grange called Colter at home. "Hey. How about some brunch? If we gotta work on a Sunday, let's at least start it off in some pleasant surroundings for a change. I got some things I want to go over with you before I go into the office."

When they were seated at the Sunrise Cafe, Grange took off his tie, unbuttoned the top three buttons of his shirt, took off his jacket and rolled up his sleeves. After he folded the jacket and tie over the next seat, he lit a cigarette and let the smoke spiral from his thick lips.

"I'm surprised you get so dressed up on a Sunday, Grange. I'm really very impressed."

"Hey. Let's have some coffee before we start our verbal combat routine. On second thought, that's just as good a way as any to make sure the synapses are connecting. Okay, don't stop now."

"That's it. I'm hungry. And I'm getting a lot of pressure to push this case forward. So it's making me ornery."

"You're so god damn preppy, Colter. Nobody would ever know you're just a bloodthirsty investigator."

"It gets me where I've got to go."

"Hey, so listen," Grange said. "This is probably off the wall, but here's a thought."

"No idea is too crazy when it comes to a criminal investigation. You know the investigator's motto. 'Dare to be stupid.' Go ahead, Grange. Be stupid."

"So I've been thinking about that song."

"Are you getting romantic in your old age, Grange?" Colter chided.

"Yeah, right. No. I'm talking about that song that Evan Strang wrote about Claudia Banks."

"It's a pretty song, and it's a major hit all over the world. My daughter wants it to be about her. She tried to get me to promise her I'd buy her a Lamborghini when she's older and match it, and everything in it, to her green eyes. That song is going to cost a lot of fathers a fortune. Maybe this Strang made a side deal with the car company on every custom car."

"Or maybe there's a clue to this case in the song."

"What do you mean, Grange?"

"Think about it. The song writer gets stabbed at a party that's celebrating his hit song. And we're looking all over the place for a motive. Maybe it has something to do with the god damn song."

"What are you getting at?"

"I'm not sure. Maybe there's a clue in the words of the song."

"Let's keep going with this one," Colter said.

"Okay. Where would you take this one?"

"Maybe he plagiarized part of the song and somebody's got it in for him over that."

"Or maybe someone to do with all the money the song is earning isn't handling something too well, you know, like keeping more than his share of the royalties."

"They're all in our files now, Grange. Anyone to do with that song was at that party and you talked to them or our boys did. I didn't see anything suspicious there but let's both have another look see with that in mind. Not a bad line of thinking, Grange. Not stupid at all."

"Hey thanks."

For the next two hours they reviewed the evidence and the interviews. Each of them had a different kind of itch. There were still too many possibilities.

When they left the coffee shop, they walked past a homeless man sleeping in the entrance of a closed office building.

"What are we gonna do with these poor bastards, Colter? This ain't Calcutta, you know? It's so fuckin' depressing."

"It's really sad, isn't it? I always think that at one time these people had mothers who loved them and who had big dreams for their kid. Who'd ever picture their child ending up like this?"

"Yeah. And for all we know maybe it's some guy like him that we're looking for."

chapter

SEVENTEEN

Halfway through the Sunday Times and her third cup of coffee, Marni called Claudia.

"How're you doing today?"

"I feel like we're all in a horror movie. Not only that, like I'm in jail. Don't get me wrong. I know I'd feel a lot worse without it, but police protection is suffocating."

"I wouldn't mind knowing someone was guarding my door today. This whole thing is really creepy."

"Do you want me to arrange it for you?"

"If that feeling comes over me again later, I might. But so far, really, I'm all right. What time do you want to go to the hospital today?"

"Had your coffee yet?"

"I'm on my third cup now. What about you?"

"Just brewing it now. Jackie called a few minutes ago. She's beginning to feel a little hopeful for the first time. Evan is breathing on his own. This is so awful for them."

"Do you want to be her daughter-in-law?"

"How could you ask me that now?"

"Evan will probably want to know the minute he wakes up. The first question he's going to ask is what happened? Then he'll ask you to marry him."

"You're such an optimist. That's why I adore you. But let's change the subject for a minute, can we? I want to be in a good mood when I see Jackie and Frank today. God knows they don't need me to make things worse than they are."

"Don't be silly. They love you for worrying about Evan as much as they are. But all right. What do you want to talk about?"

"Clothes. Anything to really change the subject and make us laugh. I have to get these cobwebs out of my head."

"All right. How about this. Remember those cotton knit sweaters we used to wear?"

"Which ones?" Claudia thought for a moment, and then she giggled. "You did it. You made me laugh. You mean the ones we banned from our closets and society as a whole?"

Both of them used to wear Marovia sweaters. But then their friends who modeled for the print ads complained that, after years of sweating under klieg lights and the baking sun they were never once offered a sample or a discount on the garments. Claudia spread the word. Her contacts around the world had so much influence on what became popular in the fashion industry that the manufacturer's sales plummeted.

"I'll never forget the designer we championed next."

"Oh right. He had been struggling for ten years and we made him an overnight success."

"Thanks for the change of subject, Marni. I think we both needed that. How about we pick you up in an hour?"

"Sounds perfect. Oh, I spoke to Eric. He said that Matty, Susan and Carl are going to meet us at the hospital today."

"That's wonderful of them. I know they've been frantic too."

"Of course Eric said he'll put any kind of publicity spin on the situation that Evan might want when he's feeling better. He said it's been getting back to him that a lot of people in the entertainment world have Evan in mind to write music for their various film and record projects, and he's ready to help Evan deal with it until he can do it himself. Carl offered to take care of any legal work that Evan might need in case there's a lawsuit or criminal situation involved. And he's prepared to work with your father's battery of lawyers if that was required."

"We have a great group of friends. We're lucky to have each other."

"One more thing, Claudia. While it's just you and me and no guards or anyone else, let me ask you something about Craig Harris. Do you remember more details about his life?"

"Yes. I do. Sorry my memory was in such a shambles yesterday. Actually I'm amazed that we were capable of having any lucid conversations at all. Craig's a wonderful guy. I could see that the two of you were getting along very nicely. You're seriously interested, I presume?"

"I'm interested, but with reservations. He phoned yesterday and I can't deny that I have at least a big crush. He seems utterly charming, sincere and intelligent. And I certainly have no complaints about his looks. But there was something a little, oh I don't know, not as bad as eerie."

"Say no more. I think I know what it is."

"Is it awful?"

"No. But I couldn't help notice how he couldn't take his eyes off you all night. It was almost melancholic, right? Is that what you're talking about?"

"That's it."

"When I first got to know him, he had already been married for about six years. His wife was killed in a skiing accident and he was still suffering terribly. Between that and his little to-do with my father over the film company investment, that's why I never mentioned him to you. And the other reason was that, well, he showed me her picture. She looked a lot like you."

"Eek. I don't know if I like this."

"He's a good man, Marni. He's got his feet on the ground now. Don't let that little story be the deal breaker, as you would say. I think he's ready to meet someone."

Just then Marni's phone gave a call-waiting beep. "Hold on a sec. Let me see who this is." She pushed her flash button and said hello.

"Hi Marni. This is Craig Harris. How are you doing today?"

"Craig. Oh, hello. Could you hold on a minute?" She pushed the call-waiting button and took a deep breath.

"Claudia. It's Craig."

"Talk to him Marni. I'll see you in an hour. And remember. I really think this could be it, and I'm thrilled for you."

"You're a dear, Claudia. I hope I'm not totally self-conscious with him now, but I'll try to remember what you said. Oh God, I don't want to be somebody's mirage."

"You're the real thing, Marni. It just means that you're the type he likes. Go get him. See you soon."

"Hi Craig. That was Claudia. We're getting ready to go back to the hospital again."

"I know you two are going through a terrible time right now. I'm trying to balance my concern for you with my selfish desire to see you again. Would you like that, Marni?"

"Yes, Craig. I would like that very much." As she said that, she realized that she was again mesmerized by the sound of his voice. Certain words that he said. The way he pronounced those words. No. It was the tone. His voice was so extraordinarily warm and moving.

"Marni? Are you still there?"

Embarrassed, she realized that she had been away on a little private journey. But to where?

"Sorry, Craig. I just poured myself another cup of coffee."

"Uh huh. Well, how does this sound to you? I thought we might do something that could relieve some of the tension you're going through. How about a game of tennis later this afternoon?"

"I can't today. I'll be at the hospital all afternoon, and I've already planned to have dinner there with Claudia and Evan's parents."

"I understand. How about tomorrow, then? By then you'll probably really need a break. I can leave work anytime after three tomorrow."

"That sounds perfect. I should be finished with my last meeting a little after three and I'll probably be like a tight rubber band. A good game of tennis sounds like the ideal change of pace."

He offered to pick her up, and she gave him the address of her last Monday meeting.

MONDAY

chapter

EIGHTEEN

At 7:30 Monday morning, Maria Lambert had just gotten comfortable in her seat on the C train from Brooklyn to her job in lower Manhattan. She was about to open her magazine when she dropped her silver rimmed ruby tinted teardrop shaped sunglasses. As she was picking them up, she saw the headline on a newspaper that someone had dropped on the floor. BANKS SOCIETY FAMILY IN SCANDAL AGAIN ATTEMPTED MURDER GRUESOME DETAILS.

She shuddered. What a violent city she lived in, she thought. Didn't anybody ever have any good news?

When the next thought hit her, she reached for the newspaper and picked it up in one beat. It had foot prints from the rush hour crowds all over it. Hmmm...I know that name, she thought. But I don't know them. So why in the world would I want to hold a dirty newspaper? She let it slide back to the floor and opened her own magazine.

She couldn't concentrate on any of the stories, or even the pictures. Something was gnawing at her. Well, sure she was distracted. She had a lot on her mind. The promotion that she had been promised could happen any day now. Maybe even today. It wouldn't put an end to her money problems, but it would help. Her sister had just moved to the West Coast, her dog was in the vet with what might be a terminal disease and she just broke up with her boyfriend.

She had had high hopes for a future with Lou. He had seemed so self-assured, like there was nothing he couldn't handle, and she liked that kind of strength and confidence in a man. But after they had been seeing each other for almost a year, she realized that he was just a dreamer, and that all his dreams were...

She grabbed for the paper again. That's where I know that name. Lou was talking about them. What was it that he had said about them?

She read the article.

> Friday night a man was found stabbed in an elevator in one of the most luxurious buildings in New York. The assailant has not been found. The victim has been identified as Evan Strang, a songwriter most recently known for penning the hit song "Claudia." He had just left a party given in his honor by Claudia Banks, the woman for whom the song was written. Miss Banks is the daughter of Jordan Alexander and Tabatha Banks, one of the wealthiest families in the United States.
>
> The police attempted to keep the story out of the press in an effort to avoid...

A knot had formed in her stomach and she couldn't read anymore. Oh my God, she thought. That's one of the men Lou liked to talk about.

Midnight Song

She ripped the article out of the paper and stuffed it into her pocketbook. Her body was trembling. Okay, relax, she told herself. Just because he talked about them doesn't mean he had anything to do with this. Why am I getting so crazy? Because I think he's crazy, that's why. But this crazy?

She tried to calm herself and review her memories in an orderly manner.

This Mr. Banks was one of the rich people Lou pointed out to her in the tabloids and society columns. He was always with different beautiful women or important world leaders or making multi-million dollar deals.

Lou would pick up the paper and show her the pictures and say things like, 'These rich men can do anything they want. Money is power, hon. Money is power. And Christ, look at him. All that and he's good looking, too. Look at me, hon. I'm great looking. I would make the perfect rich man and you'll see, one of these days I'm gonna be rich and powerful. Just give me a little more time.'

That's all he ever asked for. A little more time. He thought he had it all figured out. He said he had dreams, people to see, places to go, things to do and he would make our lives wonderful.

When she first met Lou, she was dazzled by how good looking he was and how enthusiastically he went about planning for the future. He was certain that there was nothing he couldn't accomplish. He was sure that one day he would own his own restaurant that would be the favorite place for rich people and celebrities. He knew what he would call it, he had made sketches for the interior design and he had pages and pages of menus planned. Until he had his own place, he said he could meet just the kind of contacts he needed by working in expensive restaurants and that, within a few months, he'd have the investors lined up. He had even tried to call this Mr. Banks at his office, but his call was never returned.

Okay, so he was another mistake in my life, she thought. They had had some good times together, but he turned out to be a full of shit dreamer and a little crazy. But Maria admitted to

125

herself that his enthusiasm for his dreams was, after his looks, what had made him so attractive to her.

She had never allowed herself to have dreams for herself. Ever since her parents died, the only way she was able to start functioning again was by planning her life and her work carefully. Whenever she didn't, she felt like she would derail. So yes, she had been captivated by Lou's conquer all bon vivant spirit. At least she could admit that she needed a little of that in her life and give herself credit for not letting the relationship waste more of her time.

Her thoughts were interrupted by the conductor's voice over the PA announcing that Chambers Street was next.

As she walked the few blocks to her office, she decided that she was just going through a normal post-break-up depression and that's why her thoughts had gotten so morbid.

chapter

NINETEEN

Marni had arranged for a Monday luncheon meeting between herself and GBI. Grant-Bartlet International was the company that was going to make a documentary film of Trace's up-coming international tour which was slated to kick-off in January. The last changes in their contract were now finalized after four grueling months of negotiations. Bob Grant had shaken her hand warmly, and with as much relief as she felt, but for different reasons. For him, getting this project was a major coup. To his credit, he had offered so much in their initial conversations that Marni had never felt reason to go to any of his competitors.

She had already arranged for the tour's two CD boxed set live multi-national recordings, a glossy tour magazine, and merchandising including pictures, calendars, tee shirts, caps, sweatshirts and leather bags. Also set were the film's broadcast on network television, it's subsequent runs on various cable channels, and the international distribution of the video. And of course, Eric's company would handle the worldwide publicity.

Whew. Well done. Great. Marni had told Claudia that she would happily cancel her business day to stay with her at the hospital, but Claudia had insisted that she keep her appointments, both business and personal. Evan still showed no sign of coming out of his coma, and there was nothing Marni could do but check in by phone every once and awhile.

Time for a break. She had inconspicuously checked her watch several times during the meeting. As much as she had tried, she could not deny how much she was looking forward to seeing Craig again and to playing tennis with him this afternoon.

When her meeting was over, Marni checked her watch again. She was invariably punctual for appointments and intended to meet Craig at the corner of 53rd and 6th at exactly the time they had agreed to. In spite of her ability to be cool and controlled, the anticipation of the afternoon had made her dress extra attentively today and kept her in unusually high spirits all afternoon. And, there he was, sitting in his sports car watching for her.

She usually wore slack suits to meetings. She had discovered early in her career that women in her generation had a unique opportunity to encounter what had been primarily a man's world, and so she utilized an authoritative and comfortable dress code and emotional stance that worked best for her in business situations. But today she had clearly dressed for Craig. She admitted that, at the age of thirty-six, she had an incredible crush.

She wore one of her Brelaine suits with a lime silk shell under the purple jacket and above the knee wrap skirt, with matching bag and shoes. This was only to be a tennis date, she kept reminding herself. Soon they would be in her apartment, she would change, make a quick snack for the two of them, and then they would go to the club and play tennis for an hour or two.

As Craig opened the passenger door for her, they kissed each other hello on the cheek. He looked at her admiringly.

As she got into the car, he watched her legs slide onto the seat next to him. She noticed that her skirt hiked up a bit, and as she pulled it back down towards her knees, he smiled. She felt like he was looking right through her, and her whole body felt warm.

"Have you spoken to Claudia this afternoon, Marni? Any news yet?"

"Still no change, except what you already know. He's breathing on his own, but he's still in a coma. I feel so sorry for Evan's parents. He's their only child and it's so clear how much they adore him. I can't imagine how terrified they must be. And now with everything splashed all over the papers and the news, there is no longer a feeling of peace and privacy for anyone."

"You must be drained. I can imagine how stressful this is for you, Claudia and both of the families. You two are lucky that you have each other. But it must be awful."

She wondered if he was speaking from experience. "I've certainly never been through anything like this before. Claudia's parents have hired private security around the clock for her until this is solved. They're frantic."

"How's the parking on your street?"

"There's a garage just at the corner."

"I'm glad you're taking an early break from everything, Marni. A good game of tennis should take your mind off of things for awhile and revitalize you."

"That's just what I need." When they turned onto her street, she directed him to the garage. As the doorman ushered them into the lobby, Marni realized how wonderful she felt walking with Craig by her side. It had been a long time since she'd felt this way.

Finally they were in her apartment. "Are you hungry?" she asked. "I need a quick snack before we play. I thought I'd put something together before I change."

"Fine with me."

She felt conscious of her every move.

He watched her as she put her pocketbook on the stately pink marble topped cabinet in the spacious entrance hall. He watched her as she knelt down to put her attaché case on the floor, leaning it against the wall.

"That piece," she started explaining, "belonged to my aunt. Actually, a good many pieces of furniture here are heirlooms."

Craig didn't take his eyes off Marni, but he said, "It's beautiful."

Marni looked at him. He was extremely handsome in his white tennis shorts and shirt. She was anxious to get on the courts with him because she knew that he would be a formidable player. With all that had been going on lately, she needed the diversion.

"Come, I'll show you around a bit. Then we can eat."

As she gave him a tour of her apartment, she knew that he was taken by her enthusiasm for the artistry with which she put together her very tasteful, lovely and comfortable home.

"You are obviously a woman of many talents, Marni. You have a way of making all of these diverse pieces work so well together. I am very much impressed." He continued to watch her.

At last they arrived in the kitchen. She fixed a plate of smoked oysters, crackers and cheese. As she turned and set the platter, little pearl forks and napkins on the glass topped table, she felt his arm circle her and slowly turn her towards him. She was thrown off guard, and the thought crossed her mind that this was to have been the moment when she would decide which tennis outfit to wear.

"We really should eat now, Craig. I don't know about you, but I definitely need some nutrition before we..."

Her words and thoughts began to fade as she felt the warmth of his hands on her back. His hold was so strong, yet undemanding. As he watched her eyes and started to lean towards her mouth, her thoughts became clear again and she gently pulled away, with a slightly nervous giggle.

"Tennis, Craig." But even as she said those words, she had already begun to admit that this is what they had both wanted from the moment they had met. To be this close. To be this alone. Even though she knew that her eyes were telling him the truth, she persisted anyway, because she really did not want anything to move this fast.

"I thought that...have to change into my tennis clothes... we have a reserved court and..."

He touched her face and she watched his mouth say, "Marni...Marni."

He moaned as his lips touched hers. His lips were soft, his motion so tender. He moved away to look at her again, and then he kissed her cheeks. Soft, moist, warm kisses. Then he moved to her lips again. She felt her eyes close now as his warm, smooth tongue slowly entered her mouth. She groaned as his body moved closer to hers and she let her arms circle his chest. Her legs felt weak as she floated towards him.

Then slowly he moved away from her, and this time she didn't want him to. He took off her suit jacket revealing her sleeveless silk blouse. He stared at her body, as if his eyes could see everything. His hands were on fire now, and they slowly caressed her arms, starting from her tiny wrists, and working their way slowly to her shoulders.

"I really don't think we should do this," she protested weakly.

"Just for a little while, Marni. Just for a little while...let me hold you."

As his arms enfolded her, he kissed her again, this time more insistently, this time his tongue searched her mouth hungrily. His body moved in to hers, at first gently, as he had before, and then she felt his hardness find that place between her legs that had suddenly become alive with an aching desire. His hands moved slowly up and down her back, and as they slid over her behind he pulled her against him until they were melding in to one another.

Marni's heart was pounding. In her few conscious thoughts, she could not believe that this was happening, that such feelings were possible.

Then his hands moved again, slowly gliding her away from him. As he watched her face, he gently moved his right hand up the front of her smooth silk blouse to just below where her breasts started. And then his hand cautiously moved up between her breasts, but not touching her breasts, until he held her chin and kissed her again. She heard herself purring, she wanted him to stop, this was too much too soon, but she didn't want him to stop.

As if he knew her thoughts, and all the time watching her eyes, his hand moved over the slippery fabric to her right breast and, with his hand opened he caressed her and pushed as he came to her nipple, moving up and down until he felt her nipple harden. And then his other hand reached out and touched her left breast, until he was moving both of his hands up and down and around her nipples until she cried out and grabbed for him but he didn't stop until she cried out for him again.

Before she realized what he was doing, he had lifted her and carried her into the bedroom, placing her ever so gently on the bed as if he were holding a delicate flower. He arranged her head on the pillow, removed her shoes, then his own shoes. Then he lay next to her, facing her, his elbow propping up his hand so that he could hold his head, so that his eyes could watch her.

"You are delicious, Marni. I knew you would be."

"Oh Craig. I don't feel right about this. We hardly know each other. This is only our first date...I...I know I sound like a school girl. I just don't understand what we are."

"I think we both knew everything when we first saw each other."

As he talked, he slowly lifted her blouse exposing her white lacy bra.

"I want to keep touching you, Marni. But if you don't want me to, I'll stop."

Then he kissed her, starting from the chin down to the mounds of her upper chest. When he kissed the cups of her bra, he wet his tongue and she could feel its hot wet warmth as he tried to suck on her breast through the fabric. He moved his body rhythmically against her leg as he kissed her breasts. She felt his arm go under her back to unsnap her bra and suddenly he was kissing and licking her naked breasts and sucking on her nipples as she moaned and felt her body moving with his. She wanted to scream with desire. She had never wanted a man so badly in her life. Her entire being was begging for him.

He kissed her lips again. And then he stood up, and in what seemed like one swift motion he took off his clothes. He kneeled between her legs so that his hands could rub her breasts again, and so that he could kiss her mouth. She felt like she was in a steamy pulsating bath.

Within moments he had taken off her clothes and lay beside her again. As they continued to kiss, he moved one hand slowly over her face and down her body, over her breasts, and then down, lower, until she felt him pressing on her, at first gently, and then more urgently. And then his fingers slid into her wetness and she ached for him.

He took her hand and moved it to him and she touched his manhood with trembling fingers. He was hard and he was throbbing. He knelt over her and slowly put himself into her body.

Their bodies moved together with primal heat and rhythm. He pulled himself out, then pushed in again faster and harder. Their bodies were wet, they were breathing heavily, and still they tried to get closer to each other, and they did, until they both screamed and held each other so very tightly as their bodies shuttered. And then, they could only lie there in each other's arms.

—

chapter

TWENTY

Grange picked up the phone and dialed Colter's office. He drummed his fingers on the desk top as he waited for Colter to get on the line.

"Put him on. Fast," he barked impatiently at the assistant.

His fingers rat-tat-tatted wildly and stopped when he heard Colter's voice. "I think we got our first big break. How fast can you get here?"

It was 4:45 when Colter ran into Grange's office. "What is it?"

"Sit down Colter. I think you're gonna be here awhile."

Colter sat down and studied his colleague. He had that glazed look in his eyes. Sure, that's what they all got with the first smell of who dun it. "Let's hear it, Grange."

"You know all those crazy calls we've been getting. Reiss and the guys have been talking to all of them. Everyone wants the reward money. Right before I called you, he put one of them on hold and buzzed me. He said to me 'this one's for real.' So I talked to her. She says she thinks she knows who did it. I believe her. She'll be here any minute."

Colter didn't say a word. He just nodded.

"Reiss," Grange yelled. "Get someone to bring a huge pot of coffee in here. We're gonna need it."

The coffee, cups, sugar, sweet and low, milk and stirrers were delivered. Ten minutes later, Reiss walked into Grange's office with a girl in her early to mid thirties who looked like she was about to collapse. She also looked like, under normal circumstances, she'd be a pretty good looking woman, Grange thought. No wonder Reiss was acting a little peacocky.

"Miss Lambert, this is Detective Grange, and this is Detective Colter." Reiss waited until they had all shaken hands, and then he offered her a chair. Grange noticed that her hand was damp. The poor girl was petrified. Then again, under that pretty exterior, she could turn out to be just another kook, but he doubted it.

"Miss Lambert," Grange began. "We all thank you for calling us and coming in here. We understand that this can't be easy for you. We'll have a lot of questions to ask you, so it would be helpful if you could try to relax just a little bit." She was looking at him with doey eyes that were seeing headlights. He had to make her feel comfortable. "Would you like some coffee?"

This was going to be Grange's interview with both Colter and Reiss in the room. If this was really it, they all had to hear everything right away. There was no time to waste. They had decided that they weren't going to overwhelm her with questions coming from all over the room unless they had to.

"Yes, thank you. I would like some coffee." She practically fell into the chair that Reiss had pointed her to. Her cool yellow rayon just below the knee skirt and matching long loose jacket draped the frazzled naugahyde chair in a way, Grange thought, that made the whole room look pretty.

"I'm a nervous wreck. I've never been in a police station before. What do I do?"

He liked her. When she looked at him with her green eyes about to start dropping tears, he wanted to reach out and put his arm around her. But this wasn't the time for that.

After they all had a cup of coffee in front of them, Grange started in again, for real this time. His black archless eyebrows, which should have made him look mean and evil, instead merely punctuated his dimpled smile.

"Miss Lambert..."

"Please call me Maria. It will make it easier for me to have this conversation."

"Okay, Maria. What made you call us?" He thought he better go slow and easy with her.

"I think I know who tried to kill that songwriter, Evan Strang, at Claudia Banks' apartment building." She said it with such easy authority that they all just stared at her.

"Do you think you can prove it?"

"No...I don't know. I just have a horrible strong feeling about it. There are so many things that are...coincidences."

"Okay, Maria. Why don't you tell us his name and why you think he did it." Grange had already flicked on the recorder button in his top desk drawer. He wanted to be able to review more than their notes if they had to.

"His name is Lou Stattler. He used to try to call that family. I've...we used to be...he found out something...it's all my fault...and..."

She needed help. "Maria, let's take this slowly. How long have you known him?"

"About a year." She took a deep breath, and when she did, Grange noticed her breasts for the first time because they stretched the fabric of the yellow cotton knit shell. "Okay. We had been going together. He's very good looking, and he was charming with everyone, and I mean everyone, wherever we went. He made everything feel so...so alive." With that statement, a blush crept up her face and gave her eyes a dead twinkle.

"What makes you think he did this?"

"Because I think he could do it. Because I think he's... crazy."

"Why do you think he's crazy?"

"It turned out that everything about him was a lie. A fake. And when I realized that, I realized that he was crazy. I can't believe I didn't see it right away."

"What made you realize that he was a fake? What did he lie about?"

"A few months ago, all his airs...all his big talk about the future...he stopped seeming charming to me any more. He seemed...I found out that he had been lying to me. After that, I knew that all his charm was just an act. Everything. Everything he had ever said to me had a different meaning. I mean...the magazines...the people he looked up to...no...the way he looked up to them. Oh, it's so hard to explain." She was practically hyper-ventilating.

"Take your time, Maria. What kind of work was he doing?" One thing at a time, thought Grange. I don't want to machine-gun her or she might leave something out.

"He said he was just about to be promoted from waiter to assistant manager at a very expensive restaurant in New York, in midtown. Called the Le Bon Heur Cafe. He said a lot of rich businessmen ate there, and one day, one of them would notice how bright he was and want to invest in him. But the restaurant fired him."

"Why did they fire him?"

"At first he told me that it was because he spent too much time talking to the customers, and that the owner was angry. Actually he said the owner was jealous of him, because the customers liked talking to him so much. He said some of the customers wanted to invest in his business ideas, and that made the owner furious, using his customers like that.

"But then one day I didn't feel well, so I stayed home from work and Mr. Mellard, the owner of the restaurant, called. I told him that Lou wasn't there, and that I would be happy to take a message for him."

She stopped to take a sip of her coffee.

"He told me that Lou could come in and pick up his last check. I thought that maybe I could help Lou get the job back, so I asked him if he'd rehire him, that I was sure he would stop bothering his customers and that, more than anything else, he had been looking forward to being the assistant manager.

"Mr. Mellard didn't say anything for a moment, so I thought he was considering my suggestion. But then he asked what gave me the idea that Lou was being considered for the assistant management position. I told him that's what Lou told me. He said Lou was never considered for that job, he'd gotten too many complaints about Lou because he interrupted the customers' peaceful meals and he would never consider taking him back.

"That was the first time that I knew that Lou had lied to me. Lou told me that in order to become a manager in this restaurant, you were required to be a waiter for six months so you could understand how things operated.

"I thanked Mr. Mellard for the information, told him I'd tell Lou about the check. We were just about to say good-bye when he said something strange. He said that sometimes Lou didn't know the difference between reality and the society columns he reads."

The detectives were looking at each other, wondering what this girl was talking about, and what all this had to do with a crime. Grange signaled them to give her a little more time. He could see that the memories shook her up but that she was painfully trying to be thorough. She seemed completely honest, and her over zealous determination made her seem like she needed to repent for something.

"What did you think when he said that?"

"I didn't know what to think at first. But then I saw a stack of Lou's gossip magazines, and that's when I let myself realize what kind of person Lou really was. Look, I'm not that old, but I was lonely and he seemed so exciting. But that day, when I thought about him honestly for the first time, I realized that everything that had seemed exciting about him was really sick."

"He was always reading about celebrities and millionaires, and the men who run the big corporations. He used to try to find out the phone numbers of people he read about and call them to talk about his investment ideas. None of them ever called back.

"His parents didn't have enough money to send him to college. He told me that's where the people who run the corporations and the government meet each other. And that's why they all do business with each other. So, he thought if he just went where they went, they would realize that he was really one of them.

"He was jealous of anyone who had more than he did. He was even jealous of me and my job because I earn a good salary and I have benefits. I told him to take the civil exam and work for the State too, but he said he had much bigger plans for his life than that."

"What kind of State work do you do?" Grange asked, relieved to get at least some things clarified.

"I'm an administrative assistant at the Bureau of Vital Statistics." Grange knew that that was one of the new titles being used today for secretaries. With all the cases he'd solved, he still hadn't been able to figure out why new names were being used for the same job. Must be a women's lib thing.

Colter couldn't hold himself back anymore. "It sounds like he thought a lot about money and power, Miss Lambert." Grange caught the look in Colter's eyes when he said that, and he knew where he was leading her.

"Really, that's all he thought about. I...I guess he was... well, it was more than just thinking about it all the time. It took over...it was what everything else revolved around...he's..."

"Obsessed?" Colter had hit it. But Grange needed to know more, and fast. He couldn't tell her that she had to hurry because it was getting late and a potential killer was on the loose.

"Yes. Yes, that's what he is. Oh, my God." By the time she had said those words, she had tears running down her face. She pulled a tissue out of her pocketbook to dry her eyes and, while looking in her little make-up mirror, she stopped the black line that her dripping mascara had started. "I feel so stupid for not seeing any of this sooner."

"But you're okay now, Maria." Grange wanted to hug her. Tell her that he knew that she was too good for a guy like that. But he had to keep questioning her.

"Maria, did you tell him about your conversation with Mr. Mellard?"

"Yes...and he went crazy. I had never seen him that way. It was like I had pulled a mask off his face and he knew that I saw him for what he was. I thought he was going to hit me. But then he caught himself."

"So he never hit you?"

"No...but he hit the wall and a pillow on the couch. I wanted him to get out of the apartment. When I started to tell him that, he hugged me and tried to use all the lines on me that always worked before. At that moment I was afraid of him, but I didn't want him to know it. We hadn't been exactly living together, but he had gotten used to staying with me...well...most of the time." She blushed again. "I told him I'd probably miss him so much that if he called later I'd probably ask him to come over. That made him feel better, so he took a few of his things and left. Then I called the hardware store and had the locks changed."

"Good move, Maria." Grange was pleased with her. Time to get to the nitty gritty. "Why do you think he had anything to do with stabbing Evan Strang?"

Her voice became a whisper now. "Because he knew something."

"Tell us what you mean."

"After that incident he called me every day and I wouldn't get together with him. About a week went by, and he just showed up at my office. The receptionist knew him. Oh, he had charmed everyone. She told him to go right to my office before she buzzed me, like she always had. And there he was." She was fighting back tears. "That's when he saw the papers."

"What papers?"

"In my office...he should never have been in my office that day." They could see that this interview was draining her. She was pale and shaken, and it was clear that she was using all her strength to not break down. Most of all, they knew she was getting to the good part.

"Take it slow, Maria. Tell us about the papers."

"Okay." Another deep breath. "Well, that day, some men from the systems division were in my office. They were supposed to advise the department that set up the new program about how to put all of our old records on computer. All the new ones go in automatically. But before 1980, the information used to go in the files by hand. So we had been asked to take out some files to use as samples from the 70's down to the late 1800's. There are several million files that have to go into the main computer."

She was on a roll now.

"When Lou walked into my office, I was reading out loud from the files and writing down what the men told me they needed. As soon as I saw him, I stopped reading and told him that he had to wait in the reception area for me. One of the men said that, 'no, that's not necessary, your friend is here to take you to lunch, we'll just do a few more and then go out for lunch, too.'

"So we kept going. When I read one of the names from the files, one of the men got very tense and started saying something like 'stop...wait...give me that file...I have to see that file.' He grabbed the file from me. I was thinking that's weird, but then again he had asked to see a few of the other files before, so I didn't think that much of it except that he seemed to have gotten very moody all of a sudden. He left the room, he must have xeroxed the file. When he came back he said it was time to break for lunch."

"I didn't want to start a scene in the office, so I told Lou that I would have lunch with him. I went to the ladies' room, and when I got back, we left. When we were half way down the block, Lou said that he didn't have as much time as he thought he had, that it was really good to see me, and that he'd call again soon. I was relieved that he left. I went out to lunch alone. And that was that...until this morning." Her speech was slowing, and her voice was losing strength.

They all sat looking at her, waiting. Grange thought that she looked like a little girl who was about to be punished for something horrible.

"It's okay, Maria. Please go on. You're doing fine. Tell us what happened this morning."

"When I saw...when I saw the newspaper. The story about the stabbing."

She was talking in slow-motion now, as if she were hypnotized.

"Something about it was bothering me, but I didn't realize what it was until later. I was in my office. I was working on some files. That's when I realized what was bothering me."

They thought she was going to pass out. Colter offered her more coffee. She said no, she just wanted to finish the story.

"The names in the newspaper were the same names that were in the file. The file that made the man from the computer department so upset. The day that Lou was in my office."

"What were the names, Maria?"

"Jordan and Tabatha Banks."

chapter

TWENTY ONE

"Jordan and Tabatha Banks?" It was Colter, on his feet. He and Grange looked at each other.

"Yes."

"What was in the file?" Colter had taken over. That was fine with Grange. He'd jump in when he had to. But he knew what Colter was thinking. Here, maybe, was the blackmail material he needed to find out who wrote the note. So, bingo, his case would be solved.

"I...I could get fired for this. Please don't tell them that I did this."

"Maria. Coming here and trying to help the police in a criminal investigation is the sign of a good citizen. Nobody would fire someone for that. There's nothing wrong, and everything right, about your talking to us." Colter was such a diplomat.

"No. You don't understand. These files are confidential. They're supposed to be sealed. I'm not supposed to talk about them. Nobody's supposed to know anything about them. It's against the law. Lou was there. That man. And now you."

"But this is a police investigation, Maria," Colter insisted gently. "If these files are sealed, we would have to get a court order to open them. And that could take weeks. Sometimes more. You gotta tell us what was in there."

"It's also against the law to xerox those files and take them out of the office." Maria looked straight into Grange's eyes when she said that.

"You have the file with you?" Grange could have gotten on his knees and begged her for it, but he just returned her stare.

"What will happen if they find out?"

"Nothing. You have our word." He had to say that now, and think about the consequences later.

"All right, then." With trembling hands and sweat forming on her brow, she reached into her large canvas pocketbook and pulled out a manila envelope. She looked around at all of them, then handed it to Grange.

Grange set the envelope on his desk, opened it and pulled out a set of papers, about two dozen in all, he figured. The color copies showed yellowing at the edges. By then, Colter and Reiss were standing on either side of him.

On top of the first sheet it said The United States District Court in ornate official government letters. It was a decree of some sort. They read the rest of the page together.

> On this Third day of March, Nineteen Hundred and Sixty, this court doest hereby approve the adoption petition as set forth herein.

Let it be known that this court has found in the favour of Mr. Jordan Alexander Banks and his wife Tabatha Banks as suitable and honourable adults seeking the adoption of a child in the territories of The United States of America.

The child shall be forever more known as Claudia Banks.

The Honourable Judge Arnold T. Matheson

For the first time in over two hours the room was quiet as the detectives spent the next few minutes sifting through the other papers in the file. Grange spoke first.

"Okay. If this is a piece of the puzzle, which we will assume for the moment it is, what does it have to do with your friend, excuse me, your ex-friend, Lou?"

"I don't know. I just think it does."

"Why do you think it does?"

"That day, when he was in my office. I know he came there to talk to me. I'm sure he had nothing else to do all afternoon. He was out of work. But then, just like the other man got so hot headed about this file, something affected Lou, too. I don't know why. But it did."

Now he was seeing a different Maria, and Grange liked what he saw. She was no longer the nervous, sniveling, scared child pouring her heart out. Now she was assured. Now she was acting like she was part of the team. He liked that about her.

"Who was the other man?"

"His name is, um...something Wilkens. He works for the Systems...oh, I don't know the exact name of the department. But it's a State department. He gets coordination assignments to work within any of the bureaus in the State of New York. I've seen him in our offices a few times. Roger...Roger Wilkens. That's it."

"Good. We're making progress. How long have you worked there?"

"It'll be eleven years this summer. I'm due for another pro-motion now, but what I did today will probably end my hopes for that. Not to mention my pension that I've worked so many years for. Are you sure you can protect me?"

"We'll protect you," Grange assured her again. "Where does this Lou live?"

"I'm not sure." She looked embarrassed. "I mean, when I first met him he said he was renting a room in a friend's apartment while he was looking for a new place. But then, after awhile, we were spending so much time together that he stayed with me most of the time."

"Where did he stay when he wasn't with you?"

"I'm not sure. I thought he still had that room."

"Where was it?"

"Somewhere in Queens. He never said exactly where." She just gazed straight ahead, at nothing in particular. Grange knew she felt stupid for ever having spent time with this creep and that she was trying to regain her composure and her dignity.

"I apologize if the questions seem a little personal. But I have to ask. Didn't he ever invite you there?"

She thought about this purposefully. "Yes. He did. But only at the beginning. You see, whenever we went out, it was always in the city, and it just never seemed convenient to go to Queens. Whenever the subject came up, he always said that I wouldn't like the long subway ride, or that I wasn't missing anything anyway, and that well..." she looked down, "that we wouldn't have any privacy there anyway."

She was blushing again, but kept going. "Well, you know how the beginning of relationships are. It just seemed to make sense...then." She looked at Grange who was thinking that he'd like to have a beginning of a relationship with her.

"What are his friends' names?"

"Hmmm. It was a couple. I don't remember their names." Now she got up and paced. "Wait. Just a minute. It was something like June and Jim, or Jay and Jane. Shit! Oops, I'm sorry."

Grange looked at her seriously and said, "Listen Maria. If you can't curse here, you can't curse anywhere."

That made her smile at him, and, as serious as the moment was, he couldn't help smiling back. She looked nice when she smiled. He hadn't noticed before that she had dimples and that her eyes had little lights in them.

Then she looked serious again. "Grange, he never told me their last names."

Nothing. No leads to him. What did he have here. A job that he was fired from, that was it. He told Reiss to find out everything he could about a Lou Stattler and a State employee named Roger Wilkens.

Grange got up and paced the floor. "I smell something here, but I don't know what it is I'm smelling."

Colter spoke, as if to himself, but addressing the room, in the logical way his mind worked when he was solving.

"We have here what are obviously meant to be the very private records of a husband and wife who adopted a child. It just so happens that this particular couple is one of the most prominent couples in this country. Not to mention one of the wealthiest. Why would someone seeing this information stab someone thirty-five years after the fact?"

"Even if we knew where he was, we couldn't bring him in for questioning," Grange added. "We have no grounds. It's all anecdotal, just circumstantial. Nothing really solid."

As Grange waited for Colter's next line, he got another thought. "Wait a minute. Maybe she's on the right track, but she's got the wrong man."

"What? What do you mean?" Colter asked.

"Sorry, Maria, but just because a guy is weird doesn't mean he's capable of being a criminal. If it's either of these two, it could be the Wilkens guy. We don't know yet why he reacted the way he did. Just because he works for the State doesn't mean he's perfectly sane."

"We'll see what Reiss gets." Grange could see that Colter's mind was furiously sifting and sorting all the new information.

"What happened to Evan Strang? Is he...?" This was the question Maria had been holding inside since she first picked up the phone to call the police. If Lou really did this, then she knew a criminal. She had kissed a criminal. Worse, she had made love to him and had loved it, and had thought she loved him. Had she loved a murderer?

Grange noticed her change of mood. Her different expressions were so obvious to him. He was thinking that only he could really see them.

"What are ya' thinking?"

"Oh, nothing."

"Is that woman code for 'try to guess?'"

"Not this time."

"Well anyway Maria I'm sorry. But we can't talk about his condition, even to you. Let's leave it at that for now."

She eyed Grange, really consciously noticing him for the first time since she got there. She had been too nervous to really look at these detectives, but now she was beginning to feel like she was in a cop movie on television and she felt comfortable in the part. This was insane.

"The note, Grange. The note." Colter signaled Grange to meet with him in the outer offices.

"Excuse us, Maria." With that, Colter and Grange stepped out of the room.

Colter was getting excited. "First of all, I got to call Banks. He has to know that this information has been leaked. But I want to hear this girl out first, and see what we can come up with. The more I have solved for him, the better. But I can't put that call off further than first thing in the morning. I don't know how this is going to affect him. But he's gotta know."

"Yeah. You gotta talk to the guy. Now, besides that we both know that we can't let Maria know there's also a note involved in this investigation, tell me what else you're thinking."

"All right. In the note, the guy wants money from Banks. Why does he think he can get money from him? Because he thinks he knows something that if it was public it would hurt Banks. Where's your copy of the note, Grange?"

Grange went back into his office and opened his locked desk drawer. Maria, taking advantage of being left alone a little while, was brushing her hair.

"What do I do now? Should I leave?" she asked.

"No. We might need more information from you. If you don't mind, I'd like you to wait till we get a report from Reiss. It shouldn't be much longer."

"Okay, Detective Grange. In the meantime, would you tell me where I can find the ladies' room?"

"Step this way. I'll have someone take you there." Grange had one of his men show her down the hall, then brought Colter back into the office with him to look at the note.

"In light of this new information, I still don't know what this is, Colter."

"There's a connection, Grange. We just don't see it yet. This is incredible blackmail material. Where's Reiss?"

Just as he said that, Reiss walked into the room holding some papers.

"We've got everything you'd want to know about Wilkens. Every school, his father's dead, his mother's a housekeeper, has a brother who works for the State too, he's been with the same department for thirteen years. Sounds stable, like a good boy. Sometimes they could turn into the craziest if something sets them off. But there's nothing, zero zilch, on a Lou Stattler that fits. He doesn't exist. No social security number, no driver's license, nothing. Unless he's a teenager, in his 70's or dead at the age of three, none of which sound like our man. But there is a male Francis Stattler. Fits the age, but he's been living in Los Angeles."

"Keep the boys on both of them. I want to know everything. Where's Maria? We need her to sit with the artist and get a picture of this idiot. We can get a picture of this Wilkens guy from the State. Right now, that's all we got."

chapter

TWENTY
TWO

An hour and a half later, the sketch artist was finished working with Maria. Grange looked at his watch. It was 10:30.

"You did good, Maria. You did real good. In a few minutes that picture will be out all over the country's precincts."

"I can't believe that he could be a criminal. I just can't believe it." She looked into his eyes with an intensity that shook him up. "Did you ever...uh, did you ever go out with someone who turned out to be really bad?"

"Can't say that I have. But you don't know if that's the case yet here. And even if it is, you know, we've all made bad judgments

J. E. Laine

about things. One way or another, looks like you just have to chalk this one up and...and just make sure you do better next time." He tried to look and sound serious. What, a little fatherly, maybe a little brotherly. So long as he didn't scare her away till he could get a handle on what was on his own mind about her.

"Yeah...next time. But I don't think there's going to be a next time for a long time."

"Well, you'll have plenty of time to think about that. In the meantime, Miss Maria Lambert, you look like your eyes are ready to close. I'd say it's time for you to go home and get some rest. We might need you again tomorrow or another day soon."

Maria didn't move from her cracked naugahyde chair. "This has been a strange experience, Detective Grange. And I think I've never been so scared in my life."

Grange looked at her from across his desk, his hands fidgeting with a paper clip. "First off now you've got to call me Ted, okay?" Maria nodded shyly. "And second, I'm here. The police, we're here. We'll get to the bottom of this. And here's what I'm gonna do. I'm gonna have one of our police ladies drive you home and stay with you a few days."

"Do you think I'm really in danger, Detective...I mean Ted? You think I am, don't you?"

"I don't think so, no, not now, Maria, because neither of those guys knows you've talked to us about them. But until we know what's happening, I know that I'll feel a lot better knowing someone's with you." He wished it could be him. What was it about this girl? She was a little saint compared to the overripe women he usually went for.

"Someone to stay in my apartment? Live with me there? Uh. I don't have that much room. I don't have that much food. And my God, will she have a gun?"

"Look, don't worry. All the women here are nice, they know what they're doing, they've done this before, and they're not looking for luxury here. And they'll take care of the extra food. Don't worry about it. Just relax."

"But what about work tomorrow? I have to be at work by 8:30, nine at the latest."

154

"You'll go to work. You have to act like everything's normal. And everything's gonna be normal. So listen, if you need to take a sick day or two, you'll do it, that's all. But for now, everything's normal, okay?"

"Well, all right. Whatever you say. I mean, you know what you're doing. You're the boss here." She looked at him, her eyes clouded with dread. "But what if somehow they find out, somehow, you know, that I've been here and talked to you, and they call me or come to my office. What do I do? What do I say?"

"You act cool and collected. Say what you would any other time you'd hear from either of them. That's all. And our people will be near you, so don't worry about either of them getting to you. And here," he reached into his desk and pulled out a stack of cards. "Here's my card. It has my direct line, and if for some reason I'm not here, Reiss or someone will be. And here, I'm writing my home number on it. You can call there anytime, middle of the night, anytime."

Grange got up from behind his desk and stood next to Maria's chair. Damn she smelled good, and her hair sure looked shiny and pretty under the fluorescent ceiling lights. He reached his hand out to put his card in her hand. As she took it, he took hold of her hand and patted it with his other.

"You're a nice girl, Maria. I know things are gonna work out good for you. And you did really right by coming here today. You should be proud of yourself. You did a good job."

Her skin was soft, like he knew it would be. He wanted to take her home so they could both get a good night's sleep.

Funny, he wasn't thinking that he had to get her into the sack. Well, of course he wanted to, but no, that wasn't it. Just sleeping next to her, and holding her, and telling her everything was gonna be okay. That would be fine. Jesus, this was weird.

"Sit here a minute. Let me get someone to go home with you." He went back to his desk and made a call. Now they had a few minutes together. Colter was still using one of the outer desk phones, and Reiss was watching for the results of the picture going around the country. His hand scratched his chin, and he realized that he hadn't shaved today. Um. Bad first impression.

"You know, Maria. I know life feels pretty upsetting to you right now. And you're probably feeling like you're the only one and maybe even pretty lonely about it. You might be tempted to confide in some friends about this, but I wouldn't do that just yet. Can you handle that?"

"Um. Yeah, I know that makes sense. But this will be hard not to talk about."

"Well, you'll see. You can talk to the lady that's staying with you all you want. And you can always talk to me about this. Uh, you know, anything more that you think of. Or, really, just anything that you need to talk about while this is going on. I want you to be okay. I really do." No, he didn't want to sound brotherly or fatherly. He was sure he sounded professional, and hoped that she realized he was also trying to be a friend. This was delicate. He had to be careful.

A lady cop came into the room wearing plain clothes. "Hello, Officer Katelin. This is Maria Lambert. Did Reiss fill you in?"

"Yes sir he did. We're all set. Reiss's on his way back here now, sir." She turned to Maria. "Are you okay, Miss Lambert? Are you ready to go now?"

"You're a policewoman?" She was looking at Officer Katelin with a bewildered look on her face. She was a girl around her own age, kind of cute with short brown hair and a pixy face. Dressed in jeans, sneakers, tee shirt and a denim jacket, she looked like she was going out to the movies and dinner with friends. Grange and Katelin understood Maria's curiosity and gave her benevolent smiles.

"Yes, I sure am. I'm not what you expected?"

"No, not at all. Uh, you have a gun?"

"I sure do. Right under here." She opened her jacket and raised her arm. "See? The main thing is, you'll be protected, and we won't look obvious going anywhere together. I'll go to work with you in the morning, stay for awhile. You can say I'm your friend in from South Jersey taking in the city for a week or so. Then we'll have lunch tomorrow at your office, or near your office, and I'll be right there after work. But really, I'll be nearby all day. I'll explain signals and phone procedures to you later. You ready now?"

This wasn't going to be as bad as she had thought. Maria had pictured someone bigger, older, more rugged, no one that she would feel at ease talking to. This was going to be okay.

Grange got up and came around his desk to say goodnight to them. He took Maria's hand again, this time to shake it.

"Goodnight, Maria. Don't forget. You can call me anytime. But no matter what, we'll speak in the morning."

"Thank you for everything, Detective Grange. I mean Ted. You made this experience not the nightmare it could have been. Thank you."

"Any time, Maria. And I thank you. Because of you, looks like we'll soon know what's going on here." They exchanged smiles and Maria yawned. Miss Katelin picked up her overnight case and they were gone.

"Reiss. Get Colter for me. Tell him I'm famished."

chapter

TWENTY THREE

"I swear, this is the best burger joint in the city." Grange wiped his brow with his napkin, then picked up his fork and carefully placed a few rings of onion on his hamburger.

"It's all right. A little greasy for me, though. You know how I like my steaks, but for you I'll make this one acceptable."

"Hey what a guy."

Colter was intently studying a copy of the sketch artist's drawing of Lou Stattler. "I know I haven't seen this face, Grange. And I don't think imaging is going to find anything. That's my gut."

"He doesn't look familiar to me either. But you can see how a face like this could attract a girl like Maria. Poor thing. She really fell for him."

"That's not..."

"I know, that's not what we're here to talk about. And we won't. Okay, we'll see what the computer comes up with."

"Maybe he's wanted somewhere, but I don't think so either. If he is and he's our man, he wouldn't'a been working and going out so publicly unless he thinks he's got an angel watching over him. Just in case, we're relaying everything to the FBI. I don't know about you, but I'm thinking about the other guy. That Wilkens."

"Either one of them could have written the note, given how they both reacted to that file," Colter said. "But does the stabbing fit into this new arena of information? I don't know. Right now I can't see how they're related. I think it's just a coincidence that they both happened on top of each other like that. But there is no line of speculation that we can afford to discount at this point in time."

"That's what I think too. So if it's just about the note, yeah, could be either of them, Stattler or Wilkens, fifty-fifty. On the other hand, I don't know. And if the stabbing is tied in, right now I'm at a total loss. Even with what Maria told us tonight, I'm not ready to drop the theory that the note could be about some business deal. But our possibilities are sure growing and we're getting some momentum here."

"But that file, Grange. That's personal stuff. So it's a potentially loaded situation."

"Yeah. That's certainly true enough. So let's talk on that one for now. Okay. Maybe nobody's supposed to know about this adoption. Then again, maybe everybody knows about it." Grange paused to wipe the ketchup that was dripping down his chin. "But the guy who wrote the note thinks he's got the goods on Banks. Anyway, why would it be such a secret? A lot of people are adopted. And I thought all the parents in this day and age tell their kids if they're adopted. So what's the big deal?"

"It's not a big deal unless someone is trying to keep it a big secret," Colter said. "If Banks has kept it from his daughter, then it's a big deal. And we don't know what the circumstances are. How do you judge how people chose to handle their most private concerns?"

"You can't. But I know what I've been reading and hearing. All the kids who were adopted years ago, their parents were told that they never had to think about who the original parents were. And they told the kids that they were never allowed to know anything about them. I'll tell you I think it's cruel. What is this, it's like slavery when families were pulled apart forever like that. This is supposed to be America. What's wrong with these people?"

"How come you know so much about it, Grange?"

"Cause I have a nephew. My sister's kid. She adopted him when he was a baby and we all loved him like he was our own, you know? Now he's eighteen and he's pissed at everyone. My sister's kinda insecure. And when he started asking a lot of questions about where he came from, she just shut him out. So he was going to join this group that helps adopted people find their original parents. But seems like his original mom beat him to it. She tracked him down and called him. And they got together. They're crazy about each other. Turns out she's a really nice lady. He came over to my apartment one day. He wanted to have a man to man talk about it, you know? He was afraid to tell my sister. Afraid she'd go ballistic on him."

"I've never heard a story like this. What happened?"

"I told him that it was always best to tell the truth, you know, just like I always told him. And that he should tell my sister. So he did and he was right. She went nuts. Said things like 'what do we need her for?' You know? She needed to believe that it was only him and her. That nobody else's mothering thing had to do with him but her. So this put the kid in turmoil. He really loves my sister, and more than anything he didn't want to hurt her. But this is when he really needed her to understand that this

J. E. Laine

was important to him. She refused. She just kept giving him a hard time about it."

"You'd think she'd be cooler about it. I mean, the way I am with my kids, I think you're sometimes supposed to put your kids' feelings before your own."

"We're still working on her. She's softening up a little. She's just getting out of the stage where she's putting this whole guilt trip on him. You know, like we took care of you all of your life, we gave you all this stuff, how could you turn on us like that? You know, that kind of thing."

"You'd think she'd at least have some fond feelings for the woman. After all, if it wasn't for her, she wouldn't have her son."

"Not my sister. You'd think this lady had come back from the dead to take him back the way she reacted. She just can't deal with it."

"So, how's she softening up?"

"She finally told my nephew that she'd meet the lady. That she was mentally preparing herself for it. You know what I think?"

"What's that?"

"I think she secretly feels guilty that all these years she was so happy raising her son, and she knows this other lady must have been suffering. That's why I think she can't face her."

"Did your sister tell her kid that he was adopted?"

"Yeah. She went by the book. She told him when he was little. She said she did what she was supposed to do. And then she washed her hands of it, I guess. Pretended it wasn't real. That he didn't really come from some other place. She wanted her genes to be his genes, and she couldn't deal with that they weren't. So when he got older, he didn't know why, but he knew that she never wanted to talk about it again. He thought there was some deep dark secret that she was keeping from him. Man, he didn't know what to think was going on."

"Look, if this file incident is what this whole case is about, we better figure out what's going on here."

"Maybe they never told Claudia. Banks probably thought that because he was the head of this rich and powerful family, he didn't have to do the right thing."

"That might be the whole thing right there. I've never had to talk to him about anything so personal. But it's unavoidable. Thanks for the background. At least I'm prepared for one of his reactions."

TUESDAY

chapter

TWENTY FOUR

    Colter called Jordan Banks at home at 8:15 Tuesday morn-ing and arranged to meet him for breakfast before either of them went into their offices. He used as a pretense the need for having to go over Banks' lists again. He called just on time. Banks was getting ready to leave his apartment.

    Banks had hesitated, preferring that they have their talk on the phone, but Colter insisted. He said their utmost security couldn't be guaranteed a million percent on the phone. That did it. But in fact, there was no way he could have handled this con-versation on the phone.

Banks had suggested The Dorset for breakfast, but then realized it was too public a place for a confidential meeting. So they met at Stanley's, a non-descript coffee shop in the East 40's, at 9 AM.

"Sorry we have to go to a lousy coffee shop for a meeting, Mr. Banks. I know this is not your style." Banks was wearing one of his imposingly tailored custom suits, with his trademark hand-made shoes. His full black hair was perfectly cut and combed. A little redness in his eyes indicated that he hadn't been sleeping well lately, and no wonder. Colter was dressed in his usual preppy off-the-inexpensive-rack tan slacks, plaid sports shirt and beige blazer, with a lock of his dirty blonde hair hanging on his brow.

"I've had other styles before the one you're aware of, Colter. This is fine, as long as you're sure meeting like this is necessary."

"It was either this or one of our offices. Truthfully, I wanted to meet with you in absolute privacy, and before your business day started."

"You're being kind of cryptic. Have you come up with something from the lists I've given you? As I've told you, I've run out of names. You already have everything."

"Let's order. I think we'll do better with food on the table." Colter simply wanted to get the menu reading and food ordering out of the way. They both asked for the house specialty which included a three egg omelet, home fries, toast and rolls, orange juice and coffee. As they waited for the food to arrive, Colter began the conversation that he had been dreading.

"Listen, Mr. Banks. I have to admit that I've asked you here under somewhat false pretenses."

"What are you saying?"

"We've got some new information. Some real leads that we're working on. And they have nothing at all to do with your lists."

"You sound serious. Go ahead. Let me hear it."

"Mr. Banks. Let me start by saying that we're going to get into some very personal territory here. And if I didn't think it had anything to do with the case, I would never bring it up."

"We've already gotten into some very personal territory, Detective Colter. Nobody in the world knows more about my extra-marital affairs than you do. If you have more information about that phase of my life, you'll teach me something I didn't know."

"It's not about that, and maybe I wish it was. Here, let me show you something."

Colter pulled an envelope from his inside jacket pocket, took out the piece of paper that was in it and handed it to Banks.

"Go ahead. Take a look at it."

Banks unfolded the paper and turned pale. His head continued to face the single sheet in his hands that had started shaking, while his eyes veered quickly to Colter's, then back again to the paper. Colter saw that there were tears in his eyes.

"How did you get this?"

Without using names, Colter proceeded to tell Banks what had happened at the Bureau of Vital Statistics. He gave him a brief on the two men who were in the office, and how they reacted to the file.

"Claudia doesn't know." Banks voice was a whisper. His eyes were glued to the piece of paper.

"What did you say?"

"Claudia doesn't know she's adopted. Tabatha never wanted to tell her."

"I'm sorry. I'm sorry if this is adding more pressure to your life right now."

Banks did not respond. He was hoping he could come up with a painless procedure for what lay ahead, but it was not forthcoming.

"Look, we don't know if this has anything to do with the note." He didn't want Banks to know that this might also link to the stabbing. "But I thought it would be best if you knew what happened."

Banks was lost in a private musing, as if ghosts from another world were revisiting him.

"We thought those records were sealed forever. I don't understand how a thing like this could happen."

"Mr. Banks. I think you'd better tell her. We don't know what those men were reacting to, or if anything would be made public by either of them. But it's a possibility. So, I think you'd better tell her."

"Yes. I see your point. We had better tell her." Banks' voice was strangely powerless.

"And Mr. Banks. Another thing."

"Yes. What is it?"

"Blackmail. If this information does have something to do with the note, and somebody who gets this information thinks this is a big secret, then there's an incentive for blackmail."

"Oh my God."

"Mr. Banks. I realize I've hit you with a few big things, kinda like a one-two punch. I can see that you're reeling from it, and that must be hard for you. You're a man who usually runs things, and you can't be used to something like this. You know, we've known each other for a long time, but we've never been exactly friends. But I think you might need a friend right about now. I just want to tell you that if you need to talk about this to me, you can."

"Thank you, Colter. I think I will gratefully take you up on that. Give me a minute to digest this. Let's get some more coffee." Jordan was truly thankful for Colter's offer, and welcomed the opportunity to think out loud before he determined his next steps.

They got a pot of coffee for the table and paid the bill so that they could just walk out when they were finished.

"You know, Colter. I always told Tabatha that we should tell Claudia that she was adopted. I always thought that it was something she was entitled to know. And as much as that, I've always felt so close to my daughter. I adore her. I'm afraid that she's going to hate me, and Tabatha, for not being honest with her."

"I have to admit, Banks, this is a new one for me. I've come across all kinds of inter-personal situations behind crimes and incidents, but never this. I mean, there've been crimes committed by people who we later found out were adopted, but there are more crimes committed by people who aren't adopted. And there were always letters in the newspapers tying-in the psychology of the adopted person to the crime, especially when it concerned men who serially murdered women. They say these guys are all subliminally so pent up with anger at their mothers for letting them be adopted that they take it out on every woman they meet, because they can't take it out on the actual woman herself, in some kind of healthy way. That's the extreme, and of course most people deal with things like this in healthy ways. You know, like, if they knew the woman, they could just not talk to them for awhile, or push them away for awhile. You know, to punish them a little like that, where they can exert some control over the actual situation and the actual person. At least they can get some of their negative feelings out of their systems. That's not what we're talking about here, but that's among the few things that I know about the subject."

"No, it's not what we're talking about here. What we're talking about here is that what my daughter doesn't know about herself could be the headline in tomorrow's paper. Maybe even tonight's. I think I'm going to have to forget about the office today. I better call my wife before she goes on one of her shopping sprees."

Colter stopped Banks before he went to look for the pay phone and told him about Grange's adopted nephew. "I don't know what else to say to help prepare you for this. That's everything I know about the subject."

Colter wondered if Banks was ready to handle even more in this sitting. No, he decided, this was enough for now. He'd tell him the rest of the information about the men involved in the file situation after he got over this initial hurdle. And anyway, he wanted to find out if Grange and Reiss got any more information on Lou Stattler and Roger Wilkens before he mentioned them to Banks. No use getting him crazy over false leads or dead ends.

Banks thanked him and left the table to make his call to Tabatha from the pay phone in the back of the coffee shop. When he returned, he said he was meeting his wife at their home in half an hour.

chapter

TWENTY FIVE

"Mornin' Reiss. Hear anything yet?" Grange was carrying copies of all the city's morning newspapers.

"No Grange. Waiting for reports now. So, uh...so let me ask you something, okay?"

"Yeah, okay. What d'ya want?" He knew what Reiss was going to say.

"So what about that girl? Looked like you were a little taken by her, heh Grange?"

"Well, yeah, so maybe I was. She's a nice girl. I think maybe I do kinda like her. But you know, this is a case, and I don't want to confuse the issues. But yeah, okay, I like her. So what? You like her too?"

"She's a little too old for me, Grange. You know I like them younger. Hey, I'm younger than you are," Reiss snickered. "She's more for you. But if she were closer to my age, yeah, I could go for her."

"Okay, okay. That's enough. Let me know when you got something." Grange went into his office. The used coffee cups were still out from the night before. He couldn't help but notice Maria's lipstick stain in one of them. Nice, he thought. She's got nice lips. Hmmm. Okay, time to work.

"Hey Reiss," he yelled. "Get somebody in here to clean up, would ya." He went around to his map of New York and the surrounding areas that was nestled between the file cabinets. The man could be anywhere, he thought. Could be anyone, anywhere. Who knows where people hide who do these kinds of things. Bunch of nuts. Gotta be nuts to write notes like that. Gotta be nuts to go around stabbing people like that. Nuts.

It was 9:30 AM. He hadn't heard from Maria or Officer Katelin, but decided to give them a little more time. He opened up one of the day's papers.

Damn these reporters. In The City News the story got a box on the cover, story continued on page four. The headline said, ELEVATOR STABBER ON THE LOOSE - POLICE STYMIED. "Fuck those jerks," he said out loud. He skimmed the article for anything new and insulting. God these reporters could be merciless. They're supposed to help preserve the people's faith in the police. But instead what do they do. They scare everyone to death so they can sell a few more papers.

> The police investigation into the brutal stabbing of songwriter Evan Strang remains unsolved with no end in sight. According to an unnamed source, the police department is working overtime on this case because it involves The Banks, one of the wealthiest families in the country...

The Chronicle was worse. MAD ELEVATOR STABBER
SIGHTINGS REPORTED

> Police report Mad Elevator Stabber sightings through-
> out the city as terrified New Yorkers post extra guards
> at their gates. Police Chief fears a spate of copycat
> crimes...

The worst of them all, as he knew it would be, was the
tabloid The World. VICIOUS STABBING LEAVES NEW
YORKERS PARALYZED WITH FEAR - BANKS FAMILY
IN HIDING

> The rich Jordan Banks has hidden his daughter, Clau-
> dia. The big selling song, titled "Claudia," that was writ-
> ten for her, mysteriously lead to a near hit in the form of
> a brutal stabbing at her apartment following a party she
> hosted...

The only paper that didn't sensationalize Strang's stabbing, and that was trying to keep the peace in the city, was The
Times. POLICE WORK ROUND THE CLOCK TO NAB
STABBER. This was the only paper that gave the police force
any credit at all, and at least tried to bolster the city's confidence.

> According to Police Chief Gregory Conklin, New
> York's finest are on track to determine if this was a
> random incident or one geared solely towards the vic-
> tim, Evan Strang. A sweeping effort by the Force's top
> departments is underway to...

Yesterday's papers were bad, but they weren't this bad, he
thought. And the longer it takes for us to solve this damn thing,
the worse the papers are gonna get. That's how it always goes.

"Reiss. Lemme see the overnight hospital reports." Reiss
brought them in and stayed with Grange while he read them.

There was still no change in Strang's condition. Poor guy was still in a coma.

"The trace and taps are on, all locations, Grange. And we should be getting another report from imaging any minute now. Anything else for now?"

"No. Thanks Reiss. But I'll tell you. I'm feeling really nervous today. I hate to say it, but something's gonna happen. You know the feeling."

"Yeah, I know. I wasn't gonna say it, but that's what I was thinking too. Colter should be calling in soon. I'll ring him right in to you."

"Good, that's good. Okay, just make sure everybody's on the alert. This could be a real long day. And gees, the Banks family has got to be freaking out from the papers today. They must be driving Colter crazy."

"Yeah, you're right. That's probably why we haven't heard from him yet."

We haven't heard from Maria or Officer Katelin yet either, Grange thought. He dialed Maria's office number. The receptionist sounded like she just woke up and seemed to take her time connecting him. Finally, there was her voice.

"Maria Lambert. Can I help you?"

Grange let out a sigh of relief. "Good morning, Maria. This is Detective Ted Grange. Just want to know how you're doing this mornin."

"Oh. Oh good morning Detective. I mean Ted. I'm all right. A little more tired than usual. But I'm okay. I have to tell you. That Bonnie Katelin's a really good lady. I want to thank you for that. I don't know what I would have done without her." She sounded stressed but really sweet, he thought.

"Just doing my job, Maria. I'm glad that worked out. You okay at work today?"

"Yeah, I guess so. I can't say that I really feel like being here. I'm kinda like in a daze. Like I'm waiting for something to happen and I don't know what it is. Do you know what I mean? I mean, every time the phone rings I get sweaty. I'm afraid of who it's gonna be."

"Well, just try not to worry. But listen. If one of those guys calls you, let them talk. Just talk to them like you would any other time, but try to talk for at least a minute or two. We put a tracer switch on your line so we can track 'em down if they call you." He didn't tell her about the tap. He didn't want her to feel self-conscious when she was talking to anyone.

"All right. I'll remember that. I just wish it was time to go home already. You know how some days seem to take forever? I think this day is going to feel like the longest day."

"I know exactly what you mean. But listen, I gotta go. Now don't forget. If you need me, I'm here. Okay?"

"Okay. I'll speak to you later."

"Bye, Maria. Try to make it a nice day in spite of everything."

He felt good when he got off the phone. She's an okay lady. No matter what happens, she'll get through it just fine, he thought.

Even though he knew that Officer Katelin and her support were hovering around the area, he hoped Maria didn't get any surprise visitors at the office.

chapter

TWENTY
SIX

Jordan was back in his apartment by 10:45. Tabatha greeted him in the foyer with a reflexive peck on the cheek.

"What's going on, Jordan? What is so important that you're here and not in your office? Is it something about that stabbing? Is Claudia in danger?"

"No, Tab. She's not in any danger. Not at all." He hoped with all his heart that he was justified, in every way, when he said that.

"It's something else, Tab. Why don't you have Albert make us some tea or coffee. We really need to talk. I'll meet you in the library."

The library was the most subdued room in their seventeen room Park Avenue apartment. The wood paneling, two walls of bound books, the enormous mahogany desk with leather inlays that matched the forest green leather chairs, made it a room well-disposed for serious talks and profound reflection. Jordan often sat in this room alone for hours when he had heavy decisions to make.

Tabatha arranged for Albert to bring them coffee, tea and breakfast rolls. Before Jordan got home, she had changed into a pale pink silk lounging outfit with flowing pants, a slightly scoop-necked pullover and matching leather shoes with a one inch heel. This was one of her best colors. She knew that she looked radiant with baby pink against her porcelain white skin, multi-platinum hair and green eyes. Jordan had sounded so unusually serious on the phone. She thought it important that she look her best so that at least that part of her was fortified.

When she got to the library, she was stunned to find Jordan looking so uncharacteristically forlorn. She hadn't ever remembered him looking quite like that, except when each of his parents died. For an awful moment, she thought that he might ask her for a divorce. Maybe, with all his philandering, he had met someone and actually fallen in love. Life was full of strange twists and turns, and maybe this was going to be a sharp left. But in the midst of what had just happened at Claudia's apartment?

"Albert will be just a few moments, Jordan. I asked him to knock before he came into the room."

"That's good, Tabatha. That's good. Here. Sit down across from me so that we can talk." They sat in the high-backed forest green leather chairs with brass finishing studs. Jordan was trying to be sensitive and courageous for both of them, but just getting the conversation started was proving more difficult than he had thought it would be.

"Have I told you lately how very beautiful and wonderful you are?"

"Probably not Jordan. But that's all right. I know that's what you feel. But come on, now. You didn't stay home from work this morning to drown me with compliments, did you?"

"No I didn't, Tab. It's just that what I want to talk about isn't easy for me. Or for us."

She felt the blood leave her face and a light sweat glaze her forehead and palms. Whatever it was, she would handle it. She was satisfied that, if this were indeed their final bow, she looked marvelous.

"All right, Jordan. Just tell me what's on your mind. You look awful, and that's getting me nervous. I can't imagine what you're going to say."

"Tabatha, it is about Claudia. But it's not what you think. This has nothing to do with the..." He hated the word stabbing, and he knew Tabatha was tormented by the concept, so he decided to lessen the impact. "No, Tab. This has nothing to do with what happened at the party."

"Oh dear God. Is she sick, Jordan? What...what is it?"

"No Tab. She's not sick. Listen to me." He reached across the lamp table for her hand. "Remember when we were trying so hard to have children. And we couldn't, Tabby. And then we adopted Claudia."

"Why are you...why are you talking about this?"

"You know, Tab, that I never agreed with you about not telling her that she was adopted. But, I listened to you. And, God knows why, but I can run a multi-million dollar international company, but I could never go against your decision to not tell her. Truthfully, I have felt guilty all this time. But, in fact, we never did tell her."

"What are you getting at? Is there something that you're trying to blame me for? Are you trying to explain your conduct, your extra-curricular conduct, all these years on guilt?"

"No, that's not it at all. And I don't think we should discuss that now. We truly have a few very important things to figure out, and fast."

"You don't want to tell Claudia now, do you? At her age? And while all of this horrible stuff is happening?" Tabatha was on her feet circling the forest green leather chairs.

They were startled by a knock on the door. They had both forgotten that Albert was going to bring their tea and coffee.

Albert quietly placed the sterling silver serving tray, a silver pot of coffee and another of tea, a basket of miniature breakfast rolls, two fine china cups and saucers, napkins, sugar and cream on the pale rose marble coffee table.

"Excuse me, Mrs. Banks."

"Yes, Albert?"

"Might you know where Mrs. Wilkens is this morning? Roger called hoping to be able to see her this evening."

"No, Albert. I don't have the slightest idea where she is. She's probably just out walking. It's such a beautiful day. Or perhaps she was meeting friends. I'm sorry, but I really don't know. He'll have to speak to her later."

"Thank you, Mrs. Banks. Is there anything else I can bring you?"

"Thank you, Albert." Tabatha wanted him out of the room. "This is fine for now. Please close the door again when you leave. And please, if there are any calls for either of us, we'll get the messages from you later."

"Except if it is a Detective Colter, Albert," Jordan interjected. "I'll speak to him if he calls." Jordan knew that Tabatha would relate this request only to the investigation into the stabbing. She still had no idea that there was also an ominous note in the mix.

"Very well." Albert bowed respectfully.

As soon as Albert left the room, Tabatha was on her feet, raving at her husband.

"Jordan. We haven't told her in all these years, and I can think of absolutely not one reason in the world to tell her now. She thinks she's our daughter. She is our daughter. She never has to know any different. It's better that way. Why should she ever have any questions about who she is? She's a grown and beautiful woman. She has all the poise and confidence that any woman could ever wish for. And she knows who she is. She knows she's a Banks. There is no reason for anything to change."

"Yes, Tabatha. There is a reason for some things to change."

This stopped Tabatha's tirade and pacing. She clenched the back of her chair and asked, her voice chilled and anxious, "Why? What are you saying?"

Without some of the more provocative details, like the note and the possibility of blackmail, Jordan briefly outlined what Colter had told him.

"This is impossible. Jordan, I can't take this. I don't want to lose her." Jordan took her in his arms. She was on the verge of hysterics, and he needed her to be calm so that he could lead her, rationally, to where this discussion had to lead. There were no choices today.

"First of all, Tabatha, if there is any chance, however remote, that she would find out from anybody else but us, that is what would be terrible."

"Don't expect me to answer you for awhile. You just keep talking. I'll listen. I promise. But my head is spinning. I don't know what to do or what to think."

"You're not going to lose her, Tabatha. You raised her. We raised her. She's our daughter. But she has a right to know about her own life. Think about your parents and your childhood. I think about mine very often. Look how much we took for granted. We knew who we looked like, who we took after. Those are precious and important things to know."

"But this is different, Jordan. She's not just some adopted child that you read about. She's our Claudia. Our family is special. We might not all get along all the time, but we have always loved each other very much. We have no reason to change anything. I don't want anything to change."

"I know you don't want anything to change. But Tabatha, she should be the one to decide how she wants to deal with this information. Not us. This isn't about us. It's about her. She's an adult now. I'm sure she'll be grateful to us for finally telling her. And I'm sure she'll understand why you've been so afraid for her to know. Give her some credit, Tabatha. If you really love her, you have to give her the respect she deserves."

"Of course I respect her. What are you talking about? How I feel has nothing to do with whether or not I respect her. But I'm her mother. I know what's best for her. And it's been best for her not to know."

"Are you saying that you know what's best for her, Tab, or are you really saying that you know what's best for you?"

"That wasn't fair, Jordan."

"But I have finally realized that it's true. You haven't kept this from her for her sake. You've kept this from her for your own sake. For your own insecurities and fears. I think you've always been afraid of losing her love if she knew."

"Look. The adoption agency told us that we never had to tell her. They said there was no reason for it, unless we thought she could find out from somebody else in the family or a neighbor. We were in Europe for all the months that I was supposedly pregnant. Nobody knew. Not a soul except you and me and whatever officials were involved. Damn it. Why did they have to put it in writing so that somebody could find it?"

She sank into his arms like a baby and cried. "Oh, Jordan. What are we going to do?"

"We have to be able to talk about this, Tabatha. And we have to do it now. Because in a few minutes we're going to call Claudia and have her come over here so that we can tell her."

"No, Jordan. I don't want to. I'd rather take my chances with the press finding out. Because whatever happened in that office...well...you have to have connections to get to the press. And whoever was there that day wouldn't know what to do with this information."

"Tabatha, I love you. But you're deluding yourself and you know it. I don't mean to sound cold, but you have to get a hold of yourself. Sit up and have some more coffee. We really must discuss this rationally. And right now."

She slid out of his arms and looked into his eyes.

"But Jordan. Don't you see? She won't love me as much anymore. She'll want to find out who her other mother is. And one day they'll meet each other, and she won't want to be my daughter anymore. Everything will change."

"Oh, my sweet Tabatha. That's what has been worrying you all these years. I wish to God we had talked about this before. So much time could have been saved. So much hurt could have been avoided. You would never even talk about it to me. When I wanted to talk about Claudia, and my concerns about not being honest with her, you shut me out. Really, you were shutting both Claudia and me out. It has unnecessarily driven a wedge between us for too many years."

"I'll be right back." Tabatha crossed the room and closed the bathroom door. She carefully dabbed around her eyes with cold water. When she returned to the room, she was in control of herself again. She sat in her chair and looked at her husband.

"I love you Jordan. I always have. I know what you've said is true. I've been frightened and selfish. I haven't thought about what would be right for her. I've only thought about what I could handle. I'm so ashamed."

"I can only hope that it's not too late to rectify what we have done."

"But now I must ask you, Jordan. What will happen now if we tell her? She will have so many questions. Do we have all the answers?"

"I only know that Claudia's identity is based on what we have told her. But it's not her complete story. I have put myself in her place many times. If I were adopted, I'll be damned, but I'd want to know about anything and everything that concerned me. I'd want to know who gave birth to me. What kind of person she was, what she looked like. And why she and my father didn't keep me. I suspect that, in addition to her wanting to know all of our feelings about her and the fact that she was adopted, she'll want to know all that there is to know about where she came from and the people involved. And I can't blame her. I'll even help her find out anything she wants to know."

"What do you mean?"

"You know better than most people, Tab. I have incredible resources available to me. In terms of detectives and access to records. That's all there for her. But now we have to call her. It's time for us to talk to her."

"Jordan. I have something that I have to tell you. Please just hear me out and be calm. There are a few things that I better get off my chest before we call her."

"What is it, Tabatha?"

"I have received several letters."

"What letters? What kind of letters?" Jordan's mind raced. Was the idiot that had sent him that note writing to his wife too?

"The letters were from a woman claiming to be Claudia's other mother."

"What? Why didn't you tell me? When did you get them? Who is she? What did she say?"

"She sounded like a lovely woman. She even sent a picture. She's beautiful. She looks like Claudia's mother." Tabatha wiped her tears with her baby pink silk hanky.

"I received the first one about three or four years ago. I read it over and over again, and then I put it away. I felt so guilty. She said that she had always loved her daughter, and that she hadn't wanted her to be adopted. Oh, Jordan. I know it's not what she wanted me to feel, but I felt like we had done something horrible, because this lady has suffered her whole life so that we could be happy parents."

"Did you answer her letter?"

"I almost did a few times. I vacillated between loving her for giving us Claudia, and hating her for being alive. I actually wished she was dead. I didn't want her to have the right to love our Claudia. I didn't want Claudia to have another mother. I wanted it to be like any other contract that you sign. Boom. A deal's a deal, and how dare she be a wonderful person and have feelings. But mostly, I didn't want to lose Claudia to another woman. And in my fear, I've probably driven Claudia away from me in so many ways. I guess I finally hoped that if I didn't answer, she would just go away. But she didn't.

"She wrote again. Several more times. In the last letter she said that if I didn't get in touch with her, she would try to speak directly to Claudia. That's when I finally wrote back to her. I told her not to dare. That we didn't need her. That Claudia's life was fine, rich, rewarding and full of love. And to just leave well enough alone. I was totally dismissive of her, to say the least. I haven't heard from her since then, and I've been petrified. And I felt awful about what I wrote because, really, she sounds like a wonderful person. I've been so selfish. How could I deny Claudia this woman's love because of my own fears?"

"I always took pride in us as parents, Tab. That we loved our daughter unconditionally. But it looks like we did put conditions in the way. We have a lot of healing to do with her."

"I've kept something else from you, and from Claudia."

"I can't imagine what else there could be."

"When we first took Claudia home with us, we were given two letters and a pink hand knitted sweater with matching booties. They were from that woman. I never showed them to you. I needed to pretend that they didn't exist. I needed to pretend that there was no other mother. Only me. I needed to pretend that Claudia's life started the moment we took her in our arms. One of the letters was written to us. The other was written to Claudia. She asked that we show it to her when we felt she was ready. She understood that there would come a time when, naturally, Claudia would ask questions about her other mother."

"But we never even gave her a chance to ask, did we Tab? She never even knew to ask. For all intents and purposes, we killed her past for her."

"Why is it sometimes that it takes a shock, like what you were told today, to knock sense into us? How could I have lived all these years with such blind fears?"

"Hopefully that's all behind us now. Do you...?"

"Yes. I kept everything. I've had them in a box all these years. I used to think that I'd show them to both of you one day. And then sometimes, oh so long ago, I decided that I never would. Who was I to think I could play God with her life? Oh Jordan. She is going to hate me for holding all of this from her. What have I done?"

They hugged again, and both realized that today they had the most physical contact with each other that they had had in years.

"Do you want to see the letters?"

"Of course I do. After we call Claudia."

Tabatha was so nervous she was practically babbling. "I can't make this call, Jordan. I just can't. You will have to do this. My God, I don't think I have the strength. I've never been so frightened in my life. I'm worried. I'm worried that she is going to hate us for not telling her. For keeping this a secret from her."

"Tab, listen to me. Nothing is going to change. I'm sure it will be very emotional for Claudia. For all of us. But I think we'll all be the better for it." And then he tried to create a moment of levity when he said, "And Tab, just think. You will not feel compelled to dye your hair anymore to match Claudia's. You can have your beautiful auburn hair again. I've missed it."

"Jordan. Sometimes you forget how old we are. My hair is probably half gray by now." She hugged her husband tightly. "I've missed you, Jordan. I have had so many misplaced emotions. Can you ever forgive me?" She let out a deep breath, took in another one, and let that one out slowly.

"I'll call her now, Tab, while you get the letters. It's 11:30. I hope she hasn't left for the hospital yet."

chapter

TWENTY SEVEN

Reiss ran into the room. "Hey, Grange. We got something. Listen to this. That Roger Wilkens guy. His mother was at Claudia Banks' party." He watched for Grange's reaction.

"Ya' gotta be fuckin' kidding. What the fuck are you talking about? Lemme see that report. Lemme see that." Grange grabbed the papers from Reiss.

"So, are you ready for one more piece of information?"

"What more? Yeah, yeah, come on. Let me hear it."

"She lives at the Banks' house. Ida Wilkens, Roger Wilkens' mother, has been working for them for thirty-two years."

"Holy shit. Where's Colter. He's gotta hear this. He's got so many god damn possibilities on the table now it's enough to make a guy as organized as him dizzy. He'll go crazy when he sees this. What else is in here? You're a fuckin' genius. Get Colter over here."

Within twenty minutes, Colter was running into the office and Grange raced from behind his desk to greet him.

"What's the name of the game, Detective Colter? Bingo! Bingo's the name of the game. We got our man. At least for the note. It's not Maria's friend. It's gotta be the other guy. Look at this. It's gotta be him." Grange handed him the papers.

Colter gave the sheets a once over and looked up. "Yeah. Looks like we've got something here. This is about as direct an angle as you can get, I agree," he said calmly.

"Jesus, Colter. I thought you'd jump all over this one." Grange couldn't believe that Colter wasn't at least a little enthused.

Colter's blonde brow arched. "But what's his motive, Grange? Why would Roger Wilkens look at that file and get so agitated and write Banks a note like that? And you're sure she's living there now?"

"Yeah, she's there now. They moved her in after her husband died. Sounds like she's been loyal and real close to that family." Grange sat behind his desk again and put his feet up while his hands played with a rubber band and a paper clip. "Let me ask you something Colter. You never recognized the Wilkens' name and connected it to Banks. That's not like you, Mr. Thorough."

"Her name hasn't come up in years, not since she was first listed as day help at his home. All of the notes we investigated were associated with his other life, at the office. His personal life was never involved." Colter made himself comfortable on the couch. "So what does this mean to you smart guy?"

"Okay, I see it like this," Grange continued. "For years his mother was the Banks' maid. Okay. And he doesn't like that his mother is a maid. He just never likes that. And she has to spend a lot of time with this other family and their kid instead of being home with him and her own kids, cause she helps out the Banks' nannies too. So, as close as he gets with the Banks kid from over the years he always, you know, he always resents her. So, okay, then he sees this file and he finds out something deep about this family that he thought he knew so well. And he sees a chance of getting some money from them. He wants to get money to give to his mother so that she can have her own place. She worked real hard all those years, she should have her own place."

"I don't know, Grange." Colter was still looking through the papers. "They must all be really close, I'll agree with you there. He's known that family his whole life. But if he wanted money, he probably just had to tell that to Mr. Banks. It says here that Banks bought him and his family things for years and paid for his college education. Why would Wilkens want to be so sneaky and mysterious and low life about it? It doesn't feel like he had to be that way to get money if he needed it."

"Yeah, but he's tired of having to ask for money. He just wants to have more of his own."

"But maybe his mother had a choice, Grange. Maybe she's not living at the Banks' because she has to. Maybe she wanted to live there with them. Instead of living alone. Her kids have their own places, and her husband is dead. Maybe she just doesn't want to live alone. I don't know if your theory makes sense. We have to find out more about him. I don't get the feeling from this report that there's anything but good close feelings there. Between the families."

"Yeah, but you know how resentments can get really powerful. They can turn a nice relationship into a nightmare. I still think there might be something here."

Colter read a few more sections of the report. "Look at this, Grange. She must have some money. Banks helped her sell her house after her husband died. No, your theory doesn't hold up."

"Okay, so she's living there by choice. It still doesn't mean that her son isn't upset about something. Maybe he's tired of handouts from the Banks. Ya' know, he wants to be able to afford some of the bigger things for himself and his mother. And more than anything else, he probably figures that if he wrote this note, Banks would never in a million years suppose it could be him."

"That one makes sense. I'm with you a minute. Let's take this a little further now." Colter sat far back into the cracked couch, ran his fingers through his hair and crossed his legs. "You're right. Banks would never imagine that Roger Wilkens would write that kind of note to him. And so this Wilkens guy plans to have the money dropped so that Banks never knows it's him."

Reiss had seated himself in one of the cracked naugahyde chairs and had been listening to both of them. "He's at work today."

Colter and Grange just looked at him. "So?" Grange asked. "So he's acting normal. Like nothing happened. Whatd'ya expect him to do, stay home and draw attention to himself?"

"Just thought you'd like to know."

"Okay, now we know." Grange fidgeted nervously with his paper clip and rubber band, playing with them like they were a sling shot. "So why did you say that? What are ya' thinking?"

Reiss leapt to his feet and started pacing. "Let's say Wilkens could be the man for the note. His handwriting is similar, and if he was trying to camouflage his style, what we got is something he could probably do. Then if we go along with what you said, he's got the motive, and he's got the opportunity. But, you know what? I do not think he's got the mentality for it."

"Back to square one." Grange aimed the rubber band at the file cabinet. "So then what do you think is going on here?" Ping.

Colter rifled through the set of papers on his clipboard. "What if the note and the stabbing are related. So, let's just say, for the time being, that they are. I think we're limiting our options too soon. What if Wilkens masterminded this whole thing. He wrote the note and hired someone else to do the stabbing." His fingers combed the hair from his brow. "But..."

"Yeah. But what?" Grange asked.

Colter looked up from the clipboard. "What does Evan Strang have to do with all this?"

chapter

TWENTY EIGHT

Jordan had reached Claudia's answering machine. He had tried to leave an emotionally noncommittal message so that she would not suspect that anything out of the ordinary was on his mind. But, of course, with all that was going on, she probably would not have noticed the unusual strain with which he spoke.

He was glad that he was in the library, the room that had always given him so much solace. He thought of his parents, God rest their souls. He never told them that he and Tabatha hadn't been able to produce grandchildren for them. Because of his own perceived failures his father had, certainly without meaning to, given him a tired man's view of what it meant to be a man. How silly that all seemed now. And how many years they had wasted simply not loving and enjoying each other.

And Tabatha. How much love had they let sit by the wayside while they each wrestled with their own demons. If only they had allowed themselves to speak honestly about what was on their minds. Instead, there were always only hints and symptoms.

Tabatha had never been able to get over her inability to have children, and Jordan realized now that he had always sensed that.

At the beginning, he had showered Tabatha with every material possession a woman could want. But it was never enough. Finally he was driven into the arms of other women.

He knew that even though Tabatha loved Claudia with all her heart, from the moment she first saw her, she had never been able to completely overcome her feelings of inadequacy. She sought rather to spend her life pretending that Claudia was in every way her very own, thus emotionally murdering Claudia's blood ties. She had even dyed her hair to match her daughter's natural platinum in a surface effort to erase any differences between them.

Claudia was now thirty-five years old. That meant that that was the number of years that he and his family had been living a lie and keeping secrets.

Just then there was a knock on the library door. His first thought was that Claudia might have coincidentally stopped by on her way to the hospital.

"Yes. Who is it? Come in."

The door opened slowly. "It's me." It was Tabatha. She was carrying a sterling silver canister the size of a shoe box. "Is she coming right over?"

"Her machine was on. I left a message. She's probably already at the hospital. I was just about to try her there."

The phone rang. After two rings Jordan remembered that he had told Albert to hold all calls except from Detective Colter. He ran out of the room hoping to intercept Claudia's call. When he returned to the library, his previously perfectly combed hair was falling onto his brow.

"It wasn't her, but Albert knows we're expecting to hear from her. I'll try the hospital now."

Just as he was making the call, one of the other phone lines rang.

"I know that's her," Tabatha said. "I just know it."

The buzzer on the phone console resonated throughout the room. Jordan pushed the speaker button, and Albert confirmed that it was indeed Claudia on the line.

"Hi, sweetheart. Are you at the hospital?"

Claudia loved it when her father called her sweetheart. She wondered if you were ever too old not to love sentimental words from your father.

"No. Actually I was just getting ready to leave. You must have called while I was in the shower. What's up?"

"Oh, with so much going on lately, your mom and I thought it would be nice if we all had lunch together today. Why don't you come over to the house, and then we can have Albert drop you off at the hospital later."

"I don't know, dad. I have the feeling that today's the day Evan is going to come out of his coma. It's probably just wishful thinking, but I want to be there when he does. I kind of told Jackie that I'd meet her there."

"Look, you know I don't mean to be pushy. But you're going to have to eat lunch anyway. Mightn't it just as well be here with us?"

"You know I don't like to say no to you, dad It's true, we've all been through a lot lately, and it would be nice to spend some relaxing time together. I think that would be lovely. I'll come over right away."

"Oh, that's wonderful, dear. And, Claudia?"

"Yes?"

"Just remember how much I love you."

"Oh, I know that dad. I love you too. I'll see you in a little while."

Jordan walked over to his wife and held both of her hands. "Well, Tabatha. Here we go."

"I'm going into the kitchen and have Albert help me put a tray of food together. I think it will be nice to have finger foods, coffee, tea and juice while we talk. Don't you think we should do that? You can look through this box in the meantime. I'll be back in just a few minutes."

"Give me a kiss first, Tabatha." Jordan held her in his arms in a way that he hadn't for years. He stroked her hair and then gently kissed her on the lips. "I love you, Tab. I always have. We're going to have a better life now, you and I. We have a lot of lost time to make up for."

"Let's just get through today, Jordan. I just want to get through today and know that our lives are still in one piece." And with that she returned his kiss on the lips and left the room.

He was just about to open the silver case when the buzzer on the phone console rang out. Albert announced that it was Colter.

"What's up, Colter?"

"I'm here at the station. Was just wondering how things are going there."

"We're taking care of things, Colter. I don't want to get into the details right now, but everything will be taken care of on this end by early this afternoon. You don't know it yet, but I have a lot to be grateful to you for. In the meantime, is there anything new with the investigation?"

"Yeah. Some of the leads I mentioned to you are starting to fall into place. Is this a good time to talk?"

"I'm sorry, no. Claudia is on her way here now. She could be here any minute. Is it something that can wait a few hours?"

"Yeah. It can wait. But call me the first chance you can."

"Of course. In a few hours." He felt badly that he had to put Colter off. But nothing was more important to him than getting his family through this.

Jordan considered the monumental changes that were affecting his, and his family's life in just a few hours' time. In the way that he had conditioned himself years ago for conducting business, he was able to avoid getting overwhelmed by multiple staggering circumstances, and concentrate instead on the matter at hand. He had to use this time to prepare himself for his daughter's reaction to the information that she was about to be presented with. And he had to decide how to tell her.

He knew his Claudia to be a strong woman who had always faced life's challenges in a calm and easy going way. Very unlike his wife, who tended to be severely high strung when faced with routine or extraordinary situations. He knew that Claudia felt secure with herself and in her parents' love for her. He suspected, too, that she had wondered often about the many notable differences between herself and her parents, both physically and in terms of interests and proclivities.

Her light instinctual comments about such observations that she verbalized fairly regularly all her life, he admitted to himself now, were probably really questions framed in such a way that if there was an explanation, she had cleverly and wisely opened the door for discussion. Especially when she was a teenager she'd say things like, 'everybody else I know looks more like their parents than I do,' or 'how could a mother of mine have such different tastes?' or 'I think I have another mother hidden away someplace who would be able to understand me better.'

Comments like these stung Tabatha to her core, and she showed it. In truth, both of them had reacted terribly to Claudia's comments. They ignored, made light of and denied the implications of her outbursts.

Could it be that Claudia suspected all along, and he and Tabatha had purposefully deluded themselves into thinking that she was simply going through normal adolescent angst? Could it be that she never really asked them directly whether or not she was adopted because she sensed their discomfort in even the suggestion of our not being her parents? They had rebuked her curiosity. Had they irreparably harmed their child, or their relationship with her, in any way? Certainly, there was no evidence of that. And since over time such pronouncements had tapered off, and then abruptly stopped, they felt comforted that their initial analysis of youthful woe had been correct and that their worries had been groundless.

Jordan was consumed with a guilt and fear that were foreign to his usual resolute and capable temperament. This, unlike business, was about the very substance of human beings, an area that he usually only delved into to size-up prospective clients and business associates. How could he have let his priorities disconnect so from his every day life?

His musings were interrupted by a knock on the door that opened without waiting for his invitation. In walked Claudia, looking radiant and fresh. As he walked around his desk to greet and hug his daughter, he realized that he had never opened the silver box.

"My sweet sweet Claudia. I'm so happy that you're here."

"So am I, dad. Things have been pretty awful lately. I never thought I'd experience anything like this, do you know what I mean? Plots like this are for movies and television. They're not supposed to be for real life. I'm tired of hospitals and detectives and policemen. I'm tired of worrying about Evan all the time. I just want everything to be all right again."

"I know, sweetheart. I know." He hugged his daughter again, relieved that she couldn't see the tears that were forming in his eyes. When he felt in control of himself, he offered her a seat on the couch by the coffee table, and took one of the chairs adjacent to it for himself.

"So where's mom? What's for lunch?" Leave it to Claudia to always interject nonchalance into grim moments, Jordan thought.

"She's helping Albert prepare the food. We thought we'd eat in here. I hope that's all right with you, my wonderful princess."

"I think that's nice for a change. And you were right. I'm starving, and I'll be better prepared for the day with a good meal in my belly."

"That's my sweet girl."

"You sound very sentimental today, dad. Is everything all right?"

"Yes, I feel confident that everything is going to be all right." He couldn't bring himself to say that everything was fine. No more lies or evasions, if he could possibly help it.

"What do you mean by that?"

He did not want to start the conversation until Tabatha was in the room with them. Propitiously, Claudia's attention was drawn to the silver canister.

"Where did this beautiful piece come from? I've never seen it before. Is it new?"

"No, it's not new. Actually, it's something that your mother has had for quite some time."

"Oh. It's just magnificent. Let me see it."

He tried to hide his panic. "Wait for your mother to come in, Claudia."

"You're being awfully mysterious dad. What is going on here?"

He was saved by one knock on the door followed immediately by Tabatha walking in as Albert wheeled the pewter cart with it's two glass shelves filled with trays of food, beverages and service for three. She hurried across the room to Claudia.

"Oh my dear Claudia. As always, you are the most beautiful woman on this earth. Give your mom a hug, will you?"

"My goodness, you are both so mushy today."

"We can't help it, dear. You are just too perfect for words." Tabatha was on the verge of losing control, but Jordan could see that she was trying desperately to be composed.

They all watched as Albert set the china, silver and napkins on the coffee table. When he was finished, he announced, "As you see, we have prepared a little buffet for your lunch. Please ring me if there is anything else that you need."

They all graciously thanked him, and he left the room. Tabatha took a seat across from Jordan so that they were on either side of Claudia. She looked at Jordan in a way that conveyed to him clearly that she wanted him to start the conversation. And so he did.

"Claudia, my sweetheart," he began. "You know that we always love to spend time with you, and we're so happy that you agreed to have lunch with us. But I have to admit to you that there is a very real reason why we needed to be with you today." He took a deep breath.

"What is it dad? Mom? I've had the feeling that something was on your mind since I got here. Don't make me nervous. Please, just tell me what it is."

"Claudia, there is something that your mother and I have wanted to tell you since you were a little girl. And we hope, with all of our hearts, that you will forgive us for waiting so long to have this talk with you."

Claudia was turning her head to her left and right, trying to look at both of her parents at the same time, trying to get a sense of what was on their minds from their eyes. All she could see was pain and worry. She waited for her father to continue.

"This is hard for me, Claudia. Please bear with me." Claudia couldn't believe that she saw tears forming in her father's eyes, and she couldn't help getting up off the couch, walking over to his chair and giving him a kiss on his cheek. Then she wiped his tears with his as yet unused napkin.

"It breaks my heart to see you cry, daddy. Please...please tell me what's wrong."

"I'm all right, Claudia. Really I am." He gave her a hug. "Let me pour a little coffee." Claudia moved back to the couch, and they all filled their coffee cups.

"Claudia," he continued. "When your mother and I were first married, our dream was to have children. And more than anything, we wanted a beautiful little daughter like you." He didn't want to cry again, but this was the hardest, most emotional conversation he had ever tried to have. "But, as much as we tried, your mother and I were not able to conceive. And so... well then...we looked into..."

"You're trying to tell me that I'm adopted."

Tabatha finally found her voice. "Yes, Claudia. That is what we're trying to tell you. But that shouldn't...that doesn't change anything. We just decided that this was something you had to know, and we hope you'll forgive us for waiting this long to tell you."

Claudia looked at them both and said, "You know, I love you both very very much. And you both seem to be suffering, and so nervous about this conversation. So I might as well just tell you. I already know that I'm adopted."

"You know?" Tabatha's body straightened abruptly in her seat and she nearly spilled her coffee before she was able to set it back on the table.

"Claudia," Tabatha stuttered. "How did you find out? Why didn't you ever say anything to us?"

It was Claudia's turn to take a deep breath. She stood up and walked around the room before she began. "I found out a little over four years ago."

"Four years ago?" Tabatha asked. "Jordan, that was before..."

"Tab. Let Claudia finish. Please go on, Claudia."

"Well, I received a phone call from a woman who told me that she was the woman who gave birth to me. Naturally, I assumed it was a crank call of some sort, because you had never said anything about adoption. I don't remember what I said to her, but I was just about to hang up on her when she said, in such a sweet and sincere voice, that what she was saying was true, and that she could tell that I needed time to digest what I had just heard. She said she'd call again a week from that day."

Jordan felt a lump growing in his throat. "Oh sweetheart, please forgive us. That must have been such a shocking telephone call. What did you think? What did you do? I can't believe we weren't there for you."

"When we first got off the phone, I dismissed what she had said as nonsense. But I couldn't imagine why someone would say that if it wasn't true. Unless she had just gotten the wrong number. But she knew my name, although of course so many people do. But really what got to me, and stuck with me, was the tone in her voice. The way she said what she said didn't sound at all like what I would imagine a crank caller would sound like. So, while I tried to erase the conversation from my mind, over the next days I kept thinking about it again and again. I thought of things that I hadn't thought of in so many years. You know, how in some ways I had always thought we were all really so different, and how I didn't really look like either of you."

Tabatha interrupted her. "Oh, Claudia. I'm so sorry that we didn't have the confidence, in ourselves, to tell you. I never imagined any of this could happen. Do you hate us?"

"Of course I don't hate you. Look, I guess I always knew there was something. There just seemed to be things that we were never able to talk about. And it always had to do with our differences. As a young girl, I could never understand why sometimes both of you, either together or separately, would rebuff some of my questions and concerns. It was like there were things that we just weren't allowed to discuss. It never made sense to me, because it seemed that, otherwise, we were always able to talk about anything. But on certain subjects, you both seemed very touchy." She paused, holding back her tears. "And all I wanted was to be closer to you both."

Jordan spoke with the lump in his throat. "Please tell us more about what happened with...with the woman who called you."

"All right. A few days after that first call, I came to see you both. I was going to ask you, straight out, if I was adopted. I don't remember exactly what I said, but I tried to broach the subject, I guess indirectly, at first. I remember saying something about an article I had read about adoption, and you both made repelling remarks and changed the subject. It was obviously a subject that you could not handle. It was the same kind of brick wall that was always there. So, I figured that you had probably answered my question without my really asking it. Then I decided to take the next step by myself and see what happened. By the time she called me back the next week, I had prepared myself and, I guess, not uncoincidentally, I was home when she called."

This was the topic that Tabatha dreaded the most, but she had to know. There were no more emotions or questions that they could, or should, ever hide from one another again. "So, dear, what happened when you spoke to her again, and did you meet her?"

"Why don't I make a long story short for now. I think that this is very heavy for all of us, and I don't think it's possible for us to say everything that we want to say in a short time. And really, I do have to get to the hospital."

"But we have to promise each other," Jordan interjected, "that we will spend time together so that we can all really talk about this. But please, Claudia, tell us as much as you feel comfortable talking about today."

"All right. But before I continue, I want you both to know that my feelings for you never changed. I only felt badly that there were areas of our lives that we were not able to share. And I always thought that we had missed out on something important because of that. But, as far as I'm concerned, it's never too late. I'm only glad that we can be honest with each other now. Really, I hated having a secret from you. But I didn't feel that you gave me any other choice. I feel so relieved."

For the first time in the discussion, Claudia couldn't hold back her tears. "I guess I've been keeping these tears in for a long time." Both Jordan and Tabatha got up to hug her, and they all cried.

Jordan melted whenever his daughter cried. "If you don't want to talk about this anymore now, we'll understand, sweetheart. You have so much on your mind right now."

"No, dad. I do want to talk about it now. But I'm also hungry and that food looks delicious. Can we eat a little while we talk?" She had created a moment of lightness again, and they all welcomed the chance to relax from the tensions that filled the air.

"Yes, dear," Tabatha said. "Of course. Let's all sit down again and help ourselves. As you can see, Albert and I put together your favorite brunch." They all surveyed the platters of bagels, cream cheese, nova and white fish and prepared plates for themselves. In between bites, Claudia told her story.

"I feel so much better with some food in my stomach. Okay, here I go." Claudia took a deep breath, closed her eyes and sat back with her loaded bagel. "By the time I spoke to her again, I was already pretty sure that she was telling me the truth. But this time, she had information that absolutely convinced me. She asked me if I had a copy of my birth certificate, which I did. She told me to look at the number on it, and said that it matched the number that was on my original birth certificate, the one that I was given when I was first born. You see, after you adopted me, after they put my new name with your names as my parents on my amended birth certificate, they didn't change the birth certificate number."

"By then you felt sure that she really was your original mother?"

"Pretty much so. She told me her name, and what she had named me when I was born. She told me that all I had to do was go to the New York Public Library and ask for the birth records book for the year I was born, and there I would find my original name and the same number that's on the birth certificate I have with you. I went the next day and checked and, sure enough, it was there. I phoned her that evening, and we agreed to meet each other the next week, and I have spent a lot of time with her ever since."

"What is she like, Claudia?"

"I know you feel insecure about this, mother. But you have no reason to. Yes, I do love her. I even admit that I love her very much. And of course I love you. You see, it has never changed my feelings for you. You know, if you had had more children besides me, you would have loved us all. So why aren't I just as capable of loving all of you? Anyway, she's wonderful. I know you'd like her. I think it would be good for all of us if we had lunch or dinner together here. I'd like you to meet each other. After all, we're all practically related."

"I have to tell you something, Claudia. She wrote to me. And I must admit that I wasn't very nice to her when I wrote back. I showed her no respect or consideration at all. I'm ashamed of that now. I was selfish. I didn't want competition. I wanted to be your only mother."

"I know all about it, mother. She told me. Before she wrote the last letter, I tried to talk to you again about it. I couldn't get through to you, so I thought that maybe hearing from her once more would help you calm down. But it landed up having the opposite effect."

"The two of you already knew each other," Tabatha understood.

"Yes. I didn't want it that way," Claudia said softly. "I always felt guilty about having this whole other life behind your back. But with your attitudes being how they were, you gave me no choice. Finally, it was easier for me to feel guilty, than for me to be the cause of your feeling hurt. And also, you should know, that she would have preferred speaking to you before she first spoke to me. But her every instinct told her that you would push her away, and maybe not let her know me. And she didn't want to risk that. Her instincts were right. You would have done everything in your power to stop her from meeting me, wouldn't you have?"

"Yes, I admit that's true." Tabatha looked at Jordan, then back to Claudia. "I've acted more like you were a possession of mine than an individual human being."

"All right you two." Claudia's tone became stronger. "Now it's my turn. Let me ask you a few questions. How did you adopt me without anyone finding out?"

Jordan explained that he and Tabatha used to travel through Europe for business and vacations for months at a time. After they realized they could not conceive, they had spent five months there and told everyone that Tabatha was expecting. By the time they returned to the states, they were able to pick up Claudia and bring her home with them.

Satisfied with that answer, Claudia asked another question. "Why did you want to talk about this today? This week of all weeks?"

Jordan told her what had happened at the Bureau of Vital Statistics and the very real possibility of publicity the incident might effect.

"We have all paid quite a price for being in the public eye," Jordan said, ruefully remembering the pain his tabloid affairs caused his family. "But this situation has resulted in such a joyously momentous turning point for us."

"Who were the people who saw the file?" Claudia asked.

"We don't know yet. The detectives are working on it," Jordan responded.

Claudia sat quietly watching her parents.

"What is it, dear?" Tabatha asked.

"It's ironic. All this time, the only person I told was Marni. Don't misunderstand me. I would have told everyone but I didn't want it to get back to you because I didn't think you could handle it. And now it could be headline news all over the world."

Tabatha looked at her daughter with a love and pride that burst from her heart. "You know, Claudia. I know that neither your father nor I could have loved you more if you had been truly our own child."

"And sweetheart," Jordan added. "I know that we had no right to keep this information from you. I have agonized over our decision all these years. If I were adopted, I'd want to know. I'd want to know where I came from, why my original parents didn't raise me, what kind of people they were, who I looked like. It's your life, and knowing everything about who you are is your right. We had no right to make a decision for you that denied you information about your own history, and obviously also denied you other people who also love you. This has all been too much of a secret. And damn it, except for business, secrets really are just not healthy. You know, I've dreamt about who your original parents were more times than I can tell you."

"I have too, Claudia," Tabatha said. "Do you know that this is the first time that your father and I have been able to talk openly about this? We have both been so old fashioned and stuck in our ways with our misplaced fears and insecurities. We understand now that our priorities were ourselves, not you. We were more concerned about what was good, or I should say easier, for us. We were wrong. I promise you that everything will be different now. And, I have something else to tell you. Well, actually, to show you."

Tabatha got up and brought the silver canister to Claudia. "This is where I kept her letters to me. I guess you've read copies of them already, so they're not news to you. But dad hasn't seen them yet. I never told him about them until today. But also in the box are things she made for you while she was pregnant. A little pink sweater. Booties. And a letter she wrote to you. You know, she never actually signed her letters to me. She used a post office as a return address, and a made up name. She said that before she told me her real name, she wanted to make sure that I wasn't hostile towards her. That I wouldn't try to hurt her in some way. Given the power of our family, I can understand her caution. I've been absolutely horrid to her. If it wasn't for her, there wouldn't be you. And she had to live her life without you. She sounds so nice. It must have been horrible for her. I've always wondered about her. Her tragedy was my gain. I should never have done anything to hurt her. I've always wondered what she looked like, what kind of person she is. She...she...what is her name, Claudia? Who is she?"

"Her name is Marsha Rachel Grossman."

chapter

TWENTY NINE

Marni tried to make Tuesday a fairly normal day of work, albeit a short one. She knew she would stop early to meet Claudia at the hospital again.

By 2:30 in the afternoon she admitted to herself that, between thinking about Evan and Craig, she wasn't really getting very much done. True, she had fielded some important phone calls that required quick decisions about some of her groups' recording and touring plans, but she hadn't even dented the pile of contracts that Carl Hoenig wanted her to review.

For Marni, one of the benefits of having an office at home was that she didn't have to put on a business suit and high heels unless she had a meeting. Plus she could take breaks and take care of personal matters whenever she wanted to. And, on particularly rough days, she loved her afternoon naps.

She decided to polish some of her silver, but she couldn't stop thinking about Craig. Could this be it? Had she finally met the man of her dreams? When she spoke to Claudia last night about the aborted tennis game, she hadn't been able to hide her rare level of interest.

Her train of thought was broken by the ringing phone.

"Hello." It was Craig. Her body shivered.

"Hello Marni. I'm so happy to hear your voice today. I can't stop thinking about you. What are you doing?"

"I'm just trying to get some work done before I meet Claudia at the hospital." She paused, and decided to admit the truth. "I've been thinking about you, too."

"I hoped you would say that. Is there any new news about Evan?"

"No. Nothing really."

They talked for awhile, and she again felt her body tremble every once and awhile. It was an unbelievable reaction. And this time, in spite of her resolve, she couldn't help but say what was on her mind. "Craig. I have to tell you something."

"Uh huh."

"There, you did it again. Whenever you make that sound, you know, it's crazy, but it makes me want you." She tried to sound light-hearted, and even tried to conjure a little giggle, but, damn it, she was amazed that he could do that to her.

"What sound, Marni?"

He had made that incredibly sexy guttural noise that seemed to automatically come from his throat when he said, "uh huh"...when he could have used the words "I see." It was as if, when he said that, the phone lines connected them intravenously with an aphrodisiac. The sound's melody invaded her body and made her quiver. She didn't know what to say now. She had already said too much.

"All right, Craig. Let's change the subject." The more they talked, the more he got to her. This is ridiculous, she thought. Here she was, Marni Kendell, a thirty-six year old high powered successful business woman of great style being turned into a mush of hormones by the sound of a voice on the telephone.

"Whatever you want. I'd like to see you again soon, but I understand that you have a lot on your mind. If there's any news about Evan, will you phone me from the hospital?"

"Of course I will. In the meantime, I'm still waiting to hear from Claudia. I expected a call from her by now."

"She's probably taking a much needed break. I understand that her parents are being extremely protective of her right now. They must be crazed that this happened literally within steps of her."

"Yes. She says she feels like she's living in an armed camp. Have you and her father been involved with investments together since Pandalay Films?"

"Oh. You know about that?"

"The whole world read about it."

"No. We're not right now. But that temporary misunderstanding was patched up long ago, and I'm happy to say we have utmost respect for each other. I wouldn't be surprised if another situation came up that would be commercially viable for us."

"Oh. That's great. Do you have anything in mind?"

"Uh huh."

chapter

THIRTY

Jordan had to see it for himself. After his intensely emotional lunch with Claudia and Tabatha, he was only able to sit in his office for an hour. He found it near impossible to concentrate, so he took a stroll to the New York Public Library. He stopped first at the information desk. In this vast monument filled with millions of books, he hadn't the slightest idea where to find the book that Claudia had referred to. He tried to remember exactly what she had said. She said that she had looked in a book that listed all the births from 1960, the year of her birth. When he made his inquiry, the woman who manned the desk directed him without delay to the Genealogy Department on the second floor.

There he found another information desk. The kindly gentlemen behind that desk calmly helped each person and fulfilled their requests. When it was Jordan's turn, he was asked to fill out a small requisition form, which the man took with him as he disappeared behind the racks.

Jordan walked around the room and wondered what was occupying all of these people seated at the dozens of tables, pouring over books and taking copious notes, in the genealogy section of the library. He saw old and frayed leather bound books with family crests emblazoned on the covers. There were books on the descendants of the pilgrims. People were tracing their own, and other people's histories and family lines. It seemed an extraordinary and fascinating endeavor. And here he was, preparing to look at a mere book, in this room, for the sole purpose of noting one of the first records of his daughter's existence.

He marveled at Claudia's strength and independence. At the same time he was incredibly saddened to realize that she hadn't felt that their bond was strong enough to share her journey of discovering so much about herself. Of course she was thrilled to know where she had come from, the woman who gave birth to her, where her nose, her talents, and her disposition came from. As much as he knew that she truly loved and adored he and Tabatha, he admitted that she had always had a feeling that she was not entirely connected to them. That something, and she could not fathom what, was missing. He could not, for even an instant, fault her in her quest, or for the feelings of relief that he knew she felt when her 'life story' became complete. No more questions. No more lost or missing pieces. Except why the only parents she had ever known had been so frightened to be an integral part of her truths.

His thoughts wandered to several articles that he read recently in the newspapers. One was about how the scientific community, backed by millions of dollars, excitedly announced that they had found a bone which represented a new link in the origins of man. And yet other researchers were delirious over finding dinosaur eggs and remains that indicated a new fact about their life and demise. And another decrying an Indian tribe's misery over the desecration of the graves of their ancestors.

As he looked around the room, trying to understand the individual pursuits into family histories, he related those newspaper articles to the individual searches he was witnessing. It occurred to him, too, that he and Tabatha had erected such an impenetrable wall, a true conspiracy of silence, around Claudia's adoption. They had denied her natural curiosities and her very human assurances of connectedness and continuity. If entire professional communities could give a damn about the evolution of one bone thousands of years away from themselves, of course his daughter, or anyone in that position, would long to know the biological links to their own more immediate relatives.

His cogitation was interrupted by his feeling that someone was watching him. It was the man behind the desk, trying to get his attention to let him know that the book he requested was ready for him. Jordan now saw this man as a compassionate, patient deliverer of fundamental clarification and reason.

He took the oversized weighty book to one of the few tables that had a vacant seat. This book contained the names of all the people born in the five boroughs for the year 1960. He needed some time to compose himself before he opened it, and didn't really understand why he felt at all hesitant. Before he turned to the surname that Claudia had given him, he skimmed through other pages. There were hundreds of multiple columned pages with rows and rows of very small typed names and numbers.

Finally he flipped to the section where the last names would start with the letter G. The sheer number of rows of tiny print made him dizzy. As he scanned the columns nearing the spelling of Claudia's original last name, he noticed many entries that had as a first name the word Baby. How many unimaginable tales were there in just this one corner of the planet, he wondered.

He pulled out an envelope that was in his breast pocket to use as a straight edge to help him focus on the vertiginously arranged print. There it was. The name Claudia was given when she was born. Leslie Grossman. And there was her birth date, March 3, 1960. As his eyes veered to the next column, he felt the blood drain from his flesh.

chapter

THIRTY
ONE

"Colter here."

"Colter. This is Jordan Banks. I've got to see you right away." He knew he sounded frantic, but he couldn't help it.

"What is it? Was somebody hurt?"

"No. Nothing like that. I found the link. It's the number. The number on the note."

"I'll meet you at your office within a half hour."

When Colter was seated across from his desk, Jordan handed him one of the two xerox copies he had made in the library of the page that had Claudia's birth registration listing.

"Holy shit. How did you happen to find this?"

On the piece of paper was the number 16659, the same number that was on the threatening note that Jordan had received last Friday.

Banks quickly summarized the conversation he and Tabatha had had that morning with Claudia, and his reason for going to the library.

"I wanted to see her name printed in black and white. I needed to be able to face her reality, and one of the ways I can do that is by trying to reconstruct the experience she has had with this."

"You're a good and loving father, Jordan. I don't know if many men would show that they love that much." Colter sat looking at the sheet of paper for awhile and said, "I want to fax a copy of this to Grange. It seems to point only to the note, but I want him to be aware of everything that we're finding out on this end. Just in case something ties in with the stabbing, and lately I've got an itch under my collar about there being a connection there. Excuse me while I call him."

Colter phoned Grange and filled him in on the new development and told him to expect the fax.

"Has anything shown up in the lab, or in Grange's men's interviews with the party guests, to make you think that?"

"No. Nothing there at all. It's just this itch I get. It's a professional indicator. Seems to have evolved with the job. Probably not unlike the feeling you get when you know you're about to make a smart business deal. It's a sixth sense."

Jordan combed his hand through his thick black hair. "I know what you're saying." He looked at his xerox copy again. "What does this mean to you, Colter?"

"I'm not sure yet. But let me put another interesting tidbit on the table for you."

"I don't know if I can take much more today. I can honestly say that every one of my emotions have been tapped since I got up this morning. I don't remember having another few hours quite like these. I'm drained."

"I think you'd best prepare yourself to take a lot the next few days. I'm not sure yet who, when, or how but pieces of the puzzle are coming together in such a way there is a momentum developing and something's going to pop. It's time to be in super alert and super strength mode. Know what I mean?"

"Of course I'm ready. My adrenaline is bubbling right under the surface just waiting for whatever it is I'm waiting for. I want this damn thing over with. My whole family is in an uncharacteristically reactive phase. I want things to be normal again, although normal now is going to be something very different than we've known. But I'm looking forward to it more than I've ever wanted anything in my life."

Jordan sat back in his cushy chair and looked calmly at Colter, preparing himself for the new information that he was about to hear.

"Mr. Banks. We have to talk about a few things that might surprise you. Let me ask you a few questions before I explain myself. Tell me about the woman who has been living with your family. Ida Wilkens."

"Ida Wilkens? Why in the world do you want to know about her?"

"I'll get to that. Let's just talk about her first."

Jordan gave him the history. She started working for the family thirty-two years ago as a housekeeper, helped the nannies and became very close to Claudia, has three lovely children of her own, when her husband died he helped her and her children financially, and then offered her a home with his family.

"Tell me about her children."

"I don't know what you're getting at here, but they are the sweetest, most down to earth people." Jordan's expression abruptly hardened. "I would swear on just about anything that none of them could ever be involved in anything disturbing. Are you so desperate for leads that you would pick on them?"

"Please, Mr. Banks. Just give me a brief on her kids."

"Well, all right. They're all adults now. The two oldest, Roger and Kyle, work for the State. Her daughter Peggy is married and living in New Jersey with her husband and children. They're all devoted to their mother, the boys earn good livings

J. E. Laine

and so does Peggy's husband. There's nothing at all remarkable about any of them. Now tell me what this is all about."

"It's about that information we got yesterday from the woman who works at the Bureau of Vital Statistics." He explained again the reactions of the two men who witnessed the file being read out loud. "So far, those two men are our only leads. I don't know if it means anything yet, but one of the men was Roger Wilkens."

"Why didn't you tell me about this when we were having breakfast?"

"You seemed overwhelmed enough about the adoption factor. And frankly, I wanted to see if we got anything further about them before I mentioned it to you."

"Who was the other man?"

"The boyfriend of the girl who worked there. He seems like a more sinister character, but we had to check them both out."

"If Roger had a violent reaction, it could only be because he's been close to our family all of his life and he suddenly heard very personal information about us that he was never aware of before. I'm not surprised that it shook him up. I would imagine that he was utterly shocked and desperate to protect our privacy."

"I suspect that you are accurate in your reading of this. But I haven't closed my file on him yet."

"Let's not waste our time on that family. You'll find nothing there."

"Mr. Banks. Sometimes the most normal seeming people react peculiarly when unresolved emotional pressures that they can't reconcile surface suddenly. Without a big effort, I can make a case for Roger Wilkens going off the deep end."

"Let me hear it."

"His mother works as a maid at a rich family's home. This humiliates him, but he's young and can't do anything about it. She spends her days taking care of somebody else's child when he wants his mommy home with him. His father never makes enough money for his mother not to work. He's conflicted, because he gets close to your daughter and to you and your wife, and because the families spend time together. And he's too good a boy to let anybody know that he has any hostile feelings. So they fester inside of him while everything on the surface seems fine. Then you help his mother with the bills and help send him and his brother and sister to college. He's in a position where he's beholden to you, but you are also the source of his anguish. And this creates a textbook unresolved inner conflict. All he needs is a match to light the fuse and boom. He's out of control."

Jordan was distressed by Colter's discourse. "I still say you're wasting your time. By God, if I didn't know the boy, I'd feed right into what you are saying. So I don't blame you. It sounds just about perfect in theory. But not when you know the young man as well as I do."

"I hope you're right. But please understand that we can't close his docket until we know, without a doubt, that you're right."

"I understand. But please assure me that every other possibility conceivable is being looked into with full force."

chapter

THIRTY
TWO

"He slipped up, and he knows it. He knows we're on him now." Grange's heart was beating fast. It always did when he could smell his prey. "Reiss, get Colter on the phone." He checked his watch. It was 5 o'clock.

When Reiss left his office, Grange looked out the window and hiked up the waistband of his pants. They always leave a trail, he thought. No matter how thorough they think they're being, even an individual's thoroughness has traits that are consistent.

Buzz. Reiss was on the intercom telling Grange that Colter had just coincidentally arrived. "Nice timing. Send him right in."

Colter walked in with two wrapped bialys with butter and handed one to Grange.

"Hey Colter. Glad you're here." Grange gave Colter a pat on the back and took the bag of food with his spare hand. "Okay, right about now I could really use some food. Thanks. I'm tired of sitting behind my desk. Let's sit by the coffee table on those comfortable fashionably cracked cushions, put your feet up and eat. And we'll get some coffee. Fine with you?"

He asked Reiss to get someone to bring them super strong coffee and unfolded the wax paper from his bialy.

"So now our guy is leaving trails." Grange started.

"What did he do?"

"Someone's been calling the hospital pretty regularly asking how Evan Strang is doing. We had Lieutenant Simms pick up the extension whenever anybody called to ask about him. She can do one of those real soft voices, ya know, like a concerned nurse. She made a tape and I just played it for Maria. She'd bet her life that it's Lou Stattler."

"Was there a trace on the call?"

"He called from a phone booth on 6th Avenue and 48th Street. We're checking the booth and the phone for prints now. But that's not all."

"Let's hear it."

"He attempted to get into the hospital. Said he had flowers and a get-well card for one of the patients. When he told the receptionist the patient's name, he tried to charm her. The woman at the front desk thought something was fishy 'cause he was trying too hard. The way she described him, this guy sounds exactly like Maria said he did."

"I can tell that this one doesn't have a happy ending."

"He walked out in a huff after she told him that no one was permitted in Strang's room but that he could leave the stuff with her. A real concerned person might have written an extra note or thanked her for getting the stuff to his friend. But he just kinda plunked them on her desk, so she knew he didn't really care about them. The good news is that we got the card with a little of his handwriting on it, and I can tell you it looks familiar. The lab is running it now."

"Did the men get a good description?"

"He picked the moment when our guy went to the god damn bathroom and he had no cover. Damn ass hole I should fire him. And the security guy was helping some old lady with a cane, so he missed the whole thing too."

"What was he wearing?"

"Navy sports jacket, navy pants, a white tee shirt and dark brown or black loafers. Nice looking gold watch and thick gold ring. Like Maria said, he knows how to dress like the guys at the country clubs. We showed the receptionist the police sketch. She said it looked like this guy's face."

"I have one for you too. That's why I stopped by. Someone tried to deliver another note to Jordan Banks' office this afternoon. Right after I left a meeting with him. It's got to be the same guy. He was wearing the same thing."

"Did you get him, or at least get a tail on him?"

"Close but no. Like you said, he acted real cool, like there was nothing out of the ordinary. Like he had a meeting that he had to go to. He tried his charm routine there too. As soon as he added that he also had a letter to drop off, he picked up on that someone might be onto him. He was out of there before anyone did anything."

"What are we working with...a bunch of incompetents?"

"These guys tried. One of them chased him down the street. He had his gun drawn and was going to try to shoot him in the leg. But there were too many people around so he just kept running after him. The guy ran into the subway. He was lucky. A train was just closing its doors when he got there. He managed to grab the doors, get on and poof, he was gone."

"The guy's all over the place today. He's not giving up. He desperately wants money, and he doesn't want to let anything stop him. He can't resist going for it."

"He'll probably lay low for awhile. He knows he came too close to getting caught today."

"No shit. Okay then, we have to do something. This guy is really stupid, but he's a smart ass."

Colter hesitated, then said, "We're going to have to set him up. There's no other way."

"Who's gonna be the bait?" Grange asked.

"It's gotta be either Jordan, Claudia, Maria or Evan. Any one of them is gonna be risky."

"We need a plan. Have anything in mind?"

"Not yet." Colter walked over to the window. "Do you have something?"

Grange's bushy eyebrows seemed to be trying to touch each other as his thoughts became more intent. "No. We can't put anyone in jeopardy. And this is a pretty fragile group of people we're dealing with."

"Let's eliminate Evan Strang," Colter said. "The hospital's a bad place for us to pull something unless we have a decoy in Strang's bed. But then we have a loose maniac, probably armed, walking around a hospital. Too risky."

"Right. And I'm sure neither of us like the idea of using Claudia Banks. There's no way her parents would go for it anyway. And truthfully, I don't think that she could handle it."

"What about Maria?"

"I think she could handle it, but I can't think of a scenario," Grange answered.

"That leaves Jordan Banks." Colter shook his head. "He'd do anything to help us get this thing over with."

"Okay. Like what? How do we draw this guy out?"

"We have to create a situation that Lou Stattler can't resist. A situation that plays to what we believe are his basic crazy needs. Money and high class people."

Grange was getting excited. "Okay. If we can get him back where he started, up at Jordan Banks' office, we could at least catch him trying to extort money from him. Then once we've got him, we can lock some physical evidence from the stabbing onto him."

"Only one problem," Colter reasoned. "There's no way to let him know he has an appointment with Mr. Banks. The man doesn't live anywhere. And as far as we know he's not employed right now. We have absolutely no way to track him down or get word to him. There's no way to contact him."

Grange put his feet on the coffee table, took a sip of his over milked and sugared Colombian and let his eyebrows fall back to their horizontal mode.

"Okay, then. Let's hire a plane and do some skywriting saying 'Lou Stattler call the NYPD pronto.' That way we'll cover a lot of territory fast. Or maybe we can have all the television and radio stations beg for him all day to turn himself in. Hey. I have a better idea. Maybe we can get Miss Banks to have another party."

Colter uncrossed his legs and stood up. "I think you're on to something there, Grange."

"I wasn't being exactly serious, you know."

"I know. But you gave me an idea." Colter stretched and leaned against the wall. "I want to look over the interview transcripts of all of Claudia Banks' guests and the caterers' workers. I have a feeling that that's where we'll find the answer."

"I don't know what you're on to, Colter."

"I'm not sure yet myself."

chapter

THIRTY
THREE

Colter had his sports jacket off, his plaid shirt sleeves rolled up, he didn't care that his hair was falling onto his forehead and he had summoned Grange to his office. By 6.30 Tuesday evening he was in the crime solving trenches, heavily embroiled in battle plans and solutions, and his best ideas were always hatched on his own turf.

Compared to Grange's, Colter's office was immaculate and ordered. The only things on his beige metal desk were the phone, a few neat piles of uniformly labeled folders, the beige in-out tray and a black and beige striped ceramic jar that held pencils and pens. All of his charts, maps, lists, law enforcement and investigative ledgers and office supplies were systematically organized in the desk drawers. He sat on a well-cushioned beige and black chair which coordinated with the modern couch, chairs and coffee table across the room.

As Grange entered the office with a bag full of sandwiches and coffee, Colter was methodically writing a strategy chart on the blackboard which was on the wall opposite the one painting in the room of a smiling young boy sitting on top of a huge pile of beige hay.

"Your office looks great, Colter, but I don't know how you can think in here it's so god damn neat."

"To each his own, Grange. If I had to sit in your mess all day, it'd be torture."

"You're so fuckin' civilized."

"Make yourself comfortable. I'm almost finished."

"I don't know what you're up to, but you got that mad professorial intensity in your eyes so I know you've come up with one of your usual brilliant ideas. You're an inspiration to us all, Colter. Here, I brought some sandwiches. I know you like lean roast beef with Russian dressing as much as I do. Hope you don't mind if I start without you."

After a few minutes, Colter sat down with a couple of legal pads and pens and put one set next to Grange's sandwich wrappings.

Without missing a beat of his concentration, Colter meticulously laid it out.

"This is what we know. Whoever this Lou Stattler really is, he's probably our man for both the note and the stabbing. My bet is he's still in the tri-state area, although he could have hopped a plane for anywhere by now. But he smells money, and I don't think he's ready to give up just yet. I'm figuring he's still around. We also have to assume that just because he knows we're on to him doesn't mean that his need for money and rubbing noses with the society people has diminished one bit. No, that lust seems to be what his adrenaline is made out of. The last given is that we do not have the slightest idea what his real name is, where he's staying or where he's working. So we have no way in the world to track him down."

"That being the case," Colter continued, "here's what we're down to. We have exactly two choices. We can wait indefinitely until this character feels it's safe to make another move. But you know the risks in doing that. We'll lose his smell and the momentum, and we'll have no idea how or when he's going to try something. And that could leave us sitting here for weeks or months. We can't do that. Not when the Banks family is involved. So we have to flush him out and, as far as I can tell, there's only one sure way to do that."

"What. You're gonna have Jordan Banks offer him the money on TV if he'll leave everyone alone? Then we'll grab him when he comes to pick it up?"

"No. We're going to use a version of your idea. Remember when you suggested that Claudia Banks have another party?"

"Yeah. But remember I told you I was kidding."

"I don't want her to have another party at her apartment either. But we have to create a situation that will be irresistible for him, and that will put him right into our hands."

"Okay. Okay. Don't get weird and mysterious on me. Let's hear it."

"It was all right there in the interview files, Grange," Colter teased. "You had it sitting on your desk. How'd you become one of the most decorated detectives on the force, huh?"

"Don't be a wise guy, okay? Remember I beat you to it on that Clarkson case."

"Hey, listen. If we keep solving these things like we usually do, we'll always have great health insurance. So let's keep it up."

"Yeah. I'm all for it. So let's hear what you got."

Colter got serious. "I looked through all the interview files and it's all right there. Exactly what we have to do and how to do it. Let's start with this. We know from Maria that he's been a waiter at restaurants frequented by class people. I say he probably got himself hired as a waiter at Claudia's party. A bunch of the people interviewed described someone who fits

Maria's picture of him. I say our best hope is to lure him in, using the same bait that he always falls for. Moneyed people in a situation that needs waiters."

"I hope there's more, Colter. Sounds like you're thinking of taking over The Four Seasons for a few weeks."

"We don't have a few weeks. We're going to put something together this week."

"If you stop talking in riddles, maybe I can keep up with you."

"According to the information in the interviews, the people that Miss Banks knows have a lot of talents and a lot of influence. We're going to use them to create an event that Lou Stattler will do anything to be at. Remember. He wants to get near Jordan Banks again. We don't have a phone number, an address or a place of employment. But Miss Banks' friends have the power to override that in a way that we don't, and in a way that should put this guy right under our noses. After we're finished here and we've got the plan down, we're going to call Jordan Banks for his approval and then we're going to set up a meeting with Claudia Banks' friend Eric Stanton."

"Stanton. Eric Stanton. The big publicity honcho. Yeah. He was the first one I spoke to when they found Strang in the elevator." Grange put down the quarter of sandwich that he was still chewing on and stood up. "Publicity. The media. We're going to get to Lou Stattler through the god damn media. You're a fuckin' genius, Colter. A genius." Grange paced near the couch area for a few laps.

"I pretty much have the basics of the plan worked out. We'll get the caterer that Claudia Banks used, Tommy Laten, to make the same calls he did for her party, and we'll keep him on the phone till he thinks he's got him. We'll try to get him to hire all blonde waiters, cause Lou has dark hair."

"Yeah, but with all of the descriptions of him that the press has been putting out lately, he probably dyed his hair by now."

"Maybe so. We'll get this Eric Stanton to come up with the theme for a big dinner and get him to get it publicized everywhere. He'll include the caterer's name in all his press releases. That'll help Tommy get him to work the event with him."

"That poor Tommy guy is going to be scared shitless."

"We'll have someone with him. He'll be all right."

"Let's go over the other people who could be involved."

They spent the next hour going over Colter's plan as he had charted it on the blackboard, filling in new ideas and changes as they went along. When they were done, they were impressed with the hoax they had concocted.

"I'll admit something to you, Grange."

"Yeah, what's that?"

"I don't know what this Lou thinks he can actually do if he's near Jordan Banks. That one is beyond me at the moment. But I know, I just know he wants to get to him."

"Hey, that's why he's a sicko and we're not. Then again, after what we've come up with today, your Mr. Banks might think we're ready for loony tune town."

"I think he'll go for it. He wants to get this whole thing over as fast as possible."

"Okay. So we're gonna put this big dinner type event together with waiters and we're pretty sure we'll get Lou Stattler there. What if we don't get him there? And if we do, we're gonna have all these people in the room. What if the guy goes bezerk?"

chapter

THIRTY FOUR

Eric Stanton had seventy-two hours to stage the media event of his conspicuously illustrious career. Nearly a year before they should have been reasonably ready to launch a promotion of this scale, he arranged for the publisher of Matty's best seller *Primal Evergreen*, and Susan's company, Crown Jeans, to join forces and create the most emotionally charged environmentally concerned public relations tie-in of the decade.

The program was named Global Soul, and you didn't have to be a cosmic cookie to know that the timing was auspicious. The House and Senate were threatening to dilute, limit or cancel most of the environmental protection gains made over the past fifteen years. Too many politicians didn't fathom the extent to which Americans had been educated about the ways to avoid massive chemical devastation to the planet and mankind. Over the last two weeks, the national debate had become a very partisan heated screaming match.

Finding and booking an available small ballroom for something over a hundred people was the easiest part. Making sure Tommy could get the word out beyond his usual stable of waiters was critical. Somehow, they had to attract Lou Stattler. The press would be used for this too.

Eric knew he'd have to call in every favor that he had accrued over his twenty years in worldwide promotions. He'd get the television networks, cable stations and Internet web sites to broadcast his hastily produced video clips and announcements. Every radio station and daily newspaper in the tri-state area would run the promos and press releases. He'd get the story on the national news and over the wire services in case the suspect had fled the area.

To assure a multi-media frenzy, Marni arranged for Trace to fly in on the red eye from Los Angeles after he finished taping the Gordon Lamont Show. He was to be billed as the leaked surprise entertainment.

Because Susan had been so sure that this alliance would one day take place, she had already created, and bought, the components for the dye formula for the most earthy green for the jeans. Selected retailers would receive a delivery of Leaf Jeans, which double entendre served the purpose perfectly. A photograph of Trace and a few other celebrities wearing them would be flashed around the world via satellite.

Eric's printers were ready to work over night so that Global Soul signs, flyers and posters could be distributed and hung everywhere. Carl Hoenig was prepared to put all of the contracts together.

Grange assigned one of his men, Al Pettera, to act as an assistant to Tommy who already sounded like he was about to have a nervous breakdown. He was petrified at the thought that every potential waiter he spoke to could be a man that was capable of murder.

Then there were the seating arrangements. Jordan, Tabatha and Claudia were to be seated at the main table. Colter and his policewoman date, both dressed in evening clothes, would sit with them. Grange would be at a nearby table with a blonde wigged Maria ready to identify Stattler. Most of the other tables would have specifically invited socialites, but several would have only properly attired policemen and women ready to pounce. They knew they were taking an expensive and dangerous shot, but it was better than playing the waiting game.

Jordan Banks had immediately seen the plans' merits and offered to cover the bulk of the extravaganzas costs. Garnett Publishers and Crown Jeans would cover their own expenses and split the tie-in expenditures.

If Lou Stattler did whatever he was going to do at the beginning of the party and was arrested, the guests would be invited to stay and enjoy themselves. Only then would the press be allowed in. If he waited to make his move, the ballroom was going to be a formally dressed war zone.

In less than eight hours Colter, Grange, Jordan Banks, Eric Stanton, Matty, Susan, Claudia, Marni, Carl and several major divisions of the New York police force orchestrated a miracle. If Lou Stattler didn't hear about the event, it meant he had left the planet. If he didn't take the bait, it meant that he had inexplicably stopped being a greedy sicko. Given his profile and patterns thus far, neither was plausible. They were certain he'd know his calling when he heard it.

WEDNESDAY

chapter

THIRTY
FIVE

"Let me see that beautiful face one more time." He took the woman in his arms and gave her a series of kisses that he knew would make her knees weak.

When he stopped kissing her, he nibbled her earlobe and whispered, "I'll miss you so much baby. I can't stand having a whole day without you. Maybe you could leave work a little early today," and he ground his swollen genital into her.

"Well, maybe I can come home a little early. I promise I'll try," she cooed breathlessly as she kissed his cheeks, his eyes and his neck. They had just made love. She couldn't believe he was ready to do it again.

"Come home to me soon, baby. Bobby loves you. Just remember that. You're the girl of my dreams. Let me give you a few more kisses so I know your body's thinking the same thing mine is all day, okay baby?"

No words came out of her mouth as he kissed her nipples right through her blouse, back and forth to each one while his fingers lifted her skirt and rubbed her crotch through her panty hose.

"If you don't stop I'll never leave."

"Okay baby. Whatever you say. Tell me you love me. I have to hear it one more time."

"I love you Bobby. I've never loved anyone so much in my life."

"That's my girl. Now call me in a few hours, and we'll decide what to have for dinner. We'll plan a really nice menu, just like we did last night. And I'll do the food shopping today."

"Oh no, you don't have to do that. You have too much on your mind. I'll pick up a few things on my way home from work. Did you like the wine we had last night?"

"I loved the wine. We'll plan a menu around the same wine. I'll see you later, babes. I'll go down and get the papers in a few minutes and see what interviews I can drum up. We're gonna have a beautiful life together. Just you and me."

He kissed her good-bye one more time and closed the door behind her.

What a dumb horny bitch, he thought. She doesn't have a clue. He liked using the name Bobby. It had come to him in that same kind of flash that brought all his good ideas to him.

And that was a real good idea the other night, he thought, going bar hopping looking for just the kind of girl that he found. The minute he saw Ruth Ann he recognized her hunger. He knew he could use her for a couple of weeks. The poor fool never had a man pay so much attention to her in her life.

He told her a great sob story. He said he came to New York a few days before from a small upstate town called Coolridge to find a job in the big city. He said he was an only child, that both his parents had died over the last year. First his mom, then his dad died a few months later, from a broken heart he was sure. He was too distraught to stay in the same town, too many memories there, so he sold their things and set out to make a new start.

And wouldn't you know, all the stories he had heard about New York came true. His wallet and two suitcases full of family mementos, money and clothes were stolen. His gold chain was pulled from around his neck. Said he had taken out all his savings but was lucky to have put a few wads of bills in his pants pockets.

And the worst part, he told her, was that the list of all the companies he was supposed to call for jobs was in his wallet. He acted tormented and she fell right into that sympathy maternal thing that he could always get the women in. He knew this one loved the thought of taking care of him, especially after he told her she was the most beautiful girl he had ever seen and he kissed her. After that, he knew he owned her.

Yeah, he knew he hit pay dirt. Ruth Ann was sure this was love at first sight. He had a pretty nice place to hide out, and all the sex and conveniences he wanted. The idiot believed every line he gave her. Now with all this shit about the stabbing on the news and in the papers, he'd have to make sure she didn't put four and four together. He'd just have to keep her too occupied and too happy. Ha. He knew he could do that. No problem.

She made him feel right at home in her not bad one bedroom apartment. He figured Ruth Ann for about forty years old. Not really his type, but she had great tits, an okay face and nice long bleached blonde hair. She was divorced eleven years, kept the apartment so the rent was still kinda low, no kids, worked as a secretary in the garment district and was desperate to find Mr. Right and have a baby before her biological clock blew up.

She had already spent hours telling him her life story. He listened and hugged her and let her cry on his shoulder like his life depended on it. Her parents were both dead too, and her life seemed like one big disappointment after another.

When she helped him unpack his one suitcase and sports bag that he said was all he managed to salvage from the robbery,

J. E. Laine

she ironed his shirts and jeans and offered to take everything else to the cleaners.

Last night she brought home the food and wine and he cooked her the best and most romantic meal she ever had. After dinner he told her to put on her sexiest underwear, and then he fucked her brains out. The lady thought she died and went to heaven.

Lou made himself another pot of coffee and while it was perking put on his sunglasses and went down the block to get every local newspaper to find out what was happening with the case. He liked being all over the papers. They were saying how smart he was to have alluded the police. It's about time they realized how smart he is, he thought.

He had plenty to do to keep himself occupied until Ruth Ann came home between 5:30 and 6:00, depending on how long the lines were at the supermarket. He couldn't afford to miss a single article or newscast. He intended to study every detail and plan his next move carefully. Things had gotten a little too close for comfort with the police watching for him. No, he had to come up with something really clever. He had no doubt that he would have his plan figured out by the time Ruth Ann came home tonight.

By 11:15 he had finished with all the newspapers and had made a few notes for his plan of attack. He made a tuna fish sandwich for lunch and then decided to snoop around a little before the 12 o'clock news. It never hurt to know where the jewelry and cash were hidden in case he had to make a fast escape.

There he was, the opening story. They always started the same way. With the police sketch.

Lou Stattler punched the needle point pillow that said 'Home Sweet Home' and then clicked the remote control to watch another news channel. That stupid Maria couldn't even describe me right, he moaned to himself. I'm much better looking than that shitty police sketch they keep flashing on the screen. Ignoramuses, all of them, he thought.

Then there was the segment on the Banks family, chronicling their wealth, power and influential friends.

This made Lou's body twitch. He got up and started kicking the couch, the coffee table and stopped himself before he punched the mirrored wall. God damn sons of bitches, he muttered. They think they're so much better than I am. Those spoiled brat fucks from their rich fuckin' families should choke on their silver spoons. They don't know what it's like to know you're great. I'm as good, no man, I'm better than them. Than all of them. The only thing that's in my way from living in their world is money. But I'll get my money, he thought. And then I'll make it earn more money and they'll all want to rub shoulders with me, god damn it.

He calmed himself down and hid his notes, which weren't much, under the mattress in the bedroom. I need another day of rest, he rationalized to himself. Too much on my mind today. Tomorrow I'll work out my grand plan. I just need a little inspiration. Maybe I'll watch a cop show or two. That'll do it.

He was just about to close his eyes when the famous society columnist Katherine Kellogg said she had even more news about the Banks family and their society doings. He sat up straight and paid close attention to her every word.

"Any other family would stay in hiding after the dramas that the Banks family has lived through this week. But Jordan Banks, who has bankrolled more than a few causes for his international friends, is said to be so upset by Congress' attempted reversals of the environmental laws that he jumped on the chance to use his influence in a big way, as only he can. With our Congressmen ready to vote on the new laws next week, Jordan Banks has declared this Friday Global Soul Day. He is topping the day with a bash at New York's Grand Hotel and he's inviting the richest people he knows. That alone should tell our Congressmen a thing or two. And guess who the entertainment is going to be? None other than Trace, ladies and gentlemen. Our favorite philanthropist has really outdone himself this time. More details tonight on our News at 5."

Jesus Christ. Well, this makes it real easy for me, Lou thought. I was waiting for an inspiration and instead the good Lord handed it all right to me. The man'll be there for hours, and so will I. It's a done deal. By this Friday night, I'll be a rich man. And bye bye Miss Ruth Ann. Maybe I don't have to be so nice to her anymore since I only need her for a few more days. Hmmm. No, I still might need to lay low for awhile, and a hideout couldn't get much cushier than this. Better stay with the program.

He spent the next couple of hours going over every possible scenario. This plan was going to work. Easy as pie. That idiot snitch who almost ruined everything for me is still in his fucking blackout coma, he thought. And my man Jordan Banks likes everyone to think he's so fucking perfect. He's gonna do whatever I ask him to do cause there's no way this big shot wants the world to know his magic wand doesn't work right. No way he's gonna want anybody to know this is happening to him. I got him by the balls. Lou doubled over in uncontrollable laughter, then he walked around the apartment yelling, "I'm a fucking genius. A fuckin' genius!"

Maybe I'll crash the damn party, or I'll call that Tommy catering queen and get me a little work for Friday night. He slapped his thigh with more self-congratulations when he figured it'd be real nice pay for a night's work. I'll just wait till everybody's drunk and too relaxed to give a damn about what's happening. Then I'm out of there. Gone. All I have to figure out now is where to store the cash if I'm gonna stay with my little Ruthie Ann for a few days.

At 3:30 he left the apartment to put the first part of his plan into action. At 4:15 he was on the phone with Tommy. Then he called Ruth Ann and gave her the food shopping list.

Just before the 5 o'clock news he checked around quickly to make sure the place looked good. Then he stretched his feet over the coffee table, turned on the television and waited to hear the key turn in the door. The story of Jordan Banks' bash was on every channel.

"Bobby. Bobby. What's so exciting about the news? I've been standing here talking to you and you didn't even know I was here."

"Oh, hi honey. Sorry 'bout that." He wasn't sure how long she had been watching him, so he wanted to make sure that she wouldn't connect his not noticing her with the newscast. There was only one thing to do to assure that. He jumped up, took the grocery bags out of her hands and carried her to the couch.

"I'm sorry baby. You know my mind is working overtime. I've got some serious interviews lined up for Friday, and a few more next week. I did a lot of work today. You should be proud of your Bobby. And you know what I'm going to do? When I accept one of these jobs, I'm gonna tell them that me and my lady are taking a two week vacation before I start. How does that sound to you?"

"You're so romantic. You make me feel like a princess. I've never..." and then her words were drowned by his kisses.

Might as well take advantage of this and get my rocks off now, he thought. As he carried her into the bedroom he said to her, "I've got a great idea. You know how they say that people who spend a lot of time together start looking like each other? I'll tell you a secret. I've always wanted blonde hair. So after dinner, why don't you dye my hair with the same stuff you use so we can start looking more alike right away?" He knew that after he did what he was about to do to her, she would do anything he wanted her to do. Period. No questions asked, no discussion.

chapter

THIRTY
SIX

Reiss ran into Grange's office. "Evan Strang regained consciousness. They're expecting us."

"Get O'Hara. He's driving us to the hospital now. And make sure someone tells Colter what's going on."

"Right. I'll meet you downstairs in five minutes."

Within twenty minutes they were at Springhurst Hospital meeting with Strang's doctors.

Dr. Perlstein spoke first. "You can go in and speak to him now, but these are the rules. Dr. Nelson and I will be right outside the door. We'll give you ten minutes to talk to him. Then we'll

J. E. Laine

have to ask you to leave the room while we examine him. If he seems all right, you can continue. Otherwise, we'll have to ask you to wait until we feel he can handle more questions. Most importantly, we must insist that you try not to let him get agitated or overwhelmed. If you feel that he is having an adverse reaction, or experiencing a traumatic episode, call us in immediately."

Grange assured them that their rules would be respected and adhered to absolutely. "Has he said anything to you about what happened?"

"He asked where he was and what he was doing here. We have told him where he is, and how long he's been here. We told him that he had been attacked and stabbed through the back while attending his friend Claudia Banks' party. We let him know that his parents and friends have been at the hospital, around the clock, waiting for him to wake up, and that they were all most anxious to see him. We told him that because of the nature of his injury, it was important that he speak to a detective before he speaks further to anyone else. We assured him that his interview with you would be short. We've just come from his room. He's alone and he's resting."

Dr. Grayson added, "He seemed to take what we told him calmly. But with what he has just experienced, he could have a delayed reaction to the entire circumstance."

Grange was on his feet. "I understand. We've been through this before. Now I have one very critical demand for you. The police department will do everything in its power to keep the fact that Mr. Strang has woken up out of the press. But in this case our ability to do that depends on you and your staff. No one in this hospital is to let the press know that Mr. Strang has woken up. I don't know how you have to go about it, but I must insist that you talk to everyone that's privy to his condition and tell them that every single thing that happens with this patient is confidential. If you have to threaten to fire them if they tell the wrong person, do it. Otherwise we risk having the person who stabbed him paying a little visit to your hospital. And none of us want that to happen. I don't mean to make you nervous, but we have to work together on this one. Have I made myself clear?"

Both doctors offered their full cooperation.

"Can we see him now?"

"Come this way." Dr. Perlstein led the way.

Grange could never stand the smell of hospitals. There were always the same chemical aromas that confused his senses as he walked down the halls. It was a strangely repulsive alliance of pure cleanliness, chemical medications and rotting flesh.

Grange greeted the officer guarding Strang's door and went into the room with Reiss and his concealed tape recorder close behind him.

They had looked at dozens of pictures of Evan Strang. The man they saw laying on the hospital bed looked at least ten years younger, and certainly a lot more like a healthy sleepy child than a traumatized accomplished adult. Well, after four days of total rest, with every organ functioning minimally, I'd look younger and rested too, Grange thought. Strang's eyes were opened, and he smiled uneasily.

"Mr. Strang," Grange began. "I'm Detective Ted Grange, and this is my assistant, Detective Reiss." They moved two of the guest chairs near the bed and sat down.

Strang's voice was weak, but he greeted them both and attempted to extend his arm to shake hands. The effort made him wince with pain.

"I guess I'm trying to do too much too soon." He forced a smile.

"Please. There is no reason to feel nervous with us. We don't want to get you upset, but we do need to talk to you about what happened to you. Do you feel like you're up to having a conversation like that?"

"I suppose I have to be. But honestly, right now I'm very confused."

"We just want to find out who did this to you. And maybe you can help us. I promise that we'll take it real slow. If the conversation gets too upsetting, we can stop at any time. Okay?"

"That sounds fine."

"Do you remember going to Claudia Banks' party?"

"I remember being at the party. I remember my song playing over and over again." He looked away from Grange and Reiss.

"What is it?"

"I…I don't know. It's all a little jumbled."

"Let me see if I can help you. I don't know if you were leaving the party to go home, or if you just walked into the hall for some reason. But we do know, Mr. Strang, that when one of the guests found you, you were collapsed in the elevator and whoever did this to you was already gone. Do you have any recollection of what happened?"

"I don't know. When the doctors told me that somebody stabbed me, I couldn't believe it. It was like they were talking about somebody else. But after I thought about it for awhile, I remembered feeling a horrible pain."

"Do you remember being with anyone when you felt that pain?"

"No. I can't picture being with anyone. No."

"Do you remember anything else about the moment when you felt the pain?"

"I don't think so."

"Maybe you heard sounds. Maybe you heard music or voices. It's possible that someone was talking to you."

Evan's eyes became awake and alert. "Yes. Someone was talking to me. A man's voice. I…I don't know who it was."

"What did he say to you?"

"He said he couldn't let me ruin everything for him. He said that he had plans. Important plans." Evan coughed. "Would you pour me some water please."

"Sure kid. You're doing fine. Just fine." Grange poured the water into the plastic glass that was by the bed, put a fresh straw in it and handed it to Evan. "Here you go."

"Thanks." After a few sips Evan continued. "I don't know who said those things."

"Okay. That's okay. Do you remember anything else he said?"

"He just kept saying that I was going to ruin everything he had worked his whole life for. That he had finally found what he needed and he was going to be rich and he couldn't let me get in the way."

Grange wanted to eyeball Reiss, but decided that it was more important not to distract Strang's recovering memory.

"Where were you when he was saying this to you? Did you feel him holding on to you while he was talking?"

"Yes. I remember that. He grabbed me from behind. He put my arms behind me, you know, in a hammer lock. He was covering my mouth with his other hand. We were in the hallway. He put a knife in front of my eyes and told me if I tried to scream or get away he'd kill me. That if I just stayed with him for a few minutes and told him what he wanted to know, he'd let me go and there would be nothing to worry about."

"What did he want to know?"

"I don't think he ever said. He pushed the elevator button. And when the elevator got there, he pushed me in. Then there was that pain."

"So you never saw him?"

"No. He was always behind me."

"Did it feel like he was a lot bigger than you, or about your same size?"

"Bigger."

"Did he have anything unusual about his voice? Like was it very deep or raspy?"

"No. Well, it's hard to say. He was talking to me in what I guess you would call a loud whisper. So it wasn't really his normal speaking voice."

"Did he have an accent?"

"No."

"Do you remember when his finger pushed the button to get the elevator?"

"Yes. He pushed the button. And he just kept talking."

"Do you remember what his hand or his finger looked like? Or maybe the end of his shirt sleeve? Or was his arm bare?"

"Yes. I can see it. There was black and white. A black jacket sleeve over a white cuff."

"Was he wearing any jewelry? A ring? A bracelet? A watch?"

"Yes. Yes. I remember thinking that it seemed so out of place for the situation. It looked expensive. He was wearing a gold watch with a gold band...and a big gold ring."

chapter

THIRTY
SEVEN

Reiss was assigned to bring Claudia into Evan's hospital room. Once assured that the patient was not overly jolted by the sight of this beautiful women, for whom he wrote Reiss' favorite song, he left them alone.

Tears rolled down Claudia's face at the sight of her injured friend.

"Hello lovely woman. I think one of these days I should write a song about you."

"Oh Evan," Claudia sighed as she ran to kiss his cheeks, then his forehead, then his lips. "You already wrote the most beautiful song about me. But after what's happened, I know I'll never think of it as the song you called "Claudia." I'll always think of it as "Midnight Song.""

"Why in the world would you call it "Midnight Song"?"

"Because it was right after I heard my grandfather clock chime midnight that we heard Connie screaming."

"That must have been horrible for you and our friends."

"Hearing those screams and seeing you hurt like that were the most frightening moments of my life. But I could never, ever, imagine how it must have been for you. Oh Evan. I've...everyone has been so worried. How are you? I know that you heard about everything that happened. I can't imagine how you must feel."

"These clearly haven't been my best days, my sweet lady," Evan said as he reached for her hand. "And I'll not let you change the name of my song."

She kissed his forehead again and sat in the baby blue cushioned seat a few feet from the bed. "Well, you haven't lost your charm or your sense of humor."

"No. But I think I almost lost you," Evan said as tears welled in his eyes.

"We don't have to talk about that now. I just want to say funny things to make you smile."

"Like what?"

"Like...Evan, you sure know how to make a grand party exit."

"All right, you said it. And you made me smile."

"I don't think this is the time or the place to have a major talk."

"I'm all right. I promise you that. I'm confident that the detectives will find the man that did this to me."

"I know they will, too." She wished she knew for certain. The nightmare of knowing that an insane criminal could be lurking behind any corner was more than dreadful.

"We have to talk seriously, Claudia. I get good service here. I get to see everyone I love as much as I want. And I have had time to sort out a lot of things that have been on my mind."

"Whatever you want to talk about is fine with me, Evan. It's just that...so much has happened lately. I'm a little dizzy from it all," she said, trying to cover her exhaustion with a buoyancy she didn't feel. "And I don't know if I'm ready to deal with much more."

"I just want to explain a few things to you. Like why I was so cold to you these last weeks."

"You don't have to, Evan. It was all my fault, and I can admit that to both of us. Here you were, a man whose love I should have been so happy to have, a man who wrote a wonderful song for me. And I could never give you a straight answer about my feelings. So, of course you were cross with me. I can't blame you for that."

"It's more than that, Claudia. A lot more than that. Please, sit closer to me and give me your hand again. Just while I'm telling you this story."

Claudia moved her chair close to the head of Evan's bed and took his hand.

"Prepare yourself for a pretty bizarre tale, Claudia. Let me tell you first that I've already told the police."

"What does our personal life have to do with them?"

"They think it has everything to do with what's happened."

"Good grief. You've got my head spinning now. Okay. I'm ready."

"It all started a few weeks ago. Roger Wilkens called me and said he had something very important and very personal to talk to me about."

"Roger? What was it?"

"He told me that he had accidentally been made privy to files that are usually confidential at the Bureau of Vital Statistics."

"Adoption records."

"I heard about your talk with your parents from Detective Colter. You've always known that I was adopted. Why didn't you tell me when you found out?"

"My parents. I felt so badly that it was a difficult topic for them to handle, that I never wanted to risk letting them find out that I knew. They made it clear to me that it was something they never wanted to talk about. It was like a forbidden topic. A 'conspiracy of silence' my father calls it. I love them so much, Evan. So I decided that the only way to protect their feelings was to not let people know that I knew. I told Marni. That's all. I simply never wanted to take the chance that it would get back to them and, for whatever their reasons, hurt them deeply."

"You're an extraordinary woman."

"It's not easy knowing when you're doing the best or the worst possible thing. It just seemed wise at the time. I did think it strange though. Parents are supposed to protect their children, and here I was practically living a double life so that I could protect them. But as you know, we were able to talk about it yesterday for the first time. It feels so much better now that everything is out in the open. And, I must say, it has had a wonderful effect on us all. But please tell me. What does Roger have to do with this? What did he say to you?"

"We got together for lunch one afternoon. He assumed that you and I were so close that we knew everything about each other. He hadn't known about your adoption, and he had no idea if you knew. He was going to tell your father about the incident at the Bureau, but decided against it because he was too shy to discuss something that intimate with him. So he picked me. He said he thought I'd better discuss it with you. He didn't know who the other man was that heard about it at the same time he did, and he didn't want it to get back to you from some stranger."

"Roger is such a dear, but this is beginning to sound like a real soap opera."

"I know."

"But Evan, I still don't see the connection with the police."

"Roger pulled me aside at the party. He was obviously quite nervous. He wanted to know if I had told you yet."

"Well, you certainly hadn't mentioned a thing to me. Quite the opposite. You hadn't been talking to me about much of anything at all for a few weeks. Please, keep going."

"There's something I've never told you. You know that I've been looking for my original mother, and that my mother, who absolutely adores you, has been trying to help me."

"I know. I love Jackie too. You know I do. She is wonderful. I wish my mother had her confidence and heart. And your dad is great too. You're lucky."

"I know. They've been great, understanding and supportive. I've joined all of the adoptee search groups, I've signed up with all of the international registries. So far, no luck. But here's what happened between you and me. You see, I've always known that I have a sister your age. And my original mother's description, ironically, is very much like you. So when Roger told me that you were adopted too, I totally panicked. I absolutely convinced myself that you were my sister. I was out of my mind thinking that I had fallen in love with my own sister!"

"That's why you couldn't even look at me anymore," Claudia shook her head slowly as the revelation sunk in. "I felt like I was spending time with a stranger. I couldn't imagine what was going on with you. I...I don't know what to say, Evan. That's so incredibly heavy."

"Yes I know. It was irrational, but I was out of my mind. The worst part was that I had no way of proving it either way without your suspecting something. I didn't know what to do."

"Could we be brother and sister?" she said. "What am I saying. Of course we can't be. I know who my original mother is. I know her whole story. I'll tell you more about that another time. For now, let me just say that it is incredible knowing you're looking at someone you're related to. We are so much alike, both physically and mentally. Everybody else takes these things for granted. It's amazing. I hope that you are able to have that experience some day. That's probably another reason why I didn't tell you. I didn't want you to feel bad because my mother found me. And really, it has given my life a sense of being grounded and perpetuity that I never really felt I had. Oh, don't get me started. I still don't understand what this has to do with the police."

"A Detective Grange spent time with me this morning. He asked me if I knew Roger Wilkens. After I explained how I knew him, through your family, his mother's relationship to all of you and all of that, he kept asking me more questions about him. He was very determined. And remember, everything had just started to come back to me. Finally, I told him about my conversation with Roger. And at your party, Claudia. Remember I told you that I had to speak to you later, about something very important?"

"Yes. I do remember that. I thought you were going to tell me that you couldn't take my rejections anymore, or you were going to propose. I wasn't sure which it was going to be."

"It was neither. I was going to tell you that I found out that you were adopted. I had no idea that you knew."

"I still don't understand why that is police business."

"They think the man that stabbed me was a waiter at your party. And that he overheard Roger's conversation with me, and then my conversation with you. He didn't want me to tell you. It would have ruined his sick plan."

"A waiter at my party? What plan? And how could an attempted murderer be a waiter one minute and be so insane the next?"

"Money. He was trying to extort money from your father."

THURSDAY

chapter

THIRTY
EIGHT

At 11 o' clock Thursday morning Sarah put three Federal Express packages on Jordan Banks' desk along with his regular mail and asked if he had any dictation. He said he didn't, thanked her and she left the room. He hadn't told anyone at the firm, not even his trusted secretary, about the note. Sarah didn't know why she had been told to watch for hand delivered letters. The whole company thought the extra guards on duty had only to do with the stabbing that had taken place at his daughter's party.

He called the floor security desk where Steve Crane, the special detective that Colter had assigned to him for suspicious mail and packages, was stationed with the regular guard. He also called Colter. The gala was tomorrow night and he knew the police were trying to flush the suspect out of hiding. Both Colter and Grange thought he might try something before the event. Jordan had a feeling that this was it. He greeted the young man at the door.

"How're you doing this morning, Mr. Banks?" Steve Crane seemed like an affable young man of about thirty-two, but Colter had assured Jordan that, given the right circumstances, he could be shrewd and brutal.

"Just fine, Steve, just fine thanks." Jordan noted that Steve Crane had a wide-eyed smile and a steel handshake. "Would you take a look at these FedEx packages, please. They're giving me the willies."

"Be happy to, sir. Do you recognize any of the return addresses?" Steve asked as he walked to the desk.

"I'm embarrassed to say I didn't look. I called you as soon as my secretary left the room. Sorry. I'll take a look at them now."

"Would you mind putting these gloves on first. No need to add more fingerprints."

Jordan put on the plastic gloves, sat behind his desk and studied each return address. "This is the only one that doesn't seem right. There's a company name, but it's in New York and I've never heard of it." He handed the package to Steve who had already put on his gloves.

"Let's see what's in here." He ripped the paper cord and took out the letter size envelope. And there it was. Small rigid left-leaning letters, two lines through the 'x' in Alexander. "Handwriting looks familiar, sir. I'm running this right over to the lab. You'll be notified about its contents as soon as possible."

"Thank you, Steve. I'll be waiting for the call." As the detective closed the door behind himself, the phone rang. Jordan told Colter the news.

Jordan had two hours before his luncheon meeting with several of his top buyers in the executive dining room. His hand unconsciously reached for the phone to call Karen but stopped in mid movement. He had told her this morning that their affair was over. He hadn't expected her to cry, but she did. And so did he.

chapter

THIRTY NINE

Colter's office had been transformed into the official Banks' case war room. Grange was seated comfortably on the couch reading the xerox copy of the suspect's latest note to Jordan Banks that Colter had just handed him.

I'm getting used to being on the news with you. We'll make a good team some day. Leave half a million in cash in a suitcase at the reservation desk at the Grand Hotel. One of your party guests will get the ticket from you. Listen, I know you won't miss this money and remember it's going for a good cause. Me. And your secret stays between you and me. If there is a problem, the whole world will know about your little girl. And that's a promise. I don't want to have to do that because I think we can be friends. So you know, sometimes friends have to depend on each other.

"This guy is living in some kind of dream world." Grange said. "He sees this whole thing as his red carpet to riches. Do you believe the son of a bitch?"

"We've seen worse."

"You never get ruffled, Colter. I don't know how you do it. You're neat. You're calm under any circumstances. And you get it all done every time. I can't do what I do unless things are in chaos around me. What a pair."

"So what do you think, Grange?"

"The thing about one of the party guests getting the suitcase ticket is pure bull. Nobody's touching that ticket except for Lou Stattler."

"I'm with you there. What else?"

"What is this, twenty questions? I feel like I'm applying for a job here."

"Lighten up. I'm just trying to get to something."

"The dumb fuck gave us a written confession," Grange continued. "Too bad we can't just nab him when he reports for work. Or maybe the guy thinks he's gonna be one of the guests, or maybe he'll just be hanging around the area. If we don't catch him in the act, the big boys are gonna be pissed." Grange's eyebrows were taut. "We're going to have to give Mr. Banks a bullet proof vest to wear under his tuxedo."

"No doubt he expects that."

"No press in the ballroom. No civilian goes to a rest room without a dressed up police escort clandestinely tagging along. The women on the force are going to have to be very creative fitting their weapons into their evening clothes. This should be interesting," Grange smirked.

"What about Maria? You're sure she can handle this?"

"She's all set up with her wig and we'll have someone do her make-up so she won't even recognize herself. And besides, she'll be with me."

"She'll be with you, eh?"

"Okay, cut it out. Yeah I like her. After this is over, I'm asking her out. Big deal."

"I think you're in love, Grange."

"So that's what you're getting at. You're an animal. But okay, you're probably right again. So what? It'll be good for me. Keep me off the streets."

"What do you think this guy is going to try to do?"

"I think he's going to be the waiter of the century until he pulls his move. Then no doubt he thinks he's just gonna walk right out of there with a suitcase full of cash and suddenly be a Yale graduate, a CEO of an international company and a member of the Greenwich Country Club. But we're gonna be all over him. I can't wait till we have the cuffs on this jerk."

"And if somebody screws up?"

"I think he'll have a gun with him, and he'll get crazy enough to use it."

chapter

FORTY

This was the day that all her pieces would start to come together for the first time. Claudia felt lighter than air, and not the least bit nervous. But she knew her parents, even with all of their resolve, were a bit shaky.

They planned to have a simple dinner in the small dining room so that the evening wouldn't be overwhelmed by the excess of furniture in the grand salon. Marsha had been delighted with the invitation. She had looked forward to this meeting for many years.

"Mom, dad. This is Marsha Rachel Grossman."

Only the first moment was awkward. Tabatha was unable to speak or move for the first thirty seconds that the two mothers were in each other's presence.

Marsha broke the silence when she said, "With all of my heart, I thank you for loving Claudia, and for being such a

J. E. Laine

wonderful mother." Then the two women embraced each other with a warmth, affection and respect that seemed natural given their very special bond.

Jordan greeted Marsha with joyous enthusiasm, and displayed an uncanny sensitivity to the range of feelings he knew she was experiencing.

Marsha was a tall, thin handsome women whose features were almost identical to Claudia's. The silver streaks in her straight blonde shoulder length hair were the most evident testament to her age. She had an air of incredible dignity and vitality. Around her neck she wore an exquisite gold necklace holding a bird forged in gold with a sapphire blue eye.

"You have made quite a name for yourself in the legal community, Marsha," Jordan offered. "I've been aware of your work for years. You have been a formidable champion of women's rights. I've seen you on television and read many of your articles."

"Thank you, Jordan," Marsha replied. "As you might guess, my work has been quite emotionally driven."

"Yes. I think I understand." Jordan was quick to absorb her meaning. "Please, I'd like everyone to follow me."

Jordan ushered them into the drawing room and when they were comfortably seated, he made certain that they all had the beverage of their choice as they nibbled on their hors d'oeuvres.

"One bubbly water for you, Marsha, a little rose spritzer for Claudia and Tabatha and, let's see. I think a glass of Robert Mondavi 1982 is precisely what I would like this evening. I'll have Albert bring the rest of the bottle to the dining table."

"I'm sorry, Marsha," Tabatha said. "I've been terrible to you these years. You must think I'm an awful witch."

"Not at all, Tabatha. I understood what you were going through. I didn't agree, but I understood. You were very much programmed by the old adoption philosophies in this country."

"Thank you for that latitude, but I honestly can't give myself that much credit. I did take my lead from what the adoption agency told me, but I also let myself drown in my own mis-

270

givings. It was selfish of me, to both Claudia and you, but I honestly didn't realize it until, well, only yesterday."

"I know. It seems that people who adopted years ago in this country were told that they should simply take their baby home and forget that it was adopted. I see nothing wrong with loving the child as if it were your own. But to pretend that a child doesn't have it's own origins and reality, it's own truths, under any circumstances, is to live a lie. And I can't think of anything more unfair to a child than that. To say nothing of what it creates for you as a family. Your entire relationship is then based on lies and half truths, when you could all have simply been honest and so much closer."

After a few sips of her wine spritzer, Tabatha felt open and relaxed. "A few days ago I probably would have wanted to punch you for saying that. Today, I'm just so relieved to be able to talk about it. And especially to you. You've given me so much thought and consideration, and, mostly, you've given me Claudia. I've never given you anything. Not even my kind thoughts. I'll tell you the truth. Knowing that I was raising someone else's beautiful child filled me with a guilt that I simply needed to avoid. And after I received your letters I thought that, if you were a terrific person, I would lose Claudia in some way. And I would not have been able to live with that. And that's why I was so awful to you."

"May I interrupt, ladies?" Jordan chimed in.

"First me, dad. I want you all to know how insanely happy I am today. Having you all together means so much to me." Claudia got up and gave each one of them a kiss on the cheek.

"Claudia," Jordan toasted. "In every way it's because of you that we're all here today. Ladies, let's raise our glasses to this wonderful angel that we all love with all of our hearts." And they did.

"Back to our philosophizing, if I may. Here's what I think," Jordan continued. "I think the early adoption laws and theories were based, at least partially, on the fact that nobody who made the rules realized that the babies that were being adopted were going to actually grow up. And grow up to be thinking, feeling and questioning adults, just like everyone else. I suppose they thought the kids were going to all be like perpetual little pre-programmed robots who, if they were told not to think about who gave birth to them, whose eyes and nose they had, whose talents they had, things like that that we all take for granted, well then, they wouldn't. But of course they do. And why should they be made to feel guilty for having such normal thoughts and feelings?"

"I'll tell you one of my dirtiest little secrets, Marsha," Tabatha added. "I wish someone back then had been understanding towards me, and had let me cry on their shoulder for about two years so I could mourn the fact that I could never give birth to my own child. But no. I was told that if I adopted a child, that would magically make that pain go away. I think that if you don't deal properly with something like that, it comes out in other ways. Of course they didn't have all the treatments then that they have today. But they acted like adoption was the magical cure for what was really a medical problem."

"I might add," Jordan said, "that the adoption agencies were not very kindly towards the women in your position, Marsha. They fed us stereotypes. I'm not trying to defend either Tabatha's or my actions, or lack thereof. But truthfully, they wanted us to believe that you weren't a very worthy bunch. I guess they thought that would help us eliminate you from our thoughts. Not very nice of them."

"There's so much for us to talk about," Tabatha said. "But I want to know about you, Marsha. I can't imagine what it was like to lose your child. And to never know where she was or even if she was all right and being loved and fed and clothed. Was it awful for you all those years?"

"Yes. It was worse than awful. I loved Claudia from the moment I knew she was a seed inside of me. Unfortunately, in the year when I became pregnant as a single women, the rules in our society were quite different. There were no single mothers then, only unwed mothers. There were no children in single parent homes, only bastards and illegitimate kids. The hypocrisy of semantics, you see. The ostracism and stigma is unimaginable today. There were other factors, too. The choice was hardly mine."

"I don't mean to get overly personal, but I feel like I can with you. What about Claudia's father?" Tabatha asked.

"Michael. Michael Winters. We were very much in love in college. Unfortunately, his confidence cracked and he fell apart. And he was not counseled in a positive way by the people closest to him. We should have gotten married, but the emotional reality proved too much for him, and it wasn't to be. He hurt a lot of people irreparably, including himself."

"Where is he now?"

Marsha hesitated for a moment, and then said, "He disappeared a few years ago. Before that we had never lost touch. He was consumed with guilt for his entire life for losing Claudia and myself. But he never allowed himself to be strong enough to correct the hurt. He wanted so badly to meet and to know Claudia. But the more the years went by, the more helpless he felt."

She paused and then added, "but I know I'll hear from him again soon, both because he likes to stay in touch, as do I, and because he feels as I do, that we always want to have both ourselves and our medical information available for Claudia."

"That's so very sad."

"Fortunately I'm very strong and I've been able to persevere and have a pretty outstanding life. But my truth is that I could hardly breathe until I knew where Claudia was, and if she was healthy and happy and loved."

"That's more than understandable. Did you always know that you would look for her?"

"Yes. Actually, I looked for her every day of her life until I found her. I had to tell her I loved her. I couldn't stand thinking that, if even for an instant, she would think that she was just given away for some crazy reason that kids are capable of dreaming up. And I don't mean that I needed that for me, although every fiber in me longed to see her. But my priority was for her. I couldn't imagine her having as one of her foundation truths the so untrue thought that her own mother didn't love her or want her."

J. E. Laine

"You certainly have the moral high ground, Marsha," Jordan said. "I can't imagine anything more cruel than the adoption laws that say, regardless of your circumstances, you are never to know anything about your own child ever again. I think that, in this country, only the rules of slavery were as barbaric, brutish and unnatural."

"That's why I became a lawyer."

"How in the world did you find her? With all of the records sealed, did your being a lawyer make it easy for you to track her down?" Tabatha had to know.

"That's a very long story, which I will be more than happy to tell you. But for now let me just say that the substantive part of the search took over fifteen years, and I had to go through a number of underground, and not entirely legal, channels to find her. As an attorney, I found that necessity disgraceful. As a mother and a woman, it made me furious."

"What you had to go through hardly seems fair," Jordan said.

"There are so many legal and emotional points about the adoption system that are unfair, Jordan. It has come to be viewed just about solely through the eyes and needs of adopting couples. So much so that both our legal system and our society have relegated the legal and ethical rights of both the child and the birth mother to practically inconsequential positions in comparison. Actually, the system here accommodates some of our country's most heinous secrets."

"That's an incredible statement." Jordan took another sip of his wine. "I must admit that, even though my life has been transformed because of adoption, I've never dissected what's under the surface of it. You know, the simple joy of having a child to love and raise."

"Don't feel surprised or bad about that. Most people think of it in exactly that same way. Most people would rather not ever know or confront what's really been going on to keep the system efficient and to assure that childless couples can get babies. For example, I'm representing a number of women and men who are suing various parties, including the adoption agencies today, but especially those that were doing one hell of a business in the 50's, 60's and 70's. Nobody has made them accountable for how they illegally and unethically, by the most fundamental standards, coerced children from their mothers."

"What do you mean?" Jason asked.

"Well, just for starters, try this one. You're a businessman, Jordan. Could you imagine another company's advisers or lawyer representing both that company and yours in making a deal between you?"

"Of course not. That would be preposterous. My company wouldn't have a chance for a fair outcome."

"Of course you're right. That would be a ridiculous conflict of interest. But did you know that no one involved in agency adoptions represented the mother's rights exclusively? Rather, the same people represented her as represented the adopting parents, the child and the adoption agency. What other contractual arrangement would legally permit that?"

"That's incredible."

"That's just one example. Actually, I have over sixty additional points of law and ethics on my side."

"Please, go on."

"To name just a few for now. The legal misconduct and improprieties I found are appalling. In terms of rights, criminals, by law, have been given more rights than birth mothers and their children. Then there are things like this type of maternal loss being cruel and unusual punishment. The agencies acted with bias, in conspiracy, with fraud and deceit, fraud to induce, they used false and misleading information, inflicted loss of life's pleasures, acted in breach of duty and without good faith. They acted with deliberate indifference and breach of promise. They made false expressed and implied contracts. They corruptly effected extraordinary punishment, reckless endangerment, intentional infliction of emotional damage. They made mincemeat out of intent, the right to privacy, right to know, defamation of character, confidentiality laws and the use here of a form of a life sentence where there was no crime. I have applied some interesting precedents that were meant for other industries and situations, there are constitutional issues, and I have dozens of ethical and psychological elements. One of the basic questions is, when and how is it right to take someone's child? When they're an unfit parent or they are totally informed and relinquishing absolutely voluntarily. Period."

"You sound like you're the Elie Weisel of adoption."

"Yes, I guess I am. Unless you've experienced it, it is difficult to fathom the underbelly of it. Interestingly, the issues have been quite different in the black community than they have been for the white, especially middle class, where it's usually a permanent solution for a temporary problem. Like having a wrongful or unnecessary amputation or lobotomy."

Jordan poured them all a refill. "This is really staggering. All we wanted, like thousands of other couples, was to have our own child. But then so much of it had to be so secretive, and we made it even more secretive by not even telling Claudia."

"Yes. Many parents who have told their child that they are adopted think that's enough and permanently end the conversation there. They don't want to realize that adoption is a life-long process. They want to believe that it was over the day they brought the baby home. But that is a delusion. I must add that there are many adoptive parents who are not like that, and who share and answer all their child's natural questions, concerns and searches. Their confidence and unconditional love are rewarded richly. But they are still the exception."

"Yes," Tabatha said. "I see now how our lives could have been so different. It's all very simple, really. But we made things so much more complicated than they had to be, because we thought that if we just didn't deal with or talk about things, and kept secrets, none of it had to matter."

"I understand what you're saying, Tabatha," Marsha responded. "There are so many secrets involved on every level of the legal and personal process. And secrets can never be healthy, and they always indicate that there's something to hide. Someday I hope the procedure and discussion in our society will be as open and honest as, say, divorce became. Remember, it was not that long ago that the subject of divorce was taboo, hush hush and fraught with shame and stigma, not unlike concerns about adoption are now. Not that divorce is easy, but at least there are now acceptable and public ways to be a party to it or a child of it. It should be no bigger deal for kids to openly think about and look for and know their parents, with the blessings of their adoptive parents and society. Right now there are no publicly acceptable ways for anyone to go through any of this in a healthy way. It defies all accepted tenets of the principles of mental health."

"Everything you're saying is so logical, Marsha," Jordan said. "But I guess when emotions are involved, logic can so easily get tossed to the wind. On another level, Americans always pride themselves for living in an open and forthright society. It's strange that this situation is so closed and secretive."

"Nothing happens in a vacuum, you know Jordan," Marsha responded. "And you have to view a standard in the context of the times that it took shape. There are always parallels. For instance, a lot of the laws and attitudes about it became sanctioned when women were afforded very few societal rights, and when the field of psychology considered behavior that we accept today as being deviant and punishable. Also, attitudes and laws were shaped here as other events were similarly shady, clandestine and prejudicial like the Cold War, McCarthyism Japanese internment, lack of civil rights in the black community. Some things have to be fought for. Hey, I figure if the Berlin Wall can come down, so can the inequities and misunderstandings here."

Claudia looked around the room. "You know what I think is one of the saddest things about all of this? With all of this women's lib stuff, and wanting rights equal to men's, I can't think of anything else that so uniquely and severely pits women against women. I think that is one of this situation's most abhorrent qualities and secrets. I look at the two of you, mom and mom, and I know that if you had known each other under different circumstances, you would have liked each other. But this made you feel like enemies for years, without even knowing each other."

"Yes," Marsha responded. "And society has been made complicit in this adversarial approach to the extent that there is literally a deception, almost like a mass amnesia, so that nobody has to think about the suffering and confusion this costs. Look, I understand that the desire to be a parent is so strong that most people will try anything to make that happen. But it should not be at any cost."

"What about the fathers? Couldn't they have prevented, or had a say in, their child's adoption?" Jordan asked.

"As incredible as it may sound, fathers were not given a legal voice in the decision until 1972," Marsha responded.

"I had no idea." Jordan scratched his head. "1972. That was a year before abortion was legalized."

"Yes, that's true. Perhaps you can understand why some of the politicians and the religious right trying to promote adoption instead of abortion, as a promotional slogan, no less, is so offensive to me. They have no idea what they're talking about concerning either topic."

"This is terribly personal, I know," Tabatha practically whispered. "But many women were getting illegal abortions then and..."

Marsha saw that Tabatha was uncomfortable with this subject, so she came to her aide. "I have no problem answering your question, Tabatha. I believe women must have the freedom to make this very personal decision themselves. But for me, it was not something I could do, under my particular circumstances. Under other circumstances, my decision might have been different."

"There's something else I want to say," said Claudia. "Truthfully, before I knew I was adopted I thought women in your position were, well, like white trash or promiscuous. I don't know where that stereotype came from, but as a consequence, people discard and ignore feelings or thoughts about these other human beings who are the child's original parents. And that leaves most adopted people, whether they're eight years old, eighteen, thirty-five or fifty-five conflicted, and filled with guilt, like I have been."

"I never thought I'd be able to say this," Tabatha said. "But I know now that it is so important, and lucky, that you two are able to know each other, and be in each other's lives. It's clearly true that there is no such thing as being loved by too many people. But I would guess that most people in your situation are not so lucky."

"Claudia and I are incredibly fortunate. You think the search for MIA's has been intense? There are incredibly organized adoptee search groups that have formed all over this country, and all over the world," Marsha replied. "Most adoptees want to know about, and meet, the people in their original families. Many won't admit it only because they don't want to hurt their adoptive parents. And so they have to keep it inside, or just tell friends. And most birthparents want to find their children. Look how popular reunions have gotten on the talk shows. But the laws and social understandings have not kept pace with what's right. The biggest roadblocks to change have been that adoptive parents feel unnecessarily threatened by the concept of reunions, and adoption agencies don't want their power diluted. I'm confident that all this will change because it simply is right, fair and honest for it to change."

"I see," said Tabatha. "Yes. Until the other day I would have been one of those adoptive mothers fighting against reunions."

"And the public hears that side," Marsha responded, "because they can't fathom the rest of it that isn't sugar-coated with 'and they all lived happily ever after.' No offense to either of you, but the public has traditionally been in awe of adoptive parents. For many reasons they've assumed higher standards for them than natural parents. But in fact, there is the same incidence of divorce, child abuse, spousal abuse, neglect, and poverty in adoptive as in natural homes, and there are many more failed adoptions and rejected children than the public ever hears about. So besides being drawn by love to find their children, many parents are also fueled by very rational fears."

"How did the system get this way, Marsha?" Tabatha asked.

"The study of the history of adoption in the world, and in this country in particular, is compelling, indeed. It began primarily for inheritance purposes, to assure a male heir. Later it was considered a form of punishment, an exorcism for sin, and it has been a patriarchal way of regulating women's lives. It later became a business influenced by the principles of supply and demand, just like product industries. There are many incredible facets to it's evolution. But that's a really long story for another time."

"Lets hope society is as lucky as all of us here are," Jordan said as he raised his glass. "Here's to banishing forever the injustices of the world. Now ladies, I don't know about you, but I have worked up quite an appetite. I think it's time we had our dinner."

Claudia and Tabatha rose to their feet, but Marsha hesitated. "Did you tell them, Claudia?"

"No. I haven't told them yet."

"Well, to make a long story short, just for now," Marsha went on. "A woman who worked as a housekeeper in my childhood community in Westchester, and for my parents for a number of years, actually, also worked part-time for the adoption agency in the next town. She was like an aunt to me." Marsha took a tissue from her pocketbook.

"We can talk about this later, Marsha," Tabatha said.

"No. I'd like to continue now." After dabbing at her tears, she continued. "This woman was able to look at the agency's files and find out where Claudia was. But it wasn't until I had already located Claudia that I realized...I think you should tell them this part, Claudia."

"Mom, dad. Marsha is talking about Mrs. Wilkens."

"Our Mrs. Wilkens?" they chorused.

"Yes," Claudia answered them. "I am the reason that she applied for employment with you. She wanted to be near me while I was growing up."

Jordan and Tabatha looked at each other in astonishment.

"What?" Jordan finally said. "I'm amazed that, due to your childhood closeness with her, Marsha, she never told you where Claudia was."

"She didn't know where I was. My parents moved to California many years ago, and I returned to New York years later. I had no idea what Ida had done. So I didn't know I had reason to try to locate her. If I had, that would have been a much easier and faster way to find Claudia, I can assure you."

"So," Tabatha said slowly. "That explains so many things." She lost herself in memories for a few moments, then returned to her company. "We have had two women who are very special to you with us all of these years. Jordan, I wouldn't mind another wine spritzer right about now. Care to join me Marsha?"

"I'd love to, Tabatha."

FRIDAY

chapter

FORTY ONE

Early Friday afternoon police operatives, posing as special electricians for the Global Soul event, secretly installed overhead video cameras to cover everything that went on in the ballroom, the corridors leading to it and the Grand Hotel entrance and lobby. The ballroom was to be minimally decorated so as not to block any of the cameras' sight lines.

Fortuitously, Special Police Officer Al Pettera, who had bolstered Tommy's nerve when he put the call out to the waiters, had been a restaurant waiter during school vacations, so he knew the basic ropes. But he had never worked a formal affair. Tommy had spent a lot of time tutoring him so that he could reasonably stay in constant proximity to the serving crew.

The waiters were to arrive at the Grand Hotel by 6 PM, the guests by 7. Tommy was a nervous wreck, but cool streetwise Pettera stuck close to him. As the work assignments were given out, Reiss, acting as one of the maitre'd's, spotted a waiter that looked like a blonde haired Lou Stattler. Pettera assigned Lou to the table next to Jordan Banks.

Reiss pushed the remote button to activate the video cameras and radioed the hotel room Colter was using as the pre-event headquarters. Within minutes Colter made his entrance as an early arrival, with policewoman Maxie Carpenter on his arm.

By 6:15, television cameras and reporters, banned from the ballroom, crowded the front of the hotel ready to catch a glimpse of New York's upper crust and the evening's star attraction, Trace, getting out of their limousines.

Most of the guests were in their seats by 7:15 as the dinner band played soft background music. Matty gave a brief but heartfelt environmental speech. Jordan, feeling like a football player with his armored stuffed tuxedo, welcomed the guests, spoke passionately about the need to keep stringent environmental regulations, and wished everyone a pleasant evening.

Eric, having averaged four hours of sleep the last three nights, sat bleary eyed but attentive with his overworked friends. Susan, her bright red hair deceiving the dull exhaustion she felt, had ordered a large pot of coffee for the table. Carl's bloodshot eyes showed the strain of having ravenously overseen several dozen contracts. Every guest had a copy of Trace's album, featuring "Claudia," courtesy of Hal. They had pulled it off.

Nothing appeared to be out of the ordinary. The appetizers, first course and salads were served without incident. Between courses, the band played dance music and everyone but the disguised policemen and women did the lindy, fox trot, mambo, cha cha and whatever the new dances were called. Trace was scheduled to perform at 8:40 while the dessert plates were still on the table and coffee was being served.

Maria had positively identified Lou Stattler, but the guy was acting like a boy scout, Grange thought. Everything was going too smoothly. Something was wrong. He went over the investigation's details a dozen times. We must have missed something, he admonished himself, but he couldn't figure out what it was. He knew Colter was thinking the same thing.

A few minutes later, Colter watched as Jordan Banks lifted his bowl of fresh raspberries from its under-plate and carefully removed the folded piece of paper that was hidden there. As they had planned, Jordan excused himself from the table and conspicuously explained that nature called. In less than two minutes, they met in a secured private office with video screens and special officers on duty.

Colter donned his plastic gloves and read the note aloud.

"I think we should get this over with before your snotty guests leave and we'll do it so as nobody will miss you and you can go right back to your party and your life knowing that you gave me what I deserve and our little secret is safe. Just remember. Someday you'll meet me and you'll think I'm one of your own. And you know what? You'll be right. Cause I am. At exactly 8:30 put the suitcase ticket under the cushion of the red chair in the hall that's on the way to the men's room. Have a nice life. I know I will."

Colter put the note back into the envelope and placed it in a plastic evidence bag. "He's sure making it easy for us, Mr. Banks. Are you feeling all right?"

"I'm just grateful that this whole thing is almost over. I just don't want anyone to get hurt."

"It's twenty after eight," Colter said as he watched the suspect on the video monitor. "He's looking all over for you. We don't want him to get nervous now. Better go back to your seat and keep close tabs on the time. I'll meet you back here after you do the ticket. Our boys will be ready for him." He noticed that Banks didn't move.

"You sure you're all right?"

"This is going to be a long ten minutes. I admit I'm nervous now. What if he jumps me or something?"

"Your every move is being monitored from this room. We've all got walkie talkies that look like cellular phones. And there's always someone not more than a few feet away from you."

"That's comforting."

"You're covered. All he wants is the ticket and the cash. He wants you safe and sound so he can just take his money and run. And anyway, he thinks you're buddies for life. Go back there now. It'll all be over soon."

chapter

FORTY TWO

At 8:26 sharp, Jordan Banks again excused himself from the table, checked his pocket for the ticket and walked decisively towards the hallway, diplomatically avoiding several guests who, unaware of the evening's purpose, tried to start a conversation with him.

Despite the four large columns positioned at even intervals along the hallway's path, his every move was projected on the video screens in the secured office. He could feel the sweat forming on his face and under the cumbersome bullet proof vest. An officer in a tuxedo slinked just a few feet behind him.

With a shaking hand, Jordan swiftly placed the voucher under the far right corner of the red velvet chair cushion. He felt like he was moving in slow motion. He day dreamed that all of the guests and the police had long ago deserted the ballroom and the hotel, and that he'd be left wandering the halls in a grotesque limbo. It seemed like hours, but in no time he was weaving his way back into the ballroom. And this time, relieved of his peculiar task, he attempted to act as normally as possible, and so stopped to greet his well-wishers.

As he shook the hands of his uninformed guests, a loud drum roll from the stage seemed to strangely flaunt his plight.

"Ladies and gentlemen. The moment we have all been waiting for. A man whose talent has literally dazzled the world..."

"Who's that on the screen? Beep Colter pronto."

Colter's voice was an audible whisper. "Colter here."

"Unidentified male approaching target chair. This is not, I repeat, not, the suspect."

"Get three on him pronto." Colter motioned to Grange, who immediately signaled a group of officers to hover around the Banks' table, despite it being a most untimely moment. The main event was about to begin. The MC was announcing Trace's appearance, and the audience was on its feet applauding with delighted anticipation.

Marni and Craig were seated a few tables away from Claudia. The women looked at each other now, as they had many times that evening. Marni had just seen Trace a few moments before. Where was he now? Why wasn't he on the stage? Claudia watched as her friend ran behind the backstage curtain.

As Colter hurried out of the ballroom and into the hall, he heard his portable. "Come in Colter. We have an ID on male in hallway." Just as Colter heard the message, he saw Roger Wilkens walking casually down the long hall.

"I see him." It was Grange.

Grange watched Wilkens stroll up to the red cushioned chair and look at it as if he was considering sitting comfortably for a few minutes.

Wouldn't that be fuckin' ironic, Grange thought, if we set this whole thing up for the wrong man. Then he heard a voice on his transmitter saying Wilkens was heading towards the men's room.

Colter headed back to the ballroom as he said, "Send a man in there with him to make sure he's clean."

Colter and Grange's beeper sounded again. "Something's going on backstage, sir. The entertainer isn't on stage yet. We know he was back there. No sign of him now."

As he made his way into the ballroom, heading towards the backstage area, Colter found himself in the midst of an excited audience awaiting the appearance of Trace.

Another beep. "Several individuals, men and women, exiting side ballroom door. Heading for target chair."

All that Colter wanted to know was, "Are any of them the suspect?"

"No sir. All have different physicals."

"Keep watching. He should be trying to make his move. It's good that there are some people milling around. He'll feel like he's being lost in the crowd. Just make sure some of those people milling around are our people."

"Yes sir."

"I'm heading backstage. Grange is in the hall."

The video cameras picked up a woman sitting on the red cushioned chair leafing through her copy of Matty's *Primal Evergreen*. The officer radioed to the men in the vicinity, "watch that one closely. It could be a trick."

As Colter passed the Banks' table, he noted that all, except the men and women on duty, were watching the stage expectantly. He found Marni backstage standing next to the dressing room door.

As Colter reached her he said, "What's going on, Miss Kendell? Where's Trace?"

"He'll be right out, Detective. We both apologize for the delay. Something very personal came up."

"Are you sure he's in there?"

"Yes. Of course he is."

"I need a confirmation. As you know, there's a lot going on here tonight. He's gotta come out right..."

Just then the door opened slowly. Trace came out of the room and leaned towards Marni.

As he was about to hug Marni she said, "Trace. Please say hello to Detective Colter."

J. E. Laine

"What's the matter, sir?"

"Are you performing tonight? Is everything all right?"

"Yes sir. I'm ready to go on now. Sorry for the delay."

Colter looked at them both with a look of tremendous relief.

"Break a leg, you two. Gotta go." Static on his transmitter gave way to the clear voice of Grange saying, "Colter, where the hell are you?"

"On my way to the hall. Anything up?"

"Here we go."

The mustachioed man who had taken the woman's place on the red cushioned chair was just now leisurely gliding his hand around the fabric as if he were simply feeling for it's softness. He wore a black pin-striped suit and a gold braceleted watch.

"Take off the mustache, Colter, and look who we got."

"Move in slowly, men. Wait till he picks up the suitcase." The male and female officers in the area, dressed in their evening clothes, looked like several groups of chic people having a festive night on the town.

As if on an afternoon stroll, the tactile man, keeping one hand in his jacket pocket, made his way towards the lobby.

"I believe you are holding something here for me, sir," he said as he handed the concierge the ticket. Feigning aristocratic boredom, but with a cocky smirk on his face, he rested his arms on the desk before him.

"That would be at the Reservations Desk, sir, right across the way."

"What? What did you say?"

"I said, sir, ALL packages are held at the Reservations Desk. It is directly behind you, sir."

The man stared in disbelief at the uniformed clerk, grabbed the ticket and turned on his heels without saying a word.

The one reservations attendant was busily helping another customer. The man's feet shifted uneasily. He placed his elbow on the tall desk and started ringing the bell that was glued to the counter top.

"I'm so sorry to keep you waiting sir. I'll be with you as soon as I'm finished with this gentleman."

"Miss, I know you're very busy," he huffed, "but my car is waiting for me outside. I'm a doctor and I have an emergency call. I really must have my suitcase now."

"Very well, sir. Your ticket, please."

Triumphantly he reached into his pocket and handed the little piece of paper to the harried worker. She excused herself and went through a door marked Personnel Only. Within moments she returned carrying a tan leather suitcase."

"This sure is heavy, sir. Glad I could be of service."

"So am I." The man lifted the suitcase and headed towards the door. The bell captain, noting the size and the apparent weight of the suitcase, offered to carry it for him. The man responded, "Just open the door."

"Move in. Now! Don't grab him until he's outside." Colter and Grange nodded to each other as they raced through the lobby. As they tried to bolt through the feverishly sluggish revolving door, they spotted the man hailing a cab.

"Can I help you get a taxi, sir?" Grange said as he approached the man.

"I can get one myself."

"Not as good a car as I can get you."

"I'm fine."

"Let me show you what I mean, sir," and with that, four very fancy police officers yanked the suitcase out of Lou Stattler's hand and shoved him into an unmarked car.

SUNDAY

chapter

FORTY THREE

Everyone left it to Claudia, their very own internationally renowned party planner, to organize the picnic. She thought, as she walked arm in arm with Evan, that Central Park had never felt so sweet, awash as it was in the beauty and the smells of spring.

It was Sunday, just before noon. The birds were chirping, kids were roller blading, playing baseball and volley ball. Dogs were sniffing everything while a chorus of leash grippers shouted 'drop that' as they tried to pull their pets away from barbecue droppings. The air was perfumed with the aromas of

J. E. Laine

freshly cut grass mixed with whiffs of mayonnaise. More than anything else, love was in the air.

"I'm glad that we're meeting by the boating lake. There's a ladies room nearby in the Water's Edge restaurant."

"I love you, Claudia."

"Look! There's Marni and Craig."

"Where have you two been?" Marni yelled. "Everyone's waiting for you."

"I love you too, Evan," Claudia said as she squeezed his hand and pulled him in Marni and Craig's direction.

"Careful now. I'm still a wounded man."

As they arrived at the picnic area, Tommy was finishing arranging the delicacies that he had prepared on two wooden tables. He ran to kiss Claudia hello and said, "The scrapbook for your event is in its fifth volume and I'm running out of pages again. Would you mind keeping the excitement at a minimum for awhile? Just your regular society parties for two hundred from now on, please."

"I promise, Tommy. You're a hero, you know."

"All I know is that I lived to tell the tale. And thank God we all did," he added as he greeted Evan.

Colter and Grange were huddled in the corner of the picnic blanket they shared with Colter's wife, his two kids and Maria.

"We did it again, Colter. We didn't get to play good cop bad cop this time, but that idiot is going to be locked away for years. Do you believe he left all that evidence in his stupid sports duffel? What'd he think? Nobody was going to notice that he dumped it in the locker room garbage can? The guy must a thought he had some kind of fairy godmother watching over him."

"Only us good guys have that, Grange. And it looks like you have a live one with you right now," Colter said as he nodded towards Maria sitting devotedly close to his associate.

A blanket away, Marni looked into Craig's eyes. "Do you remember this one from Herzog?"

'I feel dwarfed amidst the abundance of nature
so robust and full bodied,

with little worms that crawl from the soil after a rain, the singing birds and the squirrels, how they scamper about.
The smell of grass, the tulip cups in their array of color to delight any rainbow.
And then after all I feel more alive than I've ever known...
Could it be but Spring?'"

"No, I don't, Marni. But if I had said it to you, I would have ended it with the word 'love.'"

On this rare occasion, Marni was speechless. She was relieved that their attention was drawn to the conversation on the next blanket. And anyway, she thought, it would be more engaging to tell him later that she loved him too.

"That's what took you so long to get on the stage?" Marni heard Jackie and Frank ask. "You had just found out?"

"Yes. Her original mother is my mother's sister. Claudia and I are cousins. Everybody has always told us we look so much alike. And I have always been so especially fond of her...in a brotherly kind of way," Trace added as he winked at Evan.

"This is really too bizarre. It's like a convention of lost and found relatives," Tabatha piped in as she looked fondly at Marsha. Marsha then turned her eyes towards Ida Wilkens, who was sitting a few blankets away with Roger, Kyle, Peggy, her husband and kids.

"Well, we're probably the last lucky ones," Trace responded.

"What do you mean?" Marni asked.

"Well, what with all the mischief at the sperm banks, you know, switching vials, using the same donor's sperm for an entire city of women, egg donors, surrogate mothers. How are these kids ever going to be able to fall in love without being petrified it's their brother or sister, or ever hope to find lost relatives or the truth about who they are?"

"Maybe I'll get some publicity going on the subject. You could be the spokesman, Trace," Eric declared. "The entire world will hang on to every word you say."

"And you've just given me the subject for my next book," added Matty. "I think I'll call it that phrase you used the other day, Claudia. *The Conspiracy of Silence.*"

"When people first realize how inhuman and cruel these secret adoption laws have been," Claudia said, "maybe then they'll know how to ethically address all the new high-tech reproductive technologies."

"Here here. I'm all for that." Jordan Banks filled his glass with wine and stood up. "All right my dear friends. I propose a toast."

When everyone had their wine glasses raised, he continued. "I first want to thank everyone here for working so hard to end the nightmare for us." He looked around with tears welling in his eyes, remembering his parents, and how lucky he was to have healed his family.

He cleared his throat and said, "To love, family and friends. Fear creates secrets, and secrets create fears. If we can't share our deepest feelings with our loved ones, we will never be as close as we could be, because we will have failed to properly nurture that love. And then we risk hurting, or even losing it. There is nothing so beyond ordinary understanding or explanation, nothing that is so mysterious, that is worthy of that risk."

There wasn't a dry eye in Leaf Green jeans.